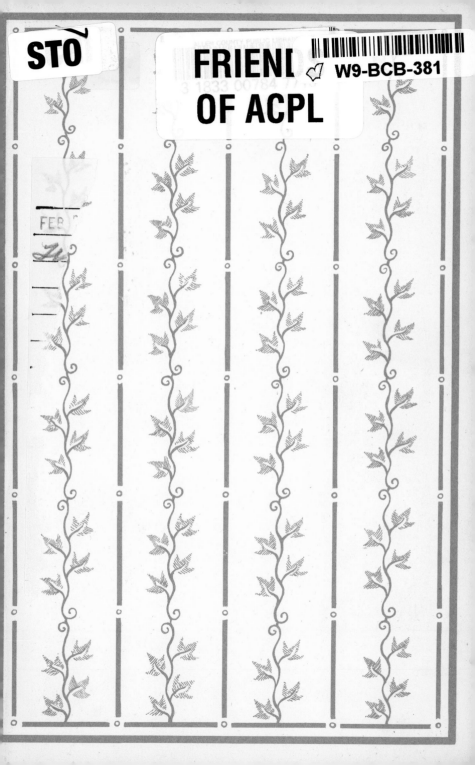

STO

FRIENDS
OF ACPL

W9-BCB-381

FEB

# Stories From Dickens

# STORIES FROM
# DICKENS

J. Walker McSpadden

*Introduction by Veronica Hutchinson*

❧

*Illustrated by Virginia Grilley*

NEW YORK
THOMAS Y. CROWELL COMPANY

Copyright, 1906
BY THOMAS Y. CROWELL & CO.

COPYRIGHT, 1924 and 1949
BY THOMAS Y. CROWELL COMPANY

Printed in the United States of America

# Introduction

U. S. 692647

In this collection of *Stories from Dickens,* the editor has selected the best known episodes about children from the novels of Charles Dickens, and has told them in the words of the author, keeping faithfully the spirit of the great storyteller. The result is that boys and girls who have lived only in books become as real to us as the most famous characters in history.

When Charles Dickens was a boy, England was a sad place for the poor and friendless to live. Children were put to work as apprentices to learn a trade when they were very young, and were often cruelly mistreated by their so-called masters. Whole families lived in debtors' prisons, sometimes for years, because their fathers could not pay their debts.

As a child, Charles Dickens knew this poverty. He was forced to go to work when quite young because his family was very poor. When he grew up and became a famous author, he wrote to expose many of the wrongs that existed at that time. One of the most appealing of Dickens' boys is David

Copperfield, probably because young David was Charles Dickens himself. Only someone who had lived through such experiences could have written in such a sympathetic manner.

He wrote vividly about the frightful slums he knew, and about the prisons and boarding schools in England. In fact, his description of school life in *Nicholas Nickleby* was so real that more than one schoolmaster thought that Dickens had written about his particular school and threatened to sue him.

Through his books he was able to reach the English reading public and tell them of conditions that they scarcely knew existed. Thoughtful people became aware of the sordid conditions, and gradually reforms took place.

These *Stories from Dickens* are intended by the editor to be an introduction to the novels of Dickens and by no means to be a substitute for them. They give the reader only brief glimpses into the lives of Dickens' children. In the novels themselves you will read much more about all of them. You will also find much kindness, laughter and fun, for the novels of Dickens are not always sad.

If you go to England sometime, you will visit the places described in these books—places that will have a special meaning to you through your reading of Charles Dickens, for he was one of the great storytellers of all time. You may stand, as I have, at the intersection of the "Seven Dials," which are seven streets that run out from a central spot right in the heart of London. And here you may imagine, as I did, that you are standing there with Oliver Twist and walking with him down the crooked streets, peopled with the characters you will read about in these *Stories from Dickens* and, later on, in his complete novels.

VERONICA HUTCHINSON

*June 24, 1949*

# Contents

# THE STORY OF

# Oliver Twist

### ❧❧

SOME years ago when the poorhouses of
England were in a bad state and the poor
people housed within them were often ill-
treated, a little waif began his life under the roof
of one of the worst of them.  His mother had
wandered there, weak, wretched and without
friends, it seemed, for she gave no clue to her
identity; and after her little boy was born she
had only strength enough to kiss him once before she breathed her last.  As no one knew
anything about her, the child became a charge
upon the parish.  He was sent with other orphans and homeless little ones to be cared for
by an elderly woman named Mrs. Mann, who
received from the parish officers but a scant
allowance for the needs of the children, to
whom she gave, in the shape of food and attention, a still shorter return.

And so the first years of this child's life were

devoted mainly to the struggle to keep body and soul together.  He won the fight by the narrowest of margins, and his ninth birthday found him a pale, thin lad, somewhat short in stature and decidedly small in girth.  But nature had placed a good sturdy spirit in his breast. It had plenty of room to expand, thanks to the spare diet, else he might not have had any ninth birthday at all.

On this momentous day he received a visitor, in the person of Mr. Bumble, the fat and pompous beadle of the workhouse, who came to see Mrs. Mann in all the glory of his cocked hat and brass buttons.

"Good morning, ma'am," said the beadle, taking out a leathern pocket-book.  "The child that was half baptized Oliver Twist is nine year old to-day."

"Bless him!" interposed Mrs. Mann, inflaming her left eye with the corner of her apron.

"And notwithstanding a offered reward of ten pound, which was afterwards increased to twenty pound; notwithstanding the most superlative, and, I may say, supernat'ral exertions on the part of this parish," said Bumble, "we have never been able to discover who is his father, or what was his mother's settlement, name, or con-dition."

Mrs. Mann raised her hands in astonishment;

but added, after a moment's reflection, "How comes he to have any name at all, then?"

The beadle drew himself up with great pride, and said, "I inwented it."

"You, Mr. Bumble!"

"I, Mrs. Mann. We name our fondlings in alphabetical order. The last was a S,—Swubble, I named him. This was a T,—Twist I named *him*. The next one as comes will be Unwin, and the next Vilkins. I have got names ready made to the end of the alphabet, and all the way through it again, when we come to Z."

"Why, you're quite a literary character, sir!" said Mrs. Mann.

"Well, well," said the beadle, evidently gratified with the compliment; "perhaps I may be. But the boy Oliver being now too old to remain here, the Board have determined to have him back into the house. I have come out myself to take him there. So let me see him at once."

"I'll fetch him directly," said Mrs. Mann, leaving the room for that purpose. And so, Oliver, having had as much of the outer coat of dirt which encrusted his face and hands removed as could be scrubbed off in one washing, was presently led into the room.

"Make a bow to the gentleman, Oliver," said Mrs. Mann.

Oliver made a bow, which was divided between the beadle on the chair and the cocked hat on the table.

"Will you go along with me, Oliver?" said Mr. Bumble, in a majestic voice.

Oliver was about to say that he would go along with anybody with great readiness, when, glancing upwards, he caught sight of Mrs. Mann, who had got behind the beadle's chair, and was shaking her fist at him with a furious countenance. He took the hint at once, for the fist had been too often impressed upon his body not to be deeply impressed upon his memory.

"Will *she* go with me?" he inquired.

"No, she can't," replied Mr. Bumble, "but she'll come and see you sometimes."

This was no very great consolation to the child. Young as he was, however, he had sense enough to pretend great regret at going away. It was no very difficult matter for the boy to call the tears into his eyes. Hunger and recent ill-usage are great assistants if you want to cry; and Oliver cried very naturally indeed. Mrs. Mann gave him a thousand embraces, and, what Oliver wanted a great deal more, a piece of bread and butter, lest he should seem too hungry when he got to the workhouse. With the slice of bread in his hand, and the little brown-cloth parish cap on his head, the boy was then led away by Mr. Bumble from the wretched home where one kind word or look had never lighted the gloom of his infant years.

Mr. Bumble walked on with long strides, and little Oliver, firmly grasping his gold-laced cuff, trotted beside him; inquiring at the end of every quarter of a mile whether they were "nearly there." To these interrogations Mr. Bumble returned very brief and snappish replies; for was he not a beadle? But at last they were there, and the boy was looking at his new home with interest not unmixed with dread.

Oliver had not been within the walls of the workhouse a quarter of an hour, and had scarcely completed the slice of bread, when Mr. Bumble, who had handed him over to the care of an old woman, returned, and, telling him it was a board night, took him before that august body forthwith.

"Bow to the Board," said Bumble. Oliver brushed away two or three tears that were lingering in his eyes, and seeing no board but the table, fortunately bowed to that.

"What's your name, boy?" said a gentleman in a high chair.

Oliver was frightened at the sight of so many fat, red-faced gentlemen, and the beadle gave him another tap behind, which made him cry.

These two causes made him answer in a very low and hesitating voice; whereupon a gentleman in a white waistcoat said he was a fool,—which was a capital way of raising his spirits and putting him quite at his ease.

"Boy," said the gentleman in the high chair, "listen to me. You know you're an orphan, I suppose?"

"What's that, sir?" inquired poor Oliver.

"The boy *is* a fool—I thought he was," said the gentleman in the white waistcoat.

"Hush!" said the gentleman who had spoken first. "You know you've got no father or mother, and that you were brought up by the parish, don't you?"

"Yes, sir," replied Oliver, weeping bitterly.

"What are you crying for?" inquired the gentleman in the white waistcoat. And, to be sure, it was very extraordinary. What *could* the boy be crying for?

"I hope you say your prayers every night," said another gentleman, in a gruff voice, "and pray for the people who feed you, and take care of you—like a Christian."

"Yes, sir," stammered the boy. The gentleman who spoke last was unconsciously right. It would have been *very* like a Christian, and a marvelously good Christian too, if Oliver had prayed for the people who fed and took care

the first six months after Oliver Twist
noved, the system was in full operation.
rather expensive at first, in consequence
increase in the undertaker's bill, and the
:y of taking in the clothes of all the
s, which fluttered loosely on their wasted,
en forms, after a week or two's gruel.
e number of workhouse inmates got thin
as the paupers, and the Board were de-

room in which the boys were fed was a
:one hall, with a copper kettle at one end,
which the master, dressed in an apron for
·pose, and assisted by one or two women,
the gruel at meal times. Of this festive
;ition each boy had one porringer, and
·e—except on occasions of great public
ıg, when he had two ounces and a quarter
ad besides. The bowls never wanted
g. The boys polished them with their
till they shone again; and when they
rformed this operation (which never took
ıng, the spoons being nearly as large as
vls), they would sit staring at the kettle,
ıger eyes, as if they could have devoured
·y bricks of which it was composed; em-
; themselves, meanwhile, in sucking their
, with the view of catching up any stray

of *him*. But he h
taught him.

"Well! You have
and taught a useful
gentleman in the hi

"So you'll begin
morning at six o'cloc
the white waistcoat.

For the combinati
in the one simple p
Oliver bowed low, by
and was hurried away
a rough hard bed, he

Poor Oliver! He li
that the Board had ju
in his and other cases
was it. The members
wise men, and when th
tention to the work-h
once, what ordinary fo
covered—that the poor

"Oho!" said the B
high living in no time
diet down to the edge
tracted with the water
limited supply of water
ply small quantities of
meals of thin gruel a
Sundays.

Fo
was r
It wa
of the
neces
paup
shrun
But
as w
light
Tl
large
out
the
ladl
com
no
rejo
of
was
spo
had
ver
the
wit
the
ple
fin

splashes of gruel that might have been cast thereon.

Boys have generally excellent appetites. Oliver Twist and his companions suffered the tortures of slow starvation for three months, until at last they got so voracious and wild with hunger that one boy, who was tall for his age and hadn't been used to that sort of thing (for his father had kept a small cook's shop), hinted darkly to his companions that unless he had another basin of gruel, he was afraid he might eat the boy who slept next him, who happened to be a weakly youth of tender age. He had a wild hungry eye, and they implicitly believed him. A council was held, and lots were cast to decide who should walk up to the master after supper that evening and ask for more; and it fell to Oliver Twist.

The evening arrived, and the boys took their places. The master, in his cook's uniform, stationed himself at the kettle; his pauper assistants ranged themselves behind him; the gruel was served out, and a long grace was said over the short rations. The gruel disappeared; the boys whispered to each other, and winked at Oliver, while his next neighbors nudged him. Child as he was, he was desperate with hunger and reckless with misery. He rose from the table and advancing to the master, basin and spoon in hand, said, somewhat alarmed at his own temerity:

"Please, sir, I want some more."

The master was a fat, healthy man, but he turned very pale. He gazed in stupefied astonishment on the small rebel for some seconds, and then clung for support to the copper. The assistants were paralyzed with wonder; the boys with fear.

"What!" said the master at length, in a faint voice.

"Please, sir," replied Oliver, "I want some more."

The master aimed a blow at Oliver's head with the ladle, pinioned him in his arms, and shrieked aloud for the beadle.

The Board were sitting in solemn conclave, when Mr. Bumble rushed into the room in great excitement, and, addressing the gentleman in the high chair, said:

"Mr. Limbkins, I beg your pardon, sir! Oliver Twist has asked for more!"

There was a general start. Horror was depicted on every countenance.

"For *more!*" said Mr. Limbkins. "Compose yourself, Bumble, and answer me distinctly. Do I understand that he asked for more, after he had eaten the supper allotted by the dietary?"

"He did, sir," replied Bumble.

"That boy will be hung," said the gentleman in the white waistcoat. "I know that boy will be hung."

Nobody disputed this opinion. An animated discussion took place. Oliver was ordered into instant confinement; and a bill was posted on the outside of the gate, offering a reward of five pounds to anybody who would take Oliver Twist off the hands of the parish. In other words, five pounds and Oliver Twist were offered to any man or woman who wanted an apprentice to any trade, business, or calling.

Oliver had a very narrow escape a few days later, as the result of this bill, from a villainous-looking man who wanted a chimney-sweep. But finally he became the apprentice of an undertaker named Sowerberry. His life here was some improvement over the workhouse, but still hard enough. Nevertheless he did get enough to eat, in the shape of broken victuals, and he slept among the coffins in the shop.

Unfortunately there was another apprentice, a great overgrown fellow named Noah Claypole, who delighted to bully Oliver in every way possible. Oliver stood it as long as he could, but Noah mistook his attitude for cowardice and added insults to rough usage. But, one day, Noah spoke ill of the boy's dead mother.

"What did you say?" asked Oliver quickly.

"A regular right-down bad 'un, she was, Work'us," repeated Noah coolly.

Crimson with fury, Oliver started up, overthrew the chair and table, seized Noah by the throat, shook him, in the violence of his rage, till his teeth chattered in his head, and, collecting his whole force into one heavy blow, felled him to the ground.

A minute ago, the boy had looked the quiet, mild, dejected creature that harsh treatment had made him. But his spirit was roused at last; the cruel insult had set his blood on fire. His breast heaved, and he defied his tormentor with an energy he had never known before.

"He'll murder me!" blubbered Noah, "Charlotte! missis! Here's the new boy a-murdering of me! Help! help! Oliver's gone mad! Char-lotte!"

His cries brought the fat maid-servant running to the scene.

"Oh, you little wretch!" screamed Charlotte, seizing Oliver with her utmost force, which was about equal to that of a strong man in good training. "Oh, you little un-grate-ful, mur-der-ous, hor-rid villain!" And between every syllable Charlotte gave Oliver a blow with all her might, accompanying it with a scream, for the benefit of society.

Charlotte's fist was by no means a light one; but lest it should not be effectual in calming Oliver's wrath, Mrs. Sowerberry plunged into the kitchen, and assisted to hold him with one hand while she scratched his face with the other. In this favorable position of affairs Noah rose from the ground and pommelled him behind.

This was rather too violent exercise to last long. When they were all three wearied out and could tear and beat no longer, they dragged Oliver, struggling and shouting but nothing daunted, into the dust-cellar, and there locked him up. This being done, Mrs. Sowerberry sank into a chair and burst into tears.

"Oh, Charlotte!" she cried! "what a mercy we have not all been murdered in our beds, with such a little villain in our house!"

And when Mr. Sowerberry presently came home, he gave Oliver a whipping on his own account for good measure.

It was not until he was left alone in the silence and stillness of the cellar that Oliver gave way to the feelings which the day's treatment had awakened. He had listened to their taunts with a look of contempt; he had borne the lash without a cry, for he felt that pride swelling in his heart which would have kept down a shriek to the last, though they had roasted him alive. But now, when there was none to see or hear him, he fell upon his knees on the floor, and, hiding his face in his hands, wept bitter tears.

For a long time Oliver remained motionless in this attitude. The candle was burning low in the socket when he rose to his feet. Having gazed cautiously round him and listened intently, he gently undid the fastenings of the door and looked abroad.

It was a cold, dark night. The stars seemed, to the boy's eyes, farther from the earth than he had ever seen them before. There was no wind, and the sombre shadows thrown by the trees upon the ground looked sepulchral and death-like, from being so still. He softly re-closed the door. He resolved to run away in the early morning—to go to that great city of London.

With the first ray of light that struggled through the crevices in the shutters, Oliver arose, and again unbarred the door. One timid look around,—one moment's pause—he had closed it behind him, and was in the open street.

He looked to the right and to the left, uncertain whither to fly. He remembered to have seen the wagons, as they went out, toiling up the hill. He took the same route, and arriving at a footpath across the fields, which he knew led out again into the road, struck into it and walked quickly on.

He was then only ten years old.

## II. OLIVER FALLS FROM BAD TO WORSE

It was seventy miles to London, a long way, and the poor boy made his way thither only with great difficulty. Begging was not allowed in many of the villages, and nearly everybody viewed him with doubt, or else shut the door in his face.

Early on the seventh morning of his flight Oliver limped slowly into the little town of Barnet, near the outskirts of London. The window-shutters were closed, the street was empty, and the boy sank down with bleeding feet and covered with dust upon a door-step.

By degrees the shutters were opened, the window-blinds were drawn up, and people began passing to and fro. Some few stopped to gaze at Oliver for a moment or two, or turned round to stare at him as they hurried by; but none relieved him, or troubled themselves to inquire how he came there. He had no heart to beg, and there he sat.

He had been crouching on the step for some time, when he was roused by observing that a boy, who had passed him carelessly some minutes before, had returned, and was now surveying him most earnestly from the opposite side of the way. He took little heed of this at first; but the boy remained in the same attitude of close observation so long that Oliver raised his head and returned his steady look. Upon this the boy crossed over, and walking close up to Oliver said:

"Hullo! my covey, what's the row?"

The boy who addressed this inquiry was about his own age, but one of the queerest-looking fellows Oliver had ever seen. He was a snub-nosed, flat-browed, common-faced boy enough, and as dirty as one would wish to see! but he had about him all the airs and manners of a man. He was short of his age, with rather bow legs, and little, sharp, ugly eyes. He wore a man's coat, which reached nearly to his heels. He had turned the cuffs back, half-way up his arm, to get his hands out of the sleeves, apparently with the ultimate view of thrusting them into the pockets of his corduroy trousers, for there he kept them. He was altogether as swaggering a young gentleman as ever stood four feet six, or something less, in his shoes.

"Hullo! my covey, what's the row?" said this strange young gentleman to Oliver.

"I am very hungry and tired," replied Oliver, the tears standing in his eyes as he spoke. "I have walked a long way. I have been walking these seven days."

The boy looked at him narrowly, and asked him some questions. He took Oliver for a va-

grant or worse, but led him into a small tavern, and gave him a feast of ham and bread; and Oliver, falling to at his new friend's bidding, made a long and hearty meal, during the progress of which the strange boy eyed him from time to time with great attention.

"Going to London?" said the strange boy, when Oliver had at length concluded.

"Yes."

"Got any lodgings?"

"No."

"Money?"

"No."

The strange boy whistled, and put his arms into his pockets as far as the big coat-sleeves would let them go.

"Do you live in London?" asked Oliver.

"Yes, I do when I'm at home," replied the strange boy. "Want to go along with me? I know and old gen'elman as lives there wot'll give you lodgings for nothink."

The unexpected offer was too tempting to be resisted, especially when Oliver was told that the old gentleman would doubtless get him a good place without loss of time. This led to a more friendly and confidential chat, in which Oliver learned that his new friend's name was Jack Dawkins, commonly called "The Artful Dodger."

As Dawkins objected to entering London before nightfall, it was nearly eleven o'clock before he piloted Oliver down some of the worst streets of the city's worst section. Finally they entered a tumbledown building, and groped their way up a rickety stairway. Then Dawkins threw open the door of a back room and drew Oliver in after him.

The walls and ceiling of the room were perfectly black with age and dirt. There was a deal table before the fire, upon which were a candle stuck in a bottle, some pewter pots, bread and butter. Several rough beds were huddled side by side upon the floor. Seated around the table were four or five boys, none older than the Dodger, smoking long clay pipes and drinking spirits with the airs of the middle-aged. But the chief figure was an old shrivelled man, whose villainous face was offset by a mass of matted red hair. He was dressed in a greasy flannel gown, and was busily at work frying sausages over a fire.

The boys crowded around Dawkins as he whispered a few words in the ear of the man. Then they all turned, as did the man, and grinned at Oliver.

"This is him, Fagin," said Jack Dawkins; "my friend Oliver Twist."

The man made a low bow to Oliver, took him

by the hand, and hoped he should have the honor of his intimate acquaintance. Upon this, the young gentlemen with the pipes came round him, and shook both his hands very hard—especially the one in which he held his little bundle. One young gentleman was very anxious to hang up his cap for him; and another was so obliging as to put his hands in Oliver's pockets, in order that, as he was very tired, he might not have the trouble of emptying them himself when he went to bed.

"We are very glad to see you, Oliver—very," said the man. "Dodger, take off the sausages, and draw a tub near the fire for Oliver."

Oliver ate his share, and the man then mixed him a glass of hot gin and water, telling him he must drink it off directly, because another gentleman wanted the tumbler. Oliver did as he was desired. Immediately afterwards, he felt himself gently lifted on to one of the sacks, and then he sank into a deep sleep.

The next morning, Oliver watched Fagin, Dawkins, and Charley Bates, another of the boys, play a curious game. The old man would place a purse and other valuables in his pockets, whereupon the boys would try to slip them out without his knowledge.

Oliver didn't understand in the least what it was all about, even when Fagin gave him some

lessons in the same game. But he was to learn
with a shock, a few days later, when Bates and
Dawkins took him with them for a walk about
town.

They were just emerging from a narrow court
not far from the open square in Clerkenwell,
when the Dodger made a sudden stop, and, laying his fingers on his lips drew his companions
back again with the greatest caution.

"What's the matter?" demanded Oliver.

"Hush!" replied the Dodger. "Do you see
that old cove at the book-stall?"

"The gentleman over the way?" said Oliver.
"Yes, I see him."

"He'll do," said the Dodger.

"A prime plant," observed Master Charley
Bates.

Oliver looked from one to the other with surprise, but he was not permitted to make any
inquiries; for the two boys walked stealthily
across the road, and slunk close behind the old
gentleman. Oliver walked a few paces after
them, and not knowing whether to advance or
retire, stood looking on in silent amazement.

The gentleman was a very respectable-looking
person who had taken up a book from the stall
and was reading away as hard as if he were in
his own study.

What was Oliver's horror and alarm as he

stood a few paces off, looking on with his eye-
lids as wide open as they would possibly go, to
see the Dodger plunge his hand into the gentleman's pocket, and draw from thence a handkerchief; to see him hand the same to Charley
Bates; and finally to behold them both running
away round the corner at full speed!

Oliver saw in a flash that they were pick-
pockets, and that he would be classed among
them! He turned to run—the worst possible
thing to do—for just then the gentleman missed
his handkerchief and glanced around in time to
see Oliver scudding away for dear life; and
shouting "Stop thief!" made off after him, book
in hand.

He was not alone in the cry, for Bates and
Dawkins, willing to divert attention from themselves, also shouted "Stop thief!" and joined
in the pursuit like good citizens.

"Stop thief! Stop thief!" There is a magic
in the sound. The tradesman leaves his counter,
and the carman his wagon; the butcher throws
down his tray; the baker his basket; the milk-
man his pail; the errand-boy his parcels; the
school-boy his marbles. Away they run, pell-
mell, helter-skelter, slap-dash, tearing, yelling,
screaming and knocking down the passengers
as they turn corners.

"Stop thief! Stop thief!" The cry is taken

up by a hundred voices, and the crowd accumulates at every turning. Away they fly, splashing through the mud and rattling along the pavements. Up go the windows, out run the people, and lend fresh vigor to the cry, "Stop thief! Stop thief!"

Stopped at last! A well-aimed blow laid Oliver upon the pavement. Then a policeman seized him by the collar and he was hustled off for trial before a magistrate.

The magistrate was a surly boor who was in the habit of committing prisoners to jail with the merest pretence of a trial. It did not take him long to decide that Oliver was a hardened criminal, in spite of the protests of the kindly old gentleman whose pocket had been picked; and the boy was, in fact, being carried away in a fainting condition, when the bookseller whose shop had been the scene of action and who had witnessed the whole thing, rushed in and declared Oliver's innocence.

The poor child was thereupon released; and the old gentleman—Mr. Brownlow by name—was so sorry for him, and so taken by his frank face, that he took him to his own home and nursed him through a severe illness, the result of all his early privations and recent trouble. Mr. Brownlow even thought of adopting him, and, as soon as he was well enough, let him have books to read out of his own well-stocked library, greatly to the eager Oliver's delight.

It did indeed seem as though the sky had cleared for the boy, but instead still darker days were threatening. For Fagin had heard of Oliver's escape with fear and anger. He knew that it would never do for the boy to tell what he knew about the thieves' den. Their one chance of safety lay in seizing him again and making him a thief like themselves, so that his mouth would be closed.

So Fagin called to his aid a burglar, a big, brutal fellow named Bill Sikes, who always went around with a knotted stick and a surly dog. Nancy, a poor girl of the streets, was also put upon the search, and soon their united efforts were successful.

One day after Oliver had begun to grow strong, he was sent by Mr. Brownlow on an errand to a bookshop. He was well dressed in a new suit, and had some books and a five-pound note of Mr. Brownlow's. It was not far, but he accidentally turned down a by-street that was not exactly in his way. He started to turn back, when he heard a girl's voice screaming, "Oh, my dear brother!" And he had hardly looked up to see what the matter was, when he was stopped by having a pair of arms thrown tight around his neck.

"Don't!" cried Oliver, struggling. "Let go of me! Who is it? What are you stopping me for?"

The only reply to this was a great number of loud lamentations from the young woman who had embraced him, and who had a little basket and a large key in her hand.

"Oh, my gracious!" said the young woman, "I've found him! Oh, Oliver! Oliver! Oh, you naughty boy, to make me suffer sich distress on your account! Come home, dear, come! Oh, I've found him! Thank gracious goodness heavins, I've found him!" With these exclamations the young woman burst into another fit of crying.

"What's the matter, ma'am?" inquired a woman.

"Oh, ma'am," replied the girl, "he ran away, near a month ago, from his parents, who are hard-working and respectable people, and went and joined a set of thieves and bad characters, and almost broke his mother's heart."

"Young wretch!" said the woman.

"I'm not," replied Oliver, greatly alarmed. "I don't know her. I haven't any sister, or father and mother either. I'm an orphan; I live at Pentonville."

"Oh, only hear him, how he braves it out!" cried the young woman.

"Why, it's Nancy!" exclaimed Oliver, who had known of her at Fagin's, and now saw her face for the first time.

"You see he knows me!" cried Nancy, appealing to the bystanders. "He can't help himself. Make him come home, there's good people, or he'll kill his dear mother and father, and break my heart!"

"What the devil's this?" said a man, bursting out of a beer-shop, with a white dog at his heels; "young Oliver! Come home to your poor mother, you young dog! Come home, directly."

"I don't belong to them. I don't know them. Help! Help!" cried Oliver, struggling in the man's powerful grasp.

"Help!" repeated the man. "Yes; I'll help you, you young rascal! What books are these? You've been a stealing 'em, have you? Give 'em here." With these words, the man tore the volumes from his grasp and struck him on the head.

"That's right!" cried a looker-on from a garret window. "That's the only way of bringing him to his senses!"

"To be sure!" cried a sleepy-faced carpenter, casting an approving look at the garret window.

"It'll do him good!" said the woman.

"And he shall have it, too!" rejoined the man, administering another blow, and seizing Oliver by the collar. "Come on, you young villain! Here, Bull's-eye, mind him, boy! Mind him!"

Weak from his recent illness and with no one in the idle crowd to befriend him, poor Oliver could only suffer himself to be led away sobbing. Bill Sikes saw his advantage, and pushed him rapidly down the street. Then, turning to Oliver, he commanded him to take hold of Nancy's hand.

"Do you hear?" growled Sikes, as Oliver hesitated, and looked round.

They were in a dark corner, quite out of the track of passengers. Oliver saw, but too plainly, that resistance would be of no avail. He held out his hand, which Nancy clasped tight in hers.

"Give me the other," said Sikes. "Here, Bull's-eye!"

The dog looked up and growled.

"See here, boy!" said Sikes, putting his other hand to Oliver's throat; "if he speaks ever so soft a word, hold him! D'ye mind?"

The dog growled again, and, licking his lips, eyed Oliver as if he were anxious to attach himself to his windpipe without delay.

And in this fashion Oliver saw with unspeakable horror that he was being taken back to Fagin's. What would the trusting Mr. Brownlow think of him? What, indeed! The hot tears blinded Oliver's eyes at the bare thought.

Presently they arrived before the house but found it perfectly dark.

"Let's have a glim," said Sikes, "or we shall go breaking our necks, or treading on the dog. Look after your legs if you do! That's all."

"Stand still a moment, and I'll get you one," replied a voice. The footsteps of the speaker were heard, and in another minute the form of Mr. John Dawkins, otherwise the Artful Dodger, appeared. He bore in his right hand a tallow candle stuck in the end of a cleft stick.

The young gentleman did not stop to bestow any other mark of recognition upon Oliver than a humorous grin; but, turning away, beckoned the visitors to follow him. As they entered the low, dingy room, they were received with a shout of laughter.

"Oh, my wig, my wig!" cried Charley Bates; "here he is! oh, cry, here he is! Oh, Fagin, look at him; Fagin, do look at him! I can't bear it; it is such a jolly game, I can't bear it! Hold me, somebody, while I laugh it out."

With this, Master Bates laid himself flat on the floor, and kicked convulsively for five minutes, in an ecstasy of joy. Then jumping to his feet he snatched the cleft stick from the Dodger, and advancing to Oliver, viewed him round and round, while Fagin, taking off his nightcap, made a great number of low bows to

the bewildered boy.  The Artful, meantime, who
seldom gave way to merriment when it inter-
fered with business, rifled Oliver's pockets thoroughly.

"Look at his togs, Fagin!" said Charley, putting the light so close to his new jacket as nearly
to set him on fire.  "Look at his togs,— super-
fine cloth, and the heavy-swell cut!  Oh, my eye,
what a game!  And his books too! nothing but
a gentleman, Fagin!"

"Delighted to see you looking so well, my
dear," said Fagin, bowing with mock humility.
"The Artful shall give you another suit, my
dear, for fear you should spoil that Sunday one.
Why didn't you write, my dear, and say you
were coming?  We'd have got something warm
for supper."

At this Master Bates roared again so loud
that Fagin himself relaxed, and even the Dodger
smiled; but as the Artful drew forth the five-
pound note at that instant, it is doubtful whether
the sally or the discovery awakened his merriment.

"Hallo! what's that?" inquired Sikes, stepping forward as old Fagin seized the note.
"That's mine, Fagin."

"No, no, my dear," said Fagin.  "Mine,
Bill, mine.  You shall have the books."

"They belong to Mr. Brownlow!" cried

Oliver, wringing his hands. "Oh, pray send them back! He'll think I stole them!"

"The boy's right," replied Fagin, with a sly wink. "He *will* think you've stolen them!"

Oliver saw by his look that all chance of rescue was gone, and shrieking wildly he made a dash for the door. But the dog arrested him with a fierce growl, while a blow laid him upon the floor.

For several days Fagin kept him hid close, for fear of searching parties. Then, resolving to get the boy deeply into crime as soon as possible, he forced him to accompany Bill Sikes upon a house-breaking expedition.

Accordingly, one raw evening they set forth —Oliver, Sikes, and another burglar, Toby Crackit—the ruffians threatening to shoot the boy if he so much as uttered one word. On account of his small size he was chosen to creep through a little window of the house which was to be robbed. The opening was about five feet from the ground, and so small that the inmates did not think it worth while to defend it securely. But it was large enough to admit a boy of Oliver's size, nevertheless.

"Now listen, you young limb," whispered Sikes, drawing a dark-lantern from his pocket and throwing the glare full in Oliver's face: "I'm going to put you through there. Take this light and go softly up the steps straight afore you, and along the little hall to the street door. Unfasten it and let us in."

So saying, the burglar boosted Oliver up on his back, and put him through the window.

"You see the stairs, don't you?"

Oliver, more dead than alive, gasped out "Yes." Sikes pointed the pistol at him, and advised him to take notice that he was within shot all the way. Nevertheless, the boy had firmly resolved that, whether he died in the attempt or not, he would make one effort to dart upstairs from the hall and alarm the family. Filled with this idea, he advanced at once, but stealthily.

"Come back!" suddenly cried Sikes aloud. "Back! back!"

Scared by the sudden breaking of the dead stillness of the place, and by a loud cry which followed it, Oliver let his lantern fall, and knew not whether to advance or fly.

The cry was repeated—a light appeared—a vision of two terrified half-dressed men at the top of the stairs swam before his eyes—a flash— a loud noise—a smoke—a crash somewhere, but where he knew not,—and he staggered back.

Sikes had disappeared for an instant; but he was up again and had him by the collar before the smoke had cleared away.

He fired his own pistol after the men, who were already retreating, and dragged the boy up.

"Clasp your arm tighter," said Sikes, as he drew him through the window. "Give me a shawl here. They've hit him. Quick! How the boy bleeds!"

Then came the loud ringing of a bell, mingled with the noise of firearms, and the shouts of men, and the sensation of being carried over uneven ground at a rapid pace. And then, the noises grew confused in the distance. A cold deadly feeling crept over the boy's heart, and he saw or heard no more.

### III.   OLIVER MAKES HIS WAY INTO GOOD SOCIETY

Bill Sikes and Toby Crackit were so hard pressed in their flight that they were soon forced to leave Oliver lying in a ditch. The hue and cry passed him to one side, leaving him alone and unconscious through the long cold night. Morning drew on apace. The rain came down thick and fast, but Oliver felt it not as it beat against him.

At length a low cry of pain broke the stillness; and uttering it, the boy awoke. His left arm, rudely bandaged in a shawl, hung heavy and useless at his side; and the bandage was saturated with blood. He was so weak that he could scarcely raise himself into a sitting posture. When he had at last done so, he looked feebly round for help, and groaned with agony. Trembling in every joint from cold and exhaustion, he made an effort to stand upright; but, shuddering from head to foot, fell prostrate on the ground.

After a short return of the stupor in which he had been so long plunged, Oliver got upon his feet, and essayed to walk. His head was dizzy, and he staggered to and fro like a drunken man. But he kept up, nevertheless, and, with his head drooping languidly on his breast, went stumbling onward, he knew not whither.

The rain was falling heavily now, but the cold drops roused him like whiplashes. He pressed forward with the last ounce of his strength, feeling that if he stopped he must surely die, and by chance reached the same house of the attempted burglary. He knew the place at once, but his strength was at an end, and he sank exhausted on the little portico by the door.

The servants who presently opened the door were immensely surprised to find the wounded boy; and two of them were certain he was the

same who had broken into the house. But in his pitiful condition they put him to bed and sent for a surgeon.

A very kind-hearted lady, Mrs. Maylie, and her adopted niece Rose, lived here. They cared for Oliver tenderly; for, like his lost friend, Mr. Brownlow, they were greatly taken by his open face, and believed in him despite the strange story which he presently found strength to tell. With the aid of their friend the surgeon, they convinced the servants that a mistake had been made, and so Oliver was not taken to jail. Instead, he was received into this kindly home, and it really seemed that now his dark days were over at last.

Oliver resumed the study of his beloved books, which he had begun with Mr. Brownlow. But he also spent much time in the open fields, and soon grew sturdy and strong, with the brown look of health in his face. Between him and Rose Maylie a tender affection sprang up. He was, in fact, her devoted knight.

One beautiful evening, when the first shades of twilight were beginning to settle upon the earth, Oliver sat at his window, intent upon his books. He had been poring over them for some time; and, as the day had been uncommonly sultry, and he had exerted himself a great deal, by slow degrees he fell asleep.

There is a kind of sleep that steals upon us sometimes, which while it holds the body prisoner, does not free the mind from a sense of things about it, or enable it to ramble at its pleasure.

Oliver knew, perfectly well, that he was in his own little room; that his books were lying on the table before him; that the sweet air was stirring among the creeping plants outside. And yet he was asleep. Suddenly, the scene changed; the air became close and confined; and he thought, with a glow of terror, that he was in old Fagin's house again. There sat the hideous old man, in his accustomed corner, pointing at him, and whispering to another man with his face averted, who sat beside him.

"Hush, my dear!" he thought he heard the thief say; "it is he, sure enough. Come away."

"He!" the other man seemed to answer; "could I mistake him, think you? If a crowd of ghosts were to put themselves into his exact shape, and he stood among them, there is something that would tell me how to point him out!"

The man seemed to say this with such dreadful hatred, that Oliver awoke with a fear and started up.

Good Heaven! what was that which sent the blood tingling to his heart, and deprived him of his voice and of power to move! There—there

—at the window—close before him—so close that he could have almost touched him before he started back—with his eyes peering into the room, and meeting his—there stood Fagin! And beside him were the scowling features of a dark man whom Oliver had seen only once, but had instinctively learned to fear.

It was but an instant, a glance, a flash, before his eyes, and they were gone. But they had recognized him, and he them. He knew they were once again lying in wait to seize him, and that his days of peace and happiness were numbered.

**U. S. 692647**

Voice and motion came back to him with the fear; and leaping from the window he called loudly for help.

Nevertheless, no trace of Fagin or the stranger could be found, though the search was pursued with haste; and Oliver's friends were forced to believe that it had been only a feverish dream.

But Oliver had not been mistaken. The two figures at the window were really Fagin and a man named Monks, who for some mysterious reason had been the boy's most vindictive enemy. It was he who had found Oliver and reported the fact to Fagin; and together they laid cunning plans to get him once more into their clutches.

At this critical moment in Oliver's welfare,

an unexpected friend to him appeared in the person of Nancy, the street-girl. She had bitterly repented her share in kidnapping him from Mr. Brownlow, and now longed for a chance to do him some service. The chance offered, when she happened to overhear the interview between Monks and Fagin. She could not understand all she heard, but she realized that the boy was in great danger unless she acted at once.

Hastening to the home of Rose Maylie, Nancy contrived to see her alone and repeated word for word the conversation she had overheard. From the dark threats of this man Monks, it seemed that Oliver's very life was in danger, because of some secret connected with his birth. Nancy knew that it meant her own death also if her visit to Miss Maylie became known, but she could not remain silent.

Miss Maylie listened to her story with horror and amazement. She realized that something must be done quickly, but did not know to whom to turn. In her perplexity Oliver made a discovery of great value to both of them. On the very day of Nancy's hurried visit and no less hurried departure he came running in, his eyes all aglow with excitement.

"I have seen him!" he exclaimed excitedly; "I knew that if I kept on looking, I should find him again, one day! I mean the gentleman who was so good to me—Mr. Brownlow!"

"Where?" asked Rose.

"Getting out of a coach," replied Oliver. "I didn't have the chance to speak to him, but I took the number of the house he went into. Here it is." And he flourished a scrap of paper delightedly. "Oh, let us go there at once!"

Rose read the address eagerly, and decided to put the discovery to account. Not alone would Oliver be gratified, but Mr. Brownlow might be the very friend they needed at this momentous time.

"Quick!" she said; "tell them to fetch a hackney-coach, and be ready to go with me. I will take you there directly, without a minute's loss of time I will only tell my aunt that we are going out for an hour, and be ready as soon as you are."

Oliver needed no prompting to hasten, and in little more than five minutes they were on their way. When they arrived at the address noted, Rose left Oliver in the coach, under pretence of preparing his friend to receive him; and sending up her card by the servant, requested to see Mr. Brownlow on very pressing business. The servant soon returned, to beg that she would walk upstairs; and following him into an upper room, Miss Maylie was presented to an elderly gentleman of benevolent appearance, in a bottle-green coat.

"Dear me," said the gentleman, hastily rising, with great politeness, "I beg your pardon, young lady—I imagined it was some importunate person who—I beg you will excuse me. Be seated, pray."

"Mr. Brownlow, I believe, sir?" said Rose.

"That is my name."

"I shall surprise you very much, I have no doubt," said Rose, naturally embarrassed; "but you once showed great kindness to a very dear young friend of mine, and I am sure you will take an interest in hearing of him again."

"Indeed!" said Mr. Brownlow.

"Oliver Twist, as you knew him," said Rose.

Mr. Brownlow was naturally surprised, but said nothing for a few moments  Then looking straight into her eyes, he remarked quietly but earnestly, "Believe me, my dear young lady, if you can tell me good news of that child, or lift the shadow which rests upon his name, you will be doing me the greatest service."

Rose at once related in a few words all that had befallen Oliver since leaving Mr. Brownlow's house; how he had searched for him but had only seen him that very day; and finally of the new danger which threatened the boy.

You may believe that Mr. Brownlow sat very

straight, upon the extreme edge of his chair, during the latter part of this recital.

"The poor lad!" he exclaimed; "but why have you not brought him with you?"

"I wished to talk with you alone about this plot. He does not know of it. But"—smilingly—"I believe he is now waiting in the coach at the door."

"At this door?" cried Mr. Brownlow. And without another word he rushed from the room.

In less than a minute he was back again, lugging Oliver in bodily and both laughing—yes, and shedding tears—at the same time.

Then after the jolliest of visits, Rose and Oliver took their leave for the present; but not before Mr. Brownlow had told Rose privately that he would turn his whole attention to the new conspiracy.

Nancy had promised to meet Rose on London Bridge, a few nights later, and Mr. Brownlow determined to be there also. In the meantime he made other plans for capturing the rogues.

## IV.  THE END OF EVIL DAYS

Now, unbeknown to poor Nancy, Fagin the thief had become suspicious of her loyalty, and had set a spy upon her heels. This spy was none other than Noah Claypole, the undertaker's apprentice, whom Oliver had so soundly thrashed. Noah had lately come to London to try his fortune in any underhand way that might arise. Now Fagin was always on the lookout for just such fellows as he. So they soon struck a bargain.

On the night when Nancy set forth to keep her appointment on the Bridge, Noah was kept busy darting from pillar to post, but all the time keeping her in sight. When she met Rose and Mr. Brownlow, the spy quickly slunk behind an abutment where he could hear every word of what she said. And you may be sure he lost no time in taking his story back to the thief.

Bill Sikes had just returned, in the early morning, from a house-breaking jaunt, and was as usual in an ugly mood. A word from Fagin about Nancy's defection set his brain on fire with hatred against the girl. He hastened to her room, and, disregarding all her appeals for mercy, struck her lifeless to the floor.

This murder proved the beginning of the end for all the gang. Mr. Brownlow had already set the police to work, and now offered a large personal reward for Sikes's arrest. The murderer was tracked in and about the city for several days, until he finally hung himself in endeavoring to escape from the roof of a house.

Horrible Fagin was captured at last, and for his share in this crime and his other wickednesses was condemned to death. A great popular clamor had been aroused against him, and he was to be hung without delay.

In the hope that the thief would throw some light upon Monks and some secret papers which Mr. Brownlow had traced, that gentleman took Oliver with him to the prison to see Fagin on his last night upon earth.

"Is the young gentleman to come, too, sir?" said the man whose duty it was to conduct them. "It's not a sight for children, sir."

"It is not indeed, my friend," rejoined Mr. Brownlow; "but my business with this man is intimately connected with him; and as this child has seen him in the full career of his success and villainy, I think it well—even at the cost of some pain and fear—that he should see him now."

These few words had been said apart, so as to be inaudible to Oliver. The man touched his hat; and glancing at Oliver with some curiosity, opened another gate, opposite to that by which they had entered, and led them on, through dark and winding ways, to the cell.

The condemned criminal was seated on his bed, rocking himself from side to side, with a countenance more like that of a snared beast than the face of a man. His mind was evidently wandering to his old life, for he continued to mutter, without appearing conscious of their presence otherwise than as a part of his vision.

"Good boy, Charley — well done!" — he mumbled. "Oliver too, ha! ha! ha! Oliver too—quite the gentleman now—quite the—take that boy away to bed!"

The jailer took the disengaged hand of Oliver, and, whispering to him not to be alarmed, looked on without speaking.

"Take him away to bed!" cried old Fagin. "Do you hear me, some of you? He has been the—the—somehow the cause of all this!"

"Fagin," said the jailer.

"That's me!" cried Fagin, falling, instantly, into the attitude of listening he had assumed upon his trial. "An old man, my Lord, a very old, old man!"

"Here," said the turnkey, laying his hand upon his breast to keep him down. "Here's somebody wants to see you, to ask you some questions, I suppose. Fagin, Fagin! Are you a man?"

"I sha'n't be one long," replied Fagin, looking up with a face retaining no human expression but rage and terror. "Strike them all dead! What right have they to butcher me?"

As he spoke he caught sight of Oliver and Mr. Brownlow. Shrinking to the farthest corner of the seat, he demanded to know what they wanted there.

"Steady," said the turnkey, still holding him down. "Now, sir, tell him what you want—quick if you please, for he grows worse as the time gets on."

"You have some papers," said Mr. Brownlow, advancing, "which were placed in your hands, for better security, by a man called Monks."

"It's all a lie together," replied the thief. "I haven't one—not one."

"For the love of God," said Mr. Brownlow, solemnly, "do not tell a lie now, upon the very verge of death; but tell me where they are. You know that Sikes is dead; and that there is no hope of any farther gain. Where are those papers?"

"Oliver," cried old Fagin, beckoning to him. "Here, here! Let me whisper to you."

"I am not afraid," said Oliver, in a firm voice, as he relinquished Mr. Brownlow's hand.

"The papers," said the thief, drawing him towards him, "are in a canvas bag, in a hole a little way up the chimney in the top front room. I want to talk to you, my dear. I want to talk to you."

"Yes, yes," returned Oliver. "Let me say a prayer. Do! Let me say one prayer. Say only one, upon your knees, with me, and we will talk till morning."

"Outside, outside," replied the thief, pushing the boy before him towards the door, and looking vacantly over his head. "Say I've gone to sleep—they'll believe you. You can get me out, if you take me so. Now then, now then!"

"Oh! God forgive this wretched man!" cried the boy, with a burst of tears.

"That's right, that's right," said old Fagin. "That'll help us on. This door first. If I shake and tremble, as we pass the gallows, don't you mind, but hurry on. Now, now, now!"

"Have you nothing else to ask him, sir?" inquired the turnkey.

"No other question," replied Mr. Brownlow. "If I hoped we could recall him to a sense of his position—"

"Nothing will do that, sir," replied the man, shaking his head. "You had better leave him."

The door of the cell opened and the attendants returned.

"Press on, press on," cried Fagin. "Softly, but not so slow. Faster, faster!"

The men laid hands upon him, and disengaging Oliver from his grasp, held him back. He struggled with the power of desperation for an

instant, and then sent up cry upon cry that pene-
trated even those massive walls and rang in
their ears until they reached the open yard.

And this—thought Oliver shudderingly—
was the last of the thief—the man from whose
clutches he had so narrowly escaped!

Noah Claypole turned state's evidence at this
time, and thus escaped the law. Dawkins, the
Artful Dodger, had been caught picking pockets
and was transported from the country. Charley
Bates was so unnerved by the fate of Nancy,
and the swift punishment of his companions, that
he reformed and became an honest, hard-working young man.

And, finally, what of Monks? He was shad-
owed and seized by Mr. Brownlow's agents, and
proved to be none other than the half-brother
of Oliver Twist! Their father was dead, but
he had left a will providing for the boy also.
And it was on this account that Monks had
wished to get him out of the way and had employed Fagin in trying to ruin the lad.

The papers were found, as Fagin had indi-
cated, and they not only cleared up Oliver's past
history, but proved his right to a share in a considerable family estate. Mr. Brownlow had
known Monk's father in their early days, and
now used this knowledge to wring a full confes-
sion from the villain.

Another strange secret came to light also, at this time. Rose Maylie was found to be a younger sister of Oliver's dead mother, and therefore the boy's own aunt.

"Not aunt!" cried Oliver, when he heard this amazing but delightful news; "I'll never call her aunt! Sister, my own dear sister, that something taught my heart to love so dearly from the first! Rose, dear darling Rose!"

And the two orphans, no longer alone but united and surrounded by loving friends, were clasped in each other's arms.

# THE STORY OF

# Smike and His Teacher

### I. HOW NICHOLAS NICKLEBY CAME TO DOTHEBOYS HALL

"EDUCATION. — At Mr. Wackford Squeers's Academy, Dotheboys Hall, at the delightful village of Dotheboys, near Greta Bridge in Yorkshire, Youth are boarded, clothed, booked, furnished with pocket-money, provided with all necessaries, instructed in all languages living and dead, mathematics, orthography, geometry, astronomy, trigonometry, the use of the globes, algebra, single stick (if required), writing, arithmetic, fortification, and every other branch of classical literature. Terms, twenty guineas per annum. No extras, no vacations, and diet unparalleled. Mr. Squeers is in town, and attends daily, from one till four, at the Saracen's Head, Snow Hill. N. B. An able assistant wanted. Annual salary £5. A Master of Arts would be preferred."

To Nicholas Nickleby, a young man of nineteen, who had come to London seeking his fortune, this advertisement in a daily paper seemed a godsend—that is, provided he could secure the

position referred to in the last two lines. It is
true the salary was not large; but he reflected
that his board and living would be included, and
that a young man of his education and ability
would be bound to rise. He even fancied himself, in a rosy-colored future, at the head of this
model school, Dotheboys Hall, in the delightful
village of Dotheboys, near Greta Bridge, in
Yorkshire.

But it would not do to sit dreaming. Some
one else might snap up this golden opportunity.
Nicholas brushed his clothes carefully and lost
no time in calling upon Mr. Squeers, at the
tavern called the Saracen's Head.

Mr. Squeers's appearance was not prepossess-
ing. He had but one eye which, while it was
unquestionably useful, was decidedly not orna-
mental, being of a greenish gray and in shape
resembling the fan-light of a street-door. The
blank side of his face was much wrinkled and
puckered up, which gave him a very sinister appearance, especially when he smiled, at which
times his expression bordered closely on the villainous. He was about two or three and fifty,
and a trifle below the middle size; and he wore a
white neckerchief with long ends, and a suit of
scholastic black.

Mr. Squeers was standing in a box by one of
the coffee-room fireplaces, fitted with one such

table as is usually seen in coffee-rooms. In a
corner of the seat was a very small deal trunk,
tied round with a scanty piece of cord; and on
the trunk was perched—his lace-up half-boots
and corduroy trousers dangling in the air—a
diminutive boy, with his shoulders drawn up to
his ears, and his hands planted on his knees, who
glanced timidly at the schoolmaster, from time
to time, with evident dread. Presently the boy
chanced to give a violent sneeze.

"Hallo, sir!" growled the schoolmaster, turning round. "What's that, sir?"

"Nothing, please, sir," replied the little boy.

"Nothing, sir!" exclaimed Mr. Squeers.

"Please, sir, I sneezed," rejoined the boy,
trembling till the little trunk shook under him.

"Oh! sneezed, did you?" retorted Mr.
Squeers. "Then what did you say 'nothing' for,
sir?"

In default of a better answer to this question,
the little boy screwed a couple of knuckles into
each of his eyes and began to cry; wherefore
Mr. Squeers knocked him off the trunk with a
blow on one side of his face, and knocked him
on again with a blow on the other.

"Wait till I get you down to Yorkshire, my
young gentleman," said Mr. Squeers, "and then
I'll give you the rest. Will you hold that noise,
sir?"

"Ye-ye-yes," sobbed the little boy, rubbing his face very hard.

"Then do so at once, sir," said Squeers. "Do you hear?"

The little boy rubbed his face harder, as if to keep the tears back; and, beyond alternately sniffing and choking, gave no farther vent to his emotions.

"Mr. Squeers," said the waiter, looking in at this juncture, "here's a gentleman asking for you at the bar."

"Show the gentleman in, Richard," replied Mr. Squeers, in a soft voice. "Put your hand-kerchief in your pocket, you little scoundrel!"

The schoolmaster had scarcely uttered these words in a fierce whisper, when the stranger entered. Affecting not to see him, Mr. Squeers feigned to be intent upon mending a pen, and offering benevolent advice to his youthful pupil.

"My dear child," said Mr. Squeers, "all people have their trials. This early trial of yours that is fit to make your little heart burst and your very eyes come out of your head with crying, what is it? Nothing; less than nothing. You are leaving your friends, but you will have a father in me, my dear, and a mother in Mrs. Squeers. At the delightful village of Dothe-boys, near Greta Bridge in Yorkshire, where youth are boarded, clothed, booked, washed, furnished with pocket-money, provided with all necessaries—"

"Mr. Squeers, I believe," said Nicholas Nickleby, as that worthy man stopped to cough.

"The same, sir. What can I do for you?"

"I came in answer to an advertisement in this morning's paper," said Nicholas. "I believe you desire an assistant."

"I do, sir," rejoined Mr. Squeers, coolly; "but if you are applying for the place, don't you think you're too young?"

"I hope not, sir, and I have a fair education. I could—"

"Could what?" interrupted the schoolmaster. "Could you lick the boys if they needed it?"

"I do not usually believe in that sort of punishment—" hesitated Nicholas.

"Could you do it?" urged Mr. Squeers.

"I think—if they needed it—I could lick anybody in your school," smiled Nicholas.

"Well, why don't you say so? I guess I had better take you. I've got to leave town at eight o'clock to-morrow morning, and haven't time to look around. So be on hand sharp!"

Nicholas thanked him and promised to be on hand.

The next day he was as good as his word, and reached the tavern a little in advance of the appointed hour.

He found Mr. Squeers sitting at breakfast, with the little boy before noticed, and four others who had turned up by some lucky chance since the interview of the previous day, ranged in a row on the opposite seat. Mr. Squeers had before him a small measure of coffee, a plate of hot toast, and a cold round of beef; but he was at that moment intent on preparing breakfast for the little boys.

"This is twopenn'orth of milk, is it, waiter?" said he, looking down into a large blue mug, and slanting it gently, so as to get an accurate view of the quantity of liquid contained in it.

"That's two-penn'orth, sir," replied the waiter.

"What a rare article milk is, to be sure, in London!" said Mr. Squeers, with a sigh. "Just fill that mug up with lukewarm water, William, will you?"

"To the wery top, sir?" inquired the waiter. "Why, the milk will be drownded."

"Never you mind that," replied Mr. Squeers. "Serve it right for being so dear! You ordered that thick bread and butter for three, did you?"

"Coming directly, sir."

"You needn't hurry yourself," said Squeers; "there's plenty of time. Conquer your passions, boys, and don't be eager after vittles." As he uttered this moral precept, Mr. Squeers took a large bite out of the cold beef, and recognized Nicholas.

"Sit down, Mr. Nickleby," said Squeers. "Here we are, a breakfasting, you see!"

Nicholas did *not* see that anybody was breakfasting except Mr. Squeers; but he bowed with all becoming reverence, and looked as cheerful as he could.

"Oh! that's the milk and water, is it, William?" said Squeers. "Very good; don't forget the bread and butter presently."

At this fresh mention of the bread and butter the five little boys looked very eager, and followed the waiter out with their eyes; meanwhile Mr. Squeers tasted the milk and water.

"Ah!" said that gentleman, smacking his lips, "here's richness! Think of the many beggars and orphans in the streets that would be glad of this, little boys. A shocking thing hunger is, isn't it, Mr. Nickleby?"

"Very shocking, sir," said Nicholas.

"When I say number one," pursued Mr. Squeers, putting the mug before the children, "the boy on the left hand nearest the window may take a drink; and when I say number two, the boy next him will go in, and so till we come to number five, which is the last boy. Are you ready?"

"Yes, sir," cried all the little boys with great eagerness.

"That's right," said Squeers, calmly getting on with his breakfast; "keep ready till I tell you to begin. Subdue your appetites, my dears, and you've conquered human nature. This is the way we inculcate strength of mind, Mr. Nickleby," said the schoolmaster, turning to Nicholas, and speaking with his mouth very full of beef and toast.

Nicholas murmured something—he knew not what—in reply; and the little boys dividing their gaze between the mug, the bread and butter (which had by this time arrived), and every morsel which Mr. Squeers took into his mouth, remained with strained eyes in torments of expectation.

"Thank God for a good breakfast," said Squeers when he had finished. "Number one may take a drink."

Number one seized the mug ravenously, and had just drunk enough to make him wish for more, when Mr. Squeers gave the signal for number two, who gave up at the same interesting moment to number three; and the process was repeated until the milk and water terminated with number five.

"And now," said the schoolmaster, dividing the bread and butter for three into as many portions as there were children, "you had better look sharp with your breakfast, for the horn will blow in a minute or two, and then every boy leaves off."

Permission being thus given to fall to, the boys began to eat voraciously and in desperate haste; while the schoolmaster (who was in high good-humor after his meal) picked his teeth with a fork, and looked smilingly on. In a very short time the horn was heard.

"I thought it wouldn't be long," said Squeers, jumping up and producing a little basket from under the seat; "put what you haven't had time to eat in here, boys! You'll want it on the road!"

Nicholas was considerably startled by these very economical arrangements; but he had no time to reflect upon them, for the little boys had to be got up to the top of the coach, and this task was in his department. But soon they were all stowed away, and the coach started off with a flourish.

The journey proved long and hard, however. They were detained several times by the bad roads and inclement weather, so that it was not until nightfall of the second day that they reached their destination.

"Jump out," said Squeers. "Hallo there! come and put this horse up. Be quick will you!"

While the schoolmaster was uttering these and

other impatient cries, Nicholas had time to observe that the school was a long cold-looking house, one story high, with a few straggling outbuildings behind, and a barn and stable adjoining. After the lapse of a minute or two, the noise of somebody unlocking the yard-gate was heard, and presently a tall, lean boy, with a lantern in his hand, issued forth.

"Is that you, Smike?" cried Squeers.

"Yes, sir," replied the boy.

"Then why the devil didn't you come before?"

"Please, sir, I fell asleep over the fire," answered Smike, with humility.

"Fire! what fire? Where's there a fire?" demanded the schoolmaster, sharply.

"Only in the kitchen, sir," replied the boy. "Missus said, as I was sitting up, I might go in there for a warm."

"Your Missus is a fool," retorted Squeers. "You'd have been a deuced deal more wakeful in the cold, I'll engage."

By this time Mr. Squeers had dismounted; and after ordering the boy to see to the pony, and to take care that he hadn't any more corn that night, he told Nicholas to wait at the front door a minute while he went round and let him in.

A host of unpleasant misgivings, which had been crowding upon Nicholas during the whole journey, thronged into his mind with redoubled force when he was left alone. And as he looked up at the dreary house and dark windows, and upon the wild country road, covered with snow, he felt a depression of heart and spirit which he had never experienced before.

Presently he was ushered into a cheerless-looking parlor where stood a large, angular woman about half a head taller than Mr. Squeers.

"This is the new young man, my dear," said that gentleman.

"Oh," replied Mrs. Squeers, nodding her head at Nicholas, and eyeing him coldly from top to toe.

"He'll take a meal with us to-night," said Squeers, "and go among the boys to-morrow morning. You can give him a shakedown here, tonight, can't you?"

"We must manage it somehow," replied the lady. "You don't much mind how you sleep, I suppose, sir?"

"No, indeed," replied Nicholas, "I am not particular."

"That's lucky," said Mrs. Squeers. And as the lady's humor was considered to lie chiefly in retort, Mr. Squeers laughed heartily, and seemed to expect that Nicholas should do the same.

After some conversation between the master

and mistress relative to the success of Mr. Squeers's trip, and the people who had paid, and the people who had made default in payment, a young servant girl brought in a Yorkshire pie and some cold beef, which being set upon the table, the boy Smike appeared with a jug of ale.

Mr. Squeers was emptying his great-coat pockets of letters to different boys, and other small documents, which he had brought down in them. The boy glanced, with an anxious and timid expression, at the papers, as if with a sickly hope that one among them might relate to him. The look was a very painful one, and went to Nicholas's heart at once, for it told a long and very sad history.

It induced him to consider the boy more attentively, and he was surprised to observe the extraordinary mixture of garments which formed his dress. Although he could not have been less than eighteen or nineteen years old, and was tall for that age, he wore a skeleton suit, such as is usually put upon very little boys, and which, though most absurdly short in the arms and legs, was quite wide enough for his thin body. In order that the lower part of his legs might be in perfect keeping with this singular dress, he had a very large pair of boots, originally made for tops, which might have been once worn by some stout farmer, but were now too patched and tattered for a beggar. He was lame; and as he feigned to be busy in arranging the table, he glanced at the letters with a look so keen, and yet so dispirited and hopeless, that Nicholas could hardly bear to watch him.

"What are you bothering about there, Smike?" cried Mrs. Squeers; "let the things alone, can't you?"

"Eh!" said Squeers, looking up. "Oh! it's you, is it?"

"Yes, sir," replied the youth, pressing his hands together, as though to control, by force, the nervous wandering of his fingers; "Is there—"

"Well!" said Squeers.

"Have you—did anybody—has nothing been heard—about me?"

"Devil a bit," replied Squeers, testily.

The lad withdrew his eyes, and, putting his hand to his face, moved towards the door.

"Not a word," resumed Squeers, "and never will be. Now, this is a pretty sort of thing, isn't it, that you should have been left here all these years, and no money paid after the first six—nor no notice taken, nor no clue to be got who you belong to? It's a pretty sort of thing that I should have to feed a great fellow like you, and never hope to get one penny for it, isn't it?"

The boy put his hand to his head as if he were making an effort to recollect something, and then, looking vacantly at his questioner, gradually broke into a smile, and limped away.

"I'll tell you what, Squeers," remarked his wife, as the door closed, "I think that young chap's turning silly."

"I hope not," said the schoolmaster; "for he's a handy fellow out-of-doors, and worth his meat and drink anyway. I should think he'd have wit enough for us, though, if he was."

Supper being over, Mr. Squeers yawned fearfully and was of opinion that it was high time to go to bed. Upon this, Mrs. Squeers and a servant dragged in a small straw mattress and a couple blankets, and arranged them into a couch for Nicholas.

"We'll put you into a regular bedroom with the boys to-morrow, Nickleby," said Squeers. "Good-night. Seven o'clock, in the morning, mind."

The next morning, when Nicholas appeared in the main room, he found Mrs. Squeers very much distressed.

"I can't find the school spoon," she said.

"Never mind it, my dear," observed Squeers in a soothing manner; "it's of no consequence."

"No consequence! why, how you talk!" retorted Mrs. Squeers, sharply; "isn't it brimstone morning?"

"I forgot, my dear," rejoined Squeers; "yes, it certainly is. We purify the boys' bloods now and then, Nickleby."

"Purify fiddlesticks' ends!" said his lady. "Don't think, young man, that we go to the expense of brimstone and molasses, just to purify them; because if you think we carry on the business in that way, you'll find yourself mistaken, and so I tell you plainly."

"My dear," said Squeers, frowning. "Hem!"

"Oh! nonsense," rejoined Mrs. Squeers. "If the young man comes to be a teacher here, let him understand, at once, that we don't want any foolery about the boys. They have the brimstone and treacle, partly because if they hadn't something or other in the way of medicine they'd be always ailing and giving a world of trouble, and partly because it spoils their appetites and comes cheaper than breakfast and dinner. So it does them good and us good at the same time, and that's fair enough, I'm sure."

A vast deal of searching and rummaging ensued, and it proving fruitless, Smike was called in, and pushed by Mrs. Squeers and boxed by Mr. Squeers; which course of treatment brightening his intellects, enabled him to suggest that possibly Mrs. Squeers might have the spoon in her pocket—as indeed turned out to be the case. But as Mrs. Squeers had previously protested that she was quite certain she had not got it, Smike received another box on the ear for presuming to contradict his mistress; so that he gained nothing of advantage by his idea.

"But come," said Squeers, "let's go to the schoolroom; and lend me a hand with my school-coat, will you?"

Nicholas assisted his master to put on an old shooting-jacket; and Squeers, arming himself with his cane, led the way across a yard, to a door in the rear of the house.

"There," said the schoolmaster, as they stepped in together; "this is our shop, Nickleby!"

It was such a crowded scene, and there were so many objects to attract attention, that, at first, Nicholas stared about him, really without seeing anything at all. By degrees, however, the place resolved itself into a bare and dirty room, with a couple of windows, stopped up with old copybooks and paper. There were two rickety desks, cut and notched, and inked in every possible way; two or three forms; a detached desk for Squeers, and another for his assistant. The ceiling was supported, like that of a barn, by crossbeams and rafters, and the walls were so stained and discolored that it was impossible to tell whether they had ever been touched with paint or whitewash.

But the pupils! How the last faint traces of hope, the remotest glimmering of any good to be derived from his efforts in this den, faded from the mind of Nicholas as he looked in dismay around! Pale and haggard faces, lank and bony figures, children with the countenances of old men, boys of stunted growth, and others whose long, meagre legs would hardly bear their stooping bodies, all crowded on the view together.

And yet this scene, painful as it was, had its grotesque features. Mrs. Squeers stood at one of the desks, presiding over an immense basin of brimstone and treacle, of which delicious compound she administered a large instalment to each boy in succession, using for the purpose a common wooden spoon, which might have been originally manufactured for some gigantic top, and which widened every young gentleman's mouth considerably; they being all obliged, under heavy penalties, to take in the whole of the bowl at a gulp.

"Now," said Squeers, giving the desk a great rap with his cane which made half the little boys nearly jump out of their boots, "is that physicking over?"

"Just over," said Mrs. Squeers, choking the last boy in her hurry, and tapping the crown of his head with the wooden spoon to restore him. "Here, you Smike; take away now. Look sharp!"

Smike shuffled out with the basin, and Mrs. Squeers having called up a little boy with a curly head and wiped her hands upon it, hurried out after him into a species of washhouse, where there was a small fire and a large kettle, together with a number of little wooden bowls which were arranged upon a board. Into these bowls Mrs. Squeers, assisted by the hungry servant, poured a brown composition, which looked like diluted pincushions without the covers, and was called porridge. A minute wedge of brown bread was inserted in each bowl, and when they had eaten their porridge by means of the bread, the boys ate the bread itself, and had finished their breakfast; whereupon Mr. Squeers said, in a solemn voice, "For what we have received, may the Lord make us truly thankful!"—and went away to his own.

Nicholas filled his stomach with a bowl of porridge, for much the same reason which induces some savages to swallow earth—lest they should be hungry when there is nothing to eat. Having disposed of a slice of bread and butter, allotted to him in virtue of his office, he sat himself down to wait for school-time.

He could not but observe how silent and sad

the boys all seemed to be. There was none of the noise and clamor of a schoolroom; none of its boisterous play or hearty mirth. The children sat crouching and shivering together, and seemed to lack the spirit to move about. The only pupil who seemed at all playful was Master Squeers, son of the master, and as his chief amusement was to tread upon the other boys' toes in his new boots, his flow of spirits was rather disagreeable than otherwise.

After some half-hour's delay Mr. Squeers reappeared, and the boys took their places and their books, of which latter there might be about one to eight learners. A few minutes having elapsed, during which Mr. Squeers looked very profound, as if he had a perfect apprehension of what was inside all the books, and could say every word of their contents by heart if he only chose to take the trouble, that gentleman called up the first class.

Obedient to this summons there ranged themselves in front of the schoolmaster's desk half a dozen scarecrows, out at knees and elbows, one of whom placed a torn and filthy book beneath his learned eye.

"This is the first class in English spelling and philosophy, Nickleby," said Squeers, beckoning Nicholas to stand beside him. "We'll get up a

Latin one, and hand that over to you. Now, then, where's the first boy?"

"Please, sir, he's cleaning the back parlor window," said the temporary head of the class.

"So he is, to be sure," rejoined Squeers. "We go upon the practical mode of teaching, Nickleby; the regular education system. C-l-e-a-n, clean, verb active, to make bright, to scour. When the boy knows this out of book, he goes and does it. Second boy, what's a horse?"

"A beast, sir," replied the boy.

"So it is," said Squeers, "and as you're perfect in that, go and look after *my* horse, and rub him down well, or I'll rub you down. The rest of the class go and draw water till somebody tells you to leave off, for it's washing-day tomorrow, and they want the coppers filled."

So saying, he dismissed the first class to their experiments in practical philosophy, and eyed Nicholas with a look, half cunning and half doubtful, as if he were not altogether certain what he might think of him by this time.

"That's the way we do it, Nickleby," he said, after a pause.

Nicholas shrugged his shoulders in a manner that was scarcely perceptible, and said he saw it was.

"And a very good way it is, too," said

Squeers. "Now, just take them fourteen little boys and hear them some reading, because, you know, you must begin to be useful. Idling about here won't do."

Mr. Squeers said this, as if it had suddenly occurred to him, either that he must not say too much to his assistant, or that his assistant did not say enough to him in praise of the establishment. The children were arranged in a semicircle round the new master, and he was soon listening to their dull, drawling recital of those stories of interest which are to be found in the spelling books.

In this exciting occupation the morning lagged heavily on. At one o'clock the boys, having previously had their appetites thoroughly taken away by stir-about and potatoes, sat down in the kitchen to some hard salt beef, of which Nicholas was graciously permitted to take his portion to his own solitary desk, to eat it there in peace. After this, there was another hour of crouching in the schoolroom and shivering with cold; and this was a fair sample of the school day at Dotheboys Hall.

There was a small stove in the corner of the room, and by it Nicholas sat down, when the school was dismissed, so heavy-hearted that it seemed to him as though every bit of joy had gone out of the world. The cruelty and coarseness of Squeers were revolting, and yet Nicholas did not know how to resent it or which way to turn. He had cast his lot here, and here he must abide.

As he was absorbed in these meditations, he all at once encountered the upturned face of Smike, who was on his knees before the stove, picking a few stray cinders from the hearth and planting them on the fire. He had paused to steal a look at Nicholas, and when he saw that he was observed, shrank back, as if expecting a blow.

"You need not fear me," said Nicholas, kindly. "Are you cold?"

"N-n-o."

"You are shivering."

"I am not cold," replied Smike, quickly. "I am used to it."

There was such an obvious fear of giving offence in his manner, and he was such a timid, broken-spirited creature, that Nicholas could not help exclaiming, "Poor fellow!"

If he had struck the drudge, he would have slunk away without a word. But now he burst into tears.

"Oh, dear, oh, dear!" he cried, covering his face with his cracked and horny hands. "My heart will break. It will, it will!"

"Hush!" said Nicholas, laying his hand upon

his shoulder. "Be a man; you are nearly one by years, God help you."

"By years!" cried Smike. "Oh dear, dear, how many of them! How many of them since I was a little child, younger than any that are here now! Where are they all?"

"Whom do you speak of?" inquired Nicholas, wishing to rouse the poor, half-witted creature to reason. "Tell me."

"My friends," he replied, "myself—my—oh! what sufferings mine have been!"

"There is always hope," said Nicholas; he knew not what to say.

"No," rejoined the other, "no; none for me. Do you remember the boy that died here?"

"I was not here, you know," said Nicholas, gently; "but what of him?"

"Why," replied the youth, drawing closer to his questioner's side, "I was with him at night, and when it was all silent he cried no more for friends he wished to come and sit with him, but began to see faces round his bed that came from home; he said they smiled, and talked to him; and he died at last lifting his head to kiss them. Do you hear?"

"Yes, yes," rejoined Nicholas.

"What faces will smile on me when I die!" cried his companion, shivering. "Who will talk to me in those long nights! They cannot come from home; they would frighten me, if they did, for I don't know what it is, and shouldn't know them. Pain and fear, pain and fear for me, alive or dead. No hope, no hope!"

The bell rang to bed, and the boy, subsiding at the sound into his usual listless state, crept away as if anxious to avoid notice. It was with a heavy heart that Nicholas soon afterwards— no, not retired; there was no retirement there— followed to his dirty and crowded dormitory.

## II.   HOW SMIKE WENT AWAY FROM DOTHEBOYS HALL

Nicholas Nickleby was of a naturally optimistic temper, however, and he lost as little time as possible brooding over his difficulties. Instead he began at once to try to make the school something more than a farce. He arranged a few regular lessons for the boys, and he treated the poor, half-starved pupils with such gentleness and sympathy that they passed from dumb amazement at the first to blind devotion. Indeed there was not one of them who would not have laid down cheerfully and let him walk over his body; and the most devoted of them all was Smike.

Nicholas was the one ray of sunlight that had ever come into this wretched creature's life. And in return, Smike now followed him to and fro, with an ever restless desire to serve or help him; anticipating such little wants as his humble ability could supply, and content only to be near him. He would sit beside him for hours, looking patiently into his face; and a word would brighten up his careworn visage, and call into it a passing gleam, even of happiness. He was an altered being; he had an object now; and that object, was, to show his attachment to the only person—that person a stranger—who had treated him, not to say with kindness, but like a human creature.

Needless to say, Squeers speedily took a dislike to Nicholas. He knew of the scarcely concealed disdain with which his assistant regarded his methods. Squeers was jealous, also, of the influence which Nicholas had so soon acquired with the boys. Smike's slavish affection was speedily discovered, and the crafty master was mean enough to strike at Nicholas through him.

Upon this poor being all the spleen and ill-humor that could not be vented on Nicholas were unceasingly bestowed. Drudgery would have been nothing—Smike was well used to that. Buffetings inflicted without cause would have been equally a matter of course; for to them also

he had served a long and weary apprenticeship;
but it was no sooner observed that he had become
attached to Nicholas, than stripes and blows,
stripes and blows, morning, noon, and night,
were his only portion.   Nicholas saw it, and
ground his teeth at every repetition of the sav-
age and cowardly attack.   But at present he
saw no way to aid the boy, for a protest would
mean his own dismissal, and the lot of Smike
and the others would become that much harder.

One day, after especially harsh treatment, the
boy sat huddled in a dark corner by himself,
sobbing as though his heart would break.   The
room was dark and deserted, when Nicholas
entered, but he heard the sound of weeping
and went over and laid his hand on the drudge's
head.

"Do not, for God's sake!" said Nicholas, in
an agitated voice; "I cannot bear to see you."

"They are more hard with me than ever,"
sobbed the boy.

"I know it," rejoined Nicholas.   "They are."

"But for you," said the outcast, "I should
die.   They would kill me, they would; I know
they would."

"You will do better, poor fellow," replied
Nicholas, shaking his head mournfully, "when
I am gone."

"Gone!" cried the other, looking intently in his face.

"Softly!" rejoined Nicholas. "Yes."

"Are you going?" demanded the boy, in an earnest whisper.

"I cannot say," replied Nicholas. "I was speaking more to my own thoughts than to you."

"Tell me," said the boy, imploringly, "oh, do tell me, *will* you go—*will* you?"

"I shall be driven to that at last!" said Nicholas. "The world is before me, after all."

"Tell me," urged Smike, "is the world as bad and dismal as this place?"

"Heaven forbid," replied Nicholas, pursuing the train of his own thoughts; "Its hardest, coarsest toil were happiness to this."

"Should I ever meet you there?" demanded the boy, speaking with unusual wildness.

"Yes," replied Nicholas, willing to soothe him.

"No, no!" said the other, clasping him by the hand. "Should I—should I—tell me that again! Say I should be sure to find you!"

"You would," replied Nicholas, with the same humane intention, "and I would help and aid you, and not bring fresh sorrow on you as I have done here."

The boy caught both the young man's hands passionately in his, and hugging them to his breast, uttered a few broken sounds which were unintelligible. Squeers entered, at the moment, and he shrank back into his old corner.

The next morning—a cold, gray day in January—Nicholas was awakened by hearing the voice of Squeers roughly demanding, "Where's that Smike?"

Nicholas looked over in the corner where the boy usually slept, but it was vacant; so he made no answer.

"Smike!" shouted Squeers.

"Do you want your head broke in a fresh place, Smike?" demanded his amiable lady, in the same key.

Still there was no reply, and still Nicholas stared about him, as did the greater part of the boys, who were by this time aroused.

"Confound his impudence!" muttered Squeers, rapping the stair-rail impatiently with his cane. "Nickleby!"

"Well, sir."

"Send that obstinate scoundrel down; don't you hear me calling?"

"He is not here, sir," replied Nicholas.

"Don't tell me a lie," retorted the schoolmaster. "He is."

"He is not," retorted Nicholas, angrily. "Don't tell me one."

"We shall soon see that," said Squeers, rushing upstairs. "I'll find him, I warrant you."

With which assurance Mr. Squeers bounced into the dormitory, and, swinging his cane in the air ready for a blow, darted into the corner. The cane descended harmlessly upon the ground. There was nobody there.

"What does this mean?" said Squeers, turning round. "Where have you hid him?"

"I have seen nothing of him since last night," replied Nicholas.

"Come," blustered Squeers, "you won't save him this way. Where is he?"

"At the bottom of the nearest pond, for aught I know," rejoined Nicholas, in a low voice, and fixing his eyes full on the master's face.

"Confound you, what do you mean by that?" retorted Squeers. Without waiting for a reply, he inquired of the boys whether any one among them knew anything of their missing schoolmate.

There was a general hum of anxious denial, in the midst of which one shrill voice was heard to say (as, indeed, everybody thought):

"Please, sir, I think Smike's run away, sir."

"Ha!" cried Squeers, turning sharp round. "Who said that?"

And, pouncing suddenly, he seized a small urchin, who was rewarded for his suggestions so soundly that he howled with pain.

"There," said Squeers. "Now if any other boy thinks Smike has run away, I shall be glad to have a talk with him."

There was, of course, a profound silence, during which Nicholas showed his disgust as plainly as looks could show it.

"Well, Nickleby," said Squeers, eyeing him maliciously. "*You* think he has run away, I suppose?"

"I think it extremely likely," replied Nicholas, in a quiet manner.

"Oh, you do, do you?" sneered Squeers. "Maybe you know he has?"

"I know nothing of the kind."

"He didn't tell you he was going, I suppose, did he?" continued Squeers.

"He did not," replied Nicholas; "I am very glad he did not, for it would then have been my duty to have warned you in time."

"Which no doubt you would have been devilish sorry to do," said Squeers, in a taunting fashion.

"I should indeed," replied Nicholas.

Meanwhile Mrs. Squeers, who had been hunting elsewhere for the boy, bustled in with great excitement.

"He is off!" said she. "The cow-house and stable are locked up, so he can't be there; and he's not downstairs anywhere, for the girl has looked. He must have gone York way, and by a public road too."

"Why must he?" inquired Squeers.

"Stupid!" said Mrs. Squeers, angrily. "He hadn't any money had he?"

"Never had a penny of his own in his whole life, that I know of," replied Squeers.

'To be sure," rejoined Mrs. Squeers, "and he didn't take anything to eat with him; that I'll answer for. So, of course, he must beg his way, and he could do that nowhere but on the public road."

"That's true," exclaimed Squeers, clapping his hands.

"True! Yes; but you would never have thought of it, for all that, if I hadn't said so," replied his wife. "Now, if you take the chaise and go one road, and I borrow Swallow's chaise and go the other, what with keeping our eyes open and asking questions, one or other of us is pretty certain to lay hold of him."

The worthy lady's plan was put into action without delay; while Nicholas remained behind in a tumult of anxiety. He realized the bitter consequences of Smike's rash act. The boy was liable to freeze or starve to death on the roadside—which could not, perhaps, be much worse than to fall again into the clutches of Mr. and Mrs. Squeers.

All that day there was no tidings of the runaway. But at daybreak the second morning the sound of wheels was heard. Nicholas hardly dared to look out of the window; but he did so, and the very first object that met his eyes was the wretched Smike: so bedabbled with mud and rain, so haggard and worn and wild, that, but for his garments being such as no scarecrow was ever seen to wear, he might have been doubtful, even then, of his identity.

"Lift him out," said Squeers, after he had literally feasted his eyes, in silence, upon the culprit. "Bring him in; bring him in!"

Smike, to all appearance more dead than alive, was brought into the house and securely locked up in a cellar until such time as Mr. Squeers should deem it expedient to operate upon him in presence of the assembled school.

After a hasty breakfast of very thin porridge, the boys were summoned to the schoolroom by resounding whacks on the desk from an ugly-looking whip in the hands of the master.

"Is every boy here?" asked Squeers, in a tremendous voice.

Every boy was there, but every boy was afraid to speak; so Squeers glared along the lines to assure himself; and every eye dropped, and every head cowered down, as he did so.

"Each boy keep his place," said Squeers, administering his favorite blow to the desk, and regarding with gloomy satisfaction the universal start which it never failed to occasion. "Nickleby! to your desk, sir!"

It was remarked by more than one small observer that there was a very curious and unusual expression in the usher's face; but he took his seat without opening his lips in reply. Squeers, casting a triumphant glance at his assistant and a scowl on the boys, left the room, and shortly afterwards returned, dragging Smike by the collar.

In any other place the appearance of the wretched, jaded, spiritless object would have occasioned a murmur of compassion and remonstrance. It had some effect, even there; for the lookers-on moved uneasily in their seats, and a few of the boldest ventured to steal looks at each other, expressive of indignation and pity.

They were lost on Squeers, however, whose gaze was fastened on the luckless Smike, as he inquired, according to custom in such cases, whether he had anything to say for himself.

"Nothing, I suppose?" said Squeers, with a diabolical grin.

Smike glanced round, and his eye rested, for an instant, on Nicholas, as if he had expected him to intercede; but his look was riveted on his desk.

"Have you anything to say?" demanded Squeers again, giving his right arm two or three flourishes to try its power and suppleness. "Stand a little out of the way, Mrs. Squeers, my dear; I've hardly got room enough."

"Spare me, sir!" cried Smike.

"Oh! that's all, is it?" said Squeers. "Yes, I'll flog you within an inch of your life, and spare you that."

"Ha, ha, ha," laughed Mrs. Squeers, "that's a good 'un!"

"I was driven to do it," said Smike, faintly, and casting another imploring look about him.

"Driven to do it, were you?" said Squeers. "Oh! it wasn't your fault; it was mine, I suppose—eh?"

Then he caught the boy firmly in his grip. One desperate cut had fallen on his body—he was wincing from the lash and uttering a scream of pain—it was raised again, and again about to fall—when Nicholas Nickleby, suddenly starting up, cried *"Stop!"* in a voice that made the rafters ring.

"Who cried stop?" said Squeers, turning savagely round.

"I," said Nicholas, stepping forward. "This must not go on."

"Must not go on!" cried Squeers, almost in a shriek.

*"No!"* thundered Nicholas.

Aghast at the boldness of this interference, Squeers released his hold of Smike, and, falling back a pace or two, gazed upon Nicholas with looks that were positively frightful.

"I say *must not!*" repeated Nicholas, nothing daunted; *"shall not!* I will prevent it!"

Squeers continued to gaze upon him, with his eyes starting out of his head; but astonishment had actually, for the moment, bereft him of speech.

"You have disregarded all my quiet interference in the miserable lad's behalf," said Nicholas; "you have returned no answer to the letter in which I begged forgiveness for him, and offered to be responsible that he would remain quietly here. Don't blame me for this public interference. You have brought it upon yourself; not I."

"Sit down, beggar!" screamed Squeers, almost beside himself with rage, and seizing Smike as he spoke.

"Wretch," rejoined Nicholas, fiercely, "touch him at your peril! I will not stand by, and see it done. My blood is up, and I have the strength of ten such men as you. Look to yourself, for by Heaven I will not spare you, if you drive me on!"

"Stand back," cried Squeers, brandishing his weapon.

"I have a long series of insults to avenge," said Nicholas, flushed with passion; "and my indignation is aggravated by the cruelties of this foul den.  Have a care; for if you rouse me farther, the consequences shall fall heavily upon your own head!"

He had scarcely spoken, when Squeers, in a violent outbreak of wrath, struck him a blow across the face which raised up a bar of livid flesh as it was inflicted.  Smarting with the agony of the blow, and concentrating into that one moment all his feelings of rage and scorn, Nicholas sprang upon him, wrested the weapon from his hand, and pinning him by the throat, beat the ruffian till he roared for mercy.

Then Nicholas left the astounded boys and the crestfallen master, and stalked out of the room. He looked anxiously around for Smike, as he closed the door, but he was nowhere to be seen.

There was nothing left for him to do.  He must face the world again; but *anything*—he told himself—would be better than this.  So he packed up a few clothes in a small valise, and, finding that nobody offered to oppose him he marched boldly out by the front door and struck into the road which led to Greta Bridge.

He did not travel far that day, as there had

been a heavy fall of snow which made the way
toilsome and hard to find.  He lay, that night,
at a cottage, where beds were let at a cheap
rate to the more humble class of travellers; and,
rising betimes next morning, made his way before night to Boroughbridge.  Passing through
that town in search of some cheap resting-place,
he stumbled upon an empty barn within a couple
of hundred yards of the roadside; in a warm
corner of which he stretched his weary limbs,
and soon fell asleep.

When he awoke next morning, and tried to
recollect his dreams, which had been all connected with his recent sojourn at Dotheboys
Hall, he sat up, rubbed his eyes, and stared—
not with the most composed countenance possible—at some motionless object which seemed
to be stationed within a few yards in front of
him.

"Strange!" cried Nicholas; "can this be
some lingering creation of the visions that have
scarcely left me!  It cannot be real— and yet
I—I am awake!  Smike!"

The form moved, rose, advanced and dropped
upon his knees at his feet.  It was Smike indeed.

"Why do you kneel to me?" said Nicholas,
hastily raising him.

"To go with you—anywhere—everywhere—
to the world's end!" replied Smike, clinging to

his hand. "Let me, oh, do let me! You are my home—my kind friend—take me with you, pray!"

"I am a friend who can do little for you," said Nicholas, kindly. "How came you here?"

He had followed him, it seemed; had never lost sight of him all the way; had watched while he slept, and when he halted for refreshment; and had feared to appear before, lest he should be sent back. He had not intended to appear now, but Nicholas had awakened more suddenly than he looked for, and he had had no time to conceal himself.

"Poor fellow!" said Nicholas, "your hard fate denies you any friend but one, and he is nearly as poor and helpless as yourself."

"May I—may I go with you?" asked Smike, timidly. "I will be your faithful, hard-working servant, I will, indeed. I want no clothes," added the poor creature, drawing his rags together; "these will do very well. I only want to be near you."

"And you shall," cried Nicholas. "And the world shall deal by you as it does by me, till one or both of us shall quit it for a better. Come!"

With these words he strapped his valise on his shoulders, and, taking his stick in one hand, extended the other to the delighted boy; and so they passed out of the old barn together.

And in the days to come—through thick and thin— Smike and Nicholas fought their battles together—and *won!*

# THE STORY OF

# Little Nell

## I. IN THE OLD CURIOSITY SHOP

IT was a queer home for a child—this place
where Little Nell lived with her grandfather. He was a dealer in all sorts of
curious old things: suits of mail which stood
like ghosts in armor here and there; fantastic
carved table and chairs; rusty weapons of various kinds; distorted figures in china and wood
and iron. And, amid it all, the oldest thing in
the shop seemed to be the little old man with the
long gray hair.

The only bit of youth was Nell herself; and
yet she had a strange intermingling of dignity
and responsibility, in spite of her small figure
and childish ways. Her fourteen yours of life
had left her undecided between childhood and
girlhood. She had not begun to grow up; and
yet she was an orphan, accustomed to doing
everything for herself.

Her grandfather tried in his way to take care
of her, for he loved her dearly. But between
the tending of his shop and the mysterious journeys which he made night after night, the child
was often sent upon strange errands or left

alone in the old house. And at all times it was she who took care of him. But the old man did not see that this lonely life was putting lines of sorrow into her face. To him she was still the child of yesterday, care-free and happy.

She had been happy once. She had gone singing through the dim rooms, and moving with gay step among their dusty treasures, making them older by her young life, and sterner and more grim by her cheerful presence. But now the chambers were cold and gloomy, and when she left her own little room to while away the tedious hours, and sat in one of them, she was still and motionless as their inanimate occupants, and had no heart to startle the echoes—hoarse from their long silence—with her voice.

In one of these rooms was a window looking into the street, where the child sat, many and many a long evening, and often far into the night, alone and thoughtful. None are so anxious as those who watch and wait; and at these times mournful fancies came flocking on her mind in crowds.

She knew instinctively that her grandfather was hiding something from her. What it was she could not guess; but these regular journeys at night, while she watched and waited, left him only the more fretful and careworn. He seemed to have a constant fever for something;

yet all he would say was that he would some day leave her a fortune. Meanwhile he had fallen into the clutches of Quilp a terrible dwarf, who had lent him money from time to time, until the entire contents of the shop were mortgaged. So it is not strange that Little Nell should have mournful thoughts.

When the night had worn away, the child would close the window and even smile, with the first dawn of light, at her night-time fears. Then after praying earnestly for her grandfather and the restoring of their former happy days, she would unlatch the door for him and fall into a troubled sleep.

One night the old man said that he would not leave home. The child's face lit up at the news, but became grave again when she saw how worried he looked.

"You took my note safely to Mr. Quilp, you say?" he asked fretfully. "What did he tell you, Nell?"

"Exactly what I told you, dear grandfather, indeed."

"True," said the old man, faintly. "Yes. But tell me again, Nell. My head fails me. What was it that he told you? Nothing more than that he would see me to-morrow or next day? That was in the note."

"Nothing more," said the child. "Shall I go

to him again to-morrow, dear grandfather? Very early? I will be there and back before breakfast."

The old man shook his head and, sighing mournfully, drew her towards him.

" 'Twould be no use, my dear, no earthly use. But if he deserts me, Nell, at this moment— if he deserts me, now, when I should, with his assistance, be recompensed for all the time and money I have lost and all the agony of mind I have undergone, which makes me what you see, I am ruined and worse,—far worse than that— I have ruined you, for whom I ventured all. If we are beggars—!"

"What if we are?" said the child, boldly. "Let us be beggars and be happy."

"Beggars—and happy!" said the old man. "Poor child!"

"Dear grandfather," cried the girl with an energy which shone in her flushed face, trembling voice, and impassioned gesture, "I am not a child in that I think, but even if I am, oh, hear me pray that we may beg, or work in open roads or fields, to earn a scanty living, rather than live as we do now."

"Nelly!" said the old man.

"Yes, yes, rather than live as we do now," the child repeated more earnestly than before. "If you are sorrowful, let me know why and be sorrowful too; if you waste away and are paler and weaker every day, let me be your nurse and try to comfort you. If you are poor, let us be poor together; but let me be with you, do let me be with you; do not let me see such change and not know why, or I shall break my heart."

The child's voice was lost in sobs, as she clasped her arms about the old man's neck; nor did she weep alone.

These were not words for other ears, nor was it a scene for other eyes. And yet other ears and eyes were there and greedily taking in all that passed, and moreover they were the ears and eyes of no less a person than Mr. Daniel Quilp, who, having entered unseen when the child first placed herself at the old man's side, stood looking on with his accustomed grin. Standing, however, being tiresome, and the dwarf being one of that kind of persons who usually make themselves at home, he soon cast his eyes upon a chair, into which he skipped with uncommon agility, and perching himself on the back with his feet upon the seat, was thus enabled to look on and listen with greater comfort to himself, besides gratifying at the same time that taste for doing something fantastic and monkey-like, which on all occasions had strong possession of him. Here, then, he sat, one leg cocked carelessly over the other, his chin resting on the palm of his hand, his head turned a little to one side, and his ugly features twisted into a complacent grimace. And in this position the old man, happening in course of time to look that way, chanced to see him.

The child uttered a suppressed shriek on beholding this figure; in their first surprise both she and the old man, not knowing what to say, and half doubting its reality, looked shrinkingly at it. Not at all disconcerted by this reception, Daniel Quilp preserved the same attitude, merely nodding twice or thrice with great condescension. At length, the old man pronounced his name and inquired how he came there.

"Through the door," said Quilp, pointing over his shoulder with his thumb. "I'm not quite small enough to get through keyholes. I wish I was. I want to have some talk with you, particularly, and in private—with nobody present, neighbor. Good-bye, little Nelly."

Nell looked at the old man, who nodded to her to retire, and kissed her cheek.

The dwarf said never a word, but watched his companion as he paced restlessly up and down the room, and presently returned to his seat. Here he remained, with his head bowed upon his breast for some time, and then suddenly raising it said,

"Once, and once for all, have you brought me any money?"

"No!" returned Quilp.

"Then," said the old man, clenching his hands desperately and looking upward, "the child and I are lost!"

"Neighbor," said Quilp, glancing sternly at him, and beating his hand twice or thrice upon the table to attract his wandering attention, "let me be plain with you, and play a fairer game than when you held all the cards, and I saw but the backs and nothing more. You have no secret from me, now."

The old man looked up, trembling.

"You are surprised," said Quilp. "Well, perhaps that's natural. You have no secret from me now, I say; no, not one. For now I know that all those sums of money, that all those loans, advances and supplies that you have had from me, have found their way to—shall I say the word?"

"Aye!" replied the old man, "say it if you will."

"To the gaming-table," rejoined Quilp, "your nightly haunt. This was the precious scheme to make your fortune, was it; this was the secret certain source of wealth in which I was to have sunk my money (if I had been the fool you took me for); this was your inexhaustible mine of gold, your El Dorado, eh?"

"Yes," cried the old man, turning upon him with gleaming eyes, "it was. It is. It will be, till I die."

"That I should have been blinded," said Quilp, looking contemptuously at him, "by a mere shallow gambler!"

"I am no gambler," cried the old man, fiercely. "I call Heaven to witness that I never played for gain of mine or love of play. It was all for *her*—for my little Nelly! I had sworn to leave her rich!"

"When did you first begin this mad career?" asked Quilp, his taunting inclination subdued, for a moment, by the old man's grief and wildness.

"When did I first begin?" he rejoined, passing his hand across his brow. "When *was* it, that I first began? When should it be, but when I began to think how little I had saved, how long a time it took to save at all, how short a time I might have, at my age, to live, and how she would be left to the rough mercies of the world with barely enough to keep her from the sorrows that wait on poverty; then it was that I began to think about it."

"Humph! the old story," said the dwarf. "You lost what money you had laid by, first, and then came to me.  While I thought you were making your fortune (as you said you were) you were making yourself a beggar, eh? Dear me!  And so it comes to pass that I hold every security you could scrape together, and a bill of sale upon the—upon the stock and property.  But did you never win?"

"Never!" groaned the old man.  "Never won back my loss!"

"I thought," sneered the dwarf, "that if a man played long enough he was sure to win at last, or, at the worst, not to come off a loser."

"And so he is!" cried the old man, "so he is; I have felt that from the first, I have always known it, I've seen it, I never felt it half so strongly as I feel it now.  Quilp, I have dreamed three nights, of winning the same large sum.  I never could dream that dream before, though I have often tried.  Do not desert me, now I have this chance!  I have no resource but you,— give me some help, let me try this one last hope."

The dwarf shrugged his shoulders and shook his head.

"Nay, Quilp, *good* Quilp!" gasped the old man, extending his hands in entreaty; "let me try just this once more.  I tell you it is not for me—it is for her!  Oh, I cannot die and leave her in poverty!"

'I couldn't do it, really," said Quilp, with

unusual politeness.   And grinning and making a
low bow he passed out of the door.

The dwarf was, for once, as good as his word.
He not only refused to lend any more money,
but he at once began to make plans for closing
the shop.   The old man was so broken-hearted
that he fell ill of a raging fever, and for days
was delirious.   Little Nell, his only nurse, gradually learned the truth about her grandfather's
evening pursuit—the gaming-table—and it added all the more to her sorrow.

At last when he was well enough to go about
again, the impatient dwarf would not be put off
any longer in regard to the sale.   An early day
was fixed for it, and the old dealer no longer
offered any objections.   Instead, he sat quietly,
dully in his chair, looking at a tiny patch of
green through his window.

To one who had been tossing on a restless bed
so long, even these few green leaves and this
tranquil light, although it languished among
chimneys and house-tops, were pleasant things.
They suggested quiet places afar off, and rest
and peace.

The child thought, more than once, that he
was moved and had forborne to speak.   But
now he shed tears—tears that it lightened her
aching heart to see—and making as though he

would fall upon his knees, he besought her to forgive him.

"Forgive you—what?" said Nell, interposing to prevent his purpose. "Oh, grandfather, what should *I* forgive?"

"All that is past, all that has come upon you, Nell," returned the old man.

"Do not talk so," said the child. "Pray do not. Let us speak of something else."

"Yes, yes, we will," he rejoined. "And it shall be of what we talked of long ago—many months—months is it, or weeks, or days? which is it, Nell?"

"I do not understand you," said the child.

"You said, let us be beggars and happy in the open fields," he answered. "Oh, let us go away—anywhere!"

"Yes, let us go," said Nell, earnestly; "there will we find happiness and peace."

And so it was arranged. On the night before the public auction they were to steal forth quietly, out into the wide world.

The old man had slept for some hours soundly in his bed, while she was busily engaged in preparing for their flight. There were a few articles of clothing for herself to carry, and a few for him; old garments, such as became their fallen fortunes, laid out to wear; and a staff to support his feeble steps, put ready for his use.

But this was not all her task, for now she must visit the old rooms for the last time.

And how different the parting with them was from any she had expected, and most of all from that which she had oftenest pictured to herself! How could she ever have thought of bidding them farewell in triumph, lonely and sad though her days had been! She sat down at the window where she had spent so many evenings—darker far, than this—and every thought of hope or cheerfulness that had occurred to her in that place came vividly upon her mind, and blotted out all its dull and mournful associations in an instant.

Her own little room, too, where she had so often knelt down and prayed at night—prayed for the time which she hoped was dawning now —the little room where she had slept so peacefully, and dreamed such pleasant dreams—it was so hard to leave it without one kind look or grateful tear.

But at last she was ready to go, and her grandfather was awakened. Just as the first rays of dawn were seen they stole forth noiselessly, hand in hand. They dared not awaken Quilp, who was sleeping that night in the shop to guard his prospective wealth. Out in the middle of the street they paused.

"Which way?" said the child.

The old man looked irresolutely and helplessly, first at her, then to the right and left,
then at her again, and shook his head. It was
plain that she was thenceforth his guide and
leader. The child felt it, but had no doubts or
misgiving, and putting her hand in his hand led
him gently away.

## II.   OUT IN THE WIDE WORLD

It was a bright morning in June when Nell
and her grandfather set forth upon their
travels. Out of the city they walked briskly,
for the desire to leave their old life— to elude
pursuit—lay strong upon them. Nell had provided a simple lunch for that day's needs; and
at night they stopped foot-sore and weary at a
hospitable farmhouse.

Late in the next day they chanced to pass a
country church. Among the tombstones, at one
side, they saw two men who were seated upon
the grass, so busily at work as not to notice the
newcomers.

It was not difficult to guess that they were
of a class of travelling showmen who went from
town to town showing Punch and his antics, for
perched upon a tombstone was a figure of that

hero himself, his nose and chin as hooked and his face as beaming as usual.

Scattered upon the ground were the other members of the play, in various stages of repair; while the two showmen were engaged with glue, hammer, and tacks, in putting their proper parts more strongly together.

The showmen raised their eyes when the old man and his young companion were close upon them, and pausing in their work, returned their looks of curiosity. One of them, the actual exhibitor, no doubt, was a little merry-faced man with a twinkling eye and a red nose, who seemed to have unconsciously imbibed something of his hero's character The other—that was he who took the money—had rather a careful and cautious look, which was perhaps inseparable from his occupation also.

The merry man was the first to greet the strangers with a nod; and following the old man's eyes, he observed that perhaps that was the first time he had ever seen a Punch off the stage.

"Why do you come here to do this?" asked the old man, after answering their greeting.

"Why, you see," rejoined the little man, "we're putting up for to-night at the public-house yonder, and it wouldn't do to let 'em see the present company undergoing repair."

"No!" cried the old man, making signs to Nell to listen, "why not, eh? why not?"

"Because it would destroy all the delusion, and take away all the interest, wouldn't it?" replied the little man. "Would you care a ha'penny for the Lord Chancellor if you know'd him in private and without his wig?—certainly not."

"Good!" said the old man, venturing to touch one of the puppets, and drawing away his hand with a shrill laugh. "Are you going to show 'em to-night? are you?"

"That is the intention, governor," replied the other. "Look here," he continued, turning to his partner, "here's all this Judy's clothes falling to pieces again. Much good *you* do at sewing things!"

Seeing that they were at a loss, the child said timidly:

"I have a needle, sir, in my basket, and thread too. Will you let me try to mend it for you? I think I can do it neater than you could."

The showman had nothing to urge against a proposal so seasonable. Nelly, kneeling down beside the box, was soon busily engaged in her task, and accomplishing it to a miracle.

While she was thus engaged, the merry little man looked at her with an interest which did not appear to be diminished when he glanced at her helpless companion. When she had finished her work he thanked her, and inquired whither they were travelling.

"N—no farther to-night, I think," said the child, looking towards her grandfather.

"If you're wanting a place to stop at," the man remarked, "I should advise you to take up at the same house with us. That's it—the long, low, white house there. It's very cheap. Come along."

The tavern was kept by a fat old landlord and landlady who made no objection to receiving their new guests, but praised Nelly's beauty and were at once prepossessed in her behalf. There was no other company in the kitchen but the two showmen, and the child felt very thankful that they had fallen upon such good quarters. The landlady was very much astonished to learn that they had come all the way from London, and appeared to have no little curiosity touching their farther destination. But Nell could give her no very clear replies.

That evening the wayfarers enjoyed the Punch show, though poor Nell was so tired that she went to sleep early in the performance.

The next morning she met the showmen at breakfast.

"And where are you going to-day?" asked the little man with the red nose.

"Indeed, I hardly know. We have not decided," replied the child.

"We're going up to the races," said the little man. "If that's your way and you'd like to have us for company, let us travel together."

"We'll go with you, and gladly," interposed Nell's grandfather, eagerly; for he had been as pleased as a child with the performance of Punch.

Nell was a trifle alarmed over the prospect of a crowded race-course; but this seemed their best chance to press forward, so she accepted the invitation thankfully.

For several days they travelled together, and despite the wearisome way the child found much novelty and interest in the wandering life. But presently she became uneasy in the changed attitude of the two showmen. From being ordinarily kind, they now seemed to watch Nell and her grandfather so closely as not to suffer them out of their sight.

The showmen had, in fact, got it into their heads that the two wayfarers were not common people, but runaways for whom a reward must even now be posted in London. And so they resolved to deliver them over to the proper authorities at the first opportunity and claim the reward.

Now, although Nell and her grandfather had

a perfect right to go where they pleased, and there was no reward offered, they were at all times fearful of being pursued by that terrible Quilp. So Nell determined to flee from these two watchful men at the earliest moment.

The chance of escape offered during one of the busy days at the race-course. While the two men were busy showing off Punch to the delighted crowd, she took her grandfather by the hand and hurriedly slipped away.

At first they pressed forward regardless of whither their steps led them, and from time to time casting fearful glances behind them to see if they were being pursued. But as they drew farther away they gained more confidence. Weariness also forced them to slacken their pace. When they had come into the middle of a little woodland they rested a short time; then encountered a path which led to the opposite side. Taking their way along it for a short distance they came to a lane, so shaded by the trees on either hand that they met together overhead, and arched the narrow way. A broken finger-post announced that this led to a village three miles off; and thither they resolved to bend their steps.

The miles appeared so long that they sometimes thought they must have missed their road. But at last, to their great joy, it led downward in a steep descent, with overhanging banks over which the footpaths led; and the clustered houses of the village peeped from the woody hollow below.

It was a very small place. The men and boys were playing at cricket on the green; and as the other folks were looking on they wandered up and down, uncertain where to seek a humble lodging. There was but one man in a little garden before his cottage, and him they were timid of approaching, for he was the schoolmaster, and had "School" written up over his window in black letters on a white board. He was a pale, simple-looking man, and sat among his flowers and beehives, smoking his pipe, in the little porch before his door.

"Speak to him, dear," the old man whispered.

"I am almost afraid to disturb him," said the child, timidly. "He does not seem to see us. Perhaps if we wait a little, he may look this way."

But as nobody else appeared and it would soon be dark, Nell at length ventured to draw near, leading her grandfather by the hand. The slight noise they made in raising the latch of the wicket-gate caught his attention. He looked at them kindly but seemed disappointed too, and slightly shook his head.

Nell dropped a courtesy, and told him they

were poor travellers who sought a shelter for
the night which they would gladly pay for, so
far as their means allowed.  The schoolmaster
looked earnestly at her as she spoke, laid aside
his pipe, and rose up directly.

"If you could direct us anywhere, sir," said
the child, "we should take it very kindly."

"You have been walking a long way," said
the schoolmaster.

"A long way, sir," the child replied.

"You're a young traveller, my child," he said,
laying his hand gently on her head.  "Your
grandchild, friend?"

"Aye, sir," cried the old man, "and the stay
and comfort of my life."

"Come in," said the schoolmaster.

Without farther preface he conducted them
into his little school-room, which was parlor and
kitchen likewise, and told them they were welcome to remain under his roof till morning.  Before they had done thanking him, he spread a
coarse white cloth upon the table, with knives
and platters; and bringing out some bread and
cold meat, besought them to eat.

They did so gladly, and the schoolmaster
showed them, soon after, to some plain but neat
sleeping chambers up close under the thatched
roof.  Here they slept the sound sleep of the

weary, and awoke refreshed and light-hearted the following day.

But the schoolmaster, while kind and courteous, was sad and quiet. He gave his small school a half-holiday that day, and Nell learned that it was because of the illness of a favorite pupil—a boy about her own age.

"If your journey is not a long one," he added to the travellers, "you're welcome to pass another night here. I should really be glad if you would do so, as I am very lonely to-day."

They accepted and thanked him with grateful hearts. Nell busied herself tidying up the rooms and trying in many little ways to add to the master's comfort. And that evening, when his pupil died, Nell's grief was almost as deep in its sympathy as the master's own.

She bade him a reluctant farewell the next morning. School had already begun, but he rose from his desk and walked with them to the gate.

It was with a trembling and reluctant hand that the child held out to him the money which a lady had given her at the races for some flowers; faltering in her thanks as she thought how small the sum was, and blushing as she offered it. But he bade her put it up, and stooping to kiss her cheek, turned back into his house.

They had not gone half-a-dozen paces when

he was at the door again; the old man retraced his steps to shake hands, and the child did the same.

"Good fortune and happiness go with you!" said the poor schoolmaster. "I am quite a solitary man now. If you ever pass this way again, you'll not forget the little village school."

"We shall never forget it, sir," rejoined Nell; "nor ever forget to be grateful to you for your kindness to us."

"I have heard such words from the lips of children very often," said the schoolmaster, shaking his head and smiling thoughtfully, "but they were soon forgotten. I had attached one young friend to me, the better friend for being young—but that's over—God bless you!"

They bade him farewell very many times and turned away, walking slowly and often looking back, until they could see him no more. At length they had left the village far behind, and even lost sight of the smoke among the trees. They trudged onward now at a quicker pace, resolving to keep the main road, and go wherever it might lead them.

But the main roads stretch a long, long way. With the exception of two or three inconsiderable clusters of cottages which they passed without stopping, and one lonely roadside public-house where they had some bread and cheese, this highway had led them to nothing—late in the afternoon—and still lengthened out, far in the distance, the same dull, tedious, winding course that they had been pursuing all day. As they had no resource, however, but to go forward, they still kept on, though at a much slower pace, being very weary and fatigued.

Finally, just at dusk, they came upon a curious little house upon wheels— a travelling show somewhat more pretentious than the Punch performance they had run away from. This little house was mounted upon a cart, with white dimity curtains at the windows and shutters of green set in panels of bright red. Altogether it was a smart little contrivance. Grazing in front of it were two comfortable-looking horses; while at its open door sat a stout lady—evidently the proprietor—sipping tea.

This lady, Mrs. Jarley by name, had seen Nell and her grandfather at the races, so hailed them and asked about the success of the Punch show. She was greatly astonished to learn that they had nothing to do with it, and were wandering about without any object in view.

Her own performance was more "classic," as she expressed it. It was a Waxwork exhibition; and as she looked at Nell's attractive face she was seized with an idea. This bright little girl was just the sort of assistant she had been needing. So she invited them to stop and have some tea with her. They did so; and when Mrs. Jarley presently unfolded her plan—which was to engage Nell to exhibit the wax figures and describe them in a set speech—Nell was delighted to accept the offer, especially since it involved no separation from her grandfather, who could dust the figures and do other light tasks.

It was really not a very hard position for Nell. At the first town where the Waxworks were to be shown, Nell was given a private view and instructed in her new duties. The figures were displayed on a raised platform some two feet from the floor, running round the room and parted from the rude public by a crimson rope breast high. They represented celebrated characters, singly and in groups, clad in glittering dresses of various climes and times, and standing more or less unsteadily upon their legs, with their eyes very wide open, and their nostrils very much inflated, and the muscles of their legs and arms very strongly developed, and all their countenances expressing great surprise. All the gentlemen were very pigeon-breasted and very blue about the beards, and all the ladies were miraculous figures; and all the ladies and all the gentlemen were looking with extraordinary earnestness at nothing at all.

Nell was taught a little speech about each

one of them, and so apt was she that one re-
hearsal rendered her able to take the willow
wand, which Mrs. Jarley had formerly wielded,
and tell the interesting history of this very select Waxwork show to the audiences which presently began to come.

Mrs. Jarley herself was delighted with the ven-
ture.    She saw at once that Nell would be a
strong drawing card.    And in order that the
child might remain contented she made her and
her grandfather as comfortable as possible, besides paying them a fair salary.

So the wanderers now rode in the van from
town to town, and lived almost happily.    Nell
carefully saved all their money, and watched
over her feeble grandfather with the tenderness
of a little mother.    She had one scare in almost
meeting face to face with Quilp, the dwarf, but
he had not recognized her.

Quilp, indeed, was a perpetual nightmare to
the child, who was constantly haunted by a
vision of his ugly face and stunted figure.    She
slept, for their better security, in the room where
the waxwork figures were, and she never retired
to this place at night but she tortured herself—
she could not help it—with imagining a resem-
blance, in some one or other of their death-like
faces, to the dwarf, and this fancy would sometimes so gain upon her that she would almost

believe he had removed the figure and stood within the clothes.

But presently a deeper and more real concern came to her. Her grandfather had never alluded to their former life, nor to his passion for gambling. He did not see the card-tables out in the country; and that was the reason why she had been so eager to wander, even without a roof over their heads. But now, as the Waxworks exhibited only in the towns, temptation came again to the poor, weak old man. He saw some men playing cards in a tavern, and instantly his slumbering passion was aroused. He would play again and win a great fortune—for Nell!

He began to play, and, of course, with the old result. He was but a tool in the hands of the sharpers, and presently he had exhausted all the slender hoard which Nell had so carefully made. She watched his actions with a bursting heart, but was powerless to stop him or keep the money out of his grasp. At last the villains who had led him on—not satisfied with their small winnings from him—urged him to get the money belonging to the Waxwork show, saying that when he won he could pay it all back.

Nell had followed her grandfather upon this visit to the gamblers, and overheard their plot. She knew there was but one thing to do, to save her grandfather. They must flee out into the world again at once. That night she roused him from his sleep, and told him they must go away.

"What does this mean?" he cried.

" I have had dreadful dreams," said the child. "If we stay here another night something awful will happen. Come!"

The old man looked at her as if she were a spirit, and trembled in every joint.

"Must we go to-night?" he asked.

"Yes, to-night," she replied. "To-morrow night will be too late. The dream will have come again. Nothing but flight can save us. Up!"

The old man rose obediently and made ready to follow. She had already packed their scanty belongings. She gave him his wallet and staff, and secretly, in the night, they fled away.

The wanderings of the next few days seemed like a nightmare to them. Nell had brought only a few pennies in her pockets and these went for a scant supply of bread and cheese. Two days and a night they rode on an open canal-boat in company with some rough but not unkind men. It was easier than walking, but the rain descended in torrents and drenched them to the skin.

Finally the boat drew up to a wharf in an ugly manufacturing town, and the travellers were cast adrift as lonely and helpless as though they had just awakened from a sleep of a thousand years.   They had not one friend, nor the least idea where to turn for shelter   But a rough stoker at one of the furnaces told them that they might pass the night in front of his fire.  It was nothing but a bed of ashes, yet they were warm and the heat dried out the poor travellers' drenched garments.

The child felt stiff and weak in every joint the next morning, but the furnace-tender told them that it was two days' journey to the open country and sweet, pure fields, and she felt that they must press forward at any cost.  So they started forth, slowly and wearily, for their journey and privations had almost exhausted them, but still with brave hearts.  Through long rows of red brick houses that looked exactly alike they wended their way, asking for bread to eat only when obliged to, and meeting little else but scowls from the dirty factory workers.

Finally, to their great joy, the open country began again to appear; and with fresh courage in their hearts they continued to press on.

They were dragging themselves along through the last street and the child felt that the time was close at hand when her enfeebled powers would bear no more; when there appeared before them, going in the same direction as themselves, a traveller on foot, who, with a portmanteau strapped to his back, leaned upon a stout stick as he walked, and read from a book which he held in his other hand.

It was not an easy matter to come up with him, and beseech his aid, for he walked fast, and was a little distance in advance. At length he stopped to look more attentively at some passage in his book. Animated with a ray of hope, the child shot on before her grandfather, and going close to the stranger without rousing him by the sound of her footsteps, began, in a few faint words, to implore his help.

He turned his head. The child clapped her hands together, uttered a wild shriek, and fell senseless at his feet.

### III.   AT THE END OF THE JOURNEY

It was the poor schoolmaster. Scarcely less moved and surprised by the sight of the child than she had been on recognizing him, he stood, for a moment, without even the presence of mind to raise her from the ground.

But quickly recovering his self-possession, he threw down his stick and book, and dropping on one knee beside her, endeavored by such simple means as occurred to him to restore her to herself; while her grandfather, standing idly by, wrung his hands, and implored her with many endearing expressions to speak to him, were it only a word.

"She is quite exhausted," said the schoolmaster, glancing upward into his face. "You have taxed her powers too far, friend."

"She is perishing of want," rejoined the old man. "I never thought how weak and ill she was till now."

Casting a look upon him, half reproachful and half compassionate, the schoolmaster took the child in his arms, and, bidding the old man gather up her little basket and follow him directly, bore her away at his utmost speed.

There was a small inn within sight, to which, it would seem, he had been directing his steps when so unexpectedly overtaken. Towards this place he hurried with his unconscious burden, and rushing into the kitchen deposited it on a chair before the fire.

A doctor was hastily called and restoratives were applied; after which Nell was given what she most needed, some warm broth and toast, and was put to bed.

The schoolmaster asked anxiously after her health the next morning, and was greatly relieved to find that she was much better, though still so weak that it would require a day's careful nursing before she could proceed upon her journey. That evening he was allowed to see her, and was greatly touched by the sight of her pale, pinched face. But she held out both hands to him.

"It makes me unhappy even in the midst of all this kindness," said the child, "to think that we should be a burden upon you. How can I ever thank you? If I had not met you so far from home, I must have died, and poor grandfather would have no one to take care of him."

"We'll not talk about dying," said the schoolmaster, "and as to burdens, I have made my fortune since you slept at my cottage."

"Indeed!" cried the child joyfully.

"Oh, yes," returned her friend. "I have been appointed clerk and schoolmaster to a village a long way from here—and a long way from the old one as you may suppose—at five-and-thirty pounds [1] a year. Five-and-thirty pounds!"

"I am very glad," said the child—"so very, very glad."

"I am on my way there now," resumed the schoolmaster. "They allowed me the stage-coach hire—outside stage-coach hire all the way. Bless you, they grudge me nothing. But as the time at which I am expected there left me ample

[1] About $175.00

leisure, I determined to walk instead. How glad I am to think I did so!"

"How glad should we be!"

"Yes, yes," said the schoolmaster, moving restlessly in his chair, "certainly, that's very true. But you—where are you going, where are you coming from, what have you been doing since you left me, what had you been doing before? Now, tell me—do tell me. I know very little of the world, and perhaps you are better fitted to advise me in its affairs than I am qualified to give advice to you; but I am very sincere, and I have a reason (you have not forgotten it) for loving you. I have felt since that time as if my love for him who died had been transferred to you."

Nell was moved in her turn by this allusion to the favorite pupil who had died, and by the plain, frank kindness of the good schoolmaster. She told him all—that they had no friend or relative—that she had fled with the old man to save him from all the miseries he dreaded— that she was flying now to save him from himself—and that she sought an asylum in some quiet place, where the temptation before which he fell would never enter, and her late sorrows and distresses could have no place.

The schoolmaster heard her with astonishment.

"This child!" he thought; "she is one of the heroines and saints of earth!"

Then he told her of a great idea which had occurred to him. They were all three to travel together to the village where his new school was located, and he made no doubt he could find them some simple and congenial employment.

The child joyfully accepted this; and the journey was made very comfortably in a stage which went that way. Stowed among the softer bundles and packages she thought this to be a drowsy, luxurious way of going, indeed.

At last they came upon a quiet, restful-looking hamlet clustered in a valley among some stately trees.

"See—here's the church!" cried the delighted schoolmaster, in a low voice; "and that old building close beside it is the school-house, I'll be sworn. Five-and-thirty pounds a year in this beautiful place!"

They admired everything—the old gray porch, the green churchyard, the ancient tower, the very weathercock; the brown thatched roofs of cottage, barn, and homestead, peeping from among the trees; the stream that rippled by the distant watermill; the blue Welsh mountains far away. It was for such a spot the child had wearied in the dense, miserable haunts of labor. Upon her bed of ashes, and amidst the squalid horrors through which they had forced their way, visions of such scenes—beautiful indeed, but not more beautiful than this sweet reality—had been always present to her mind. They had seemed to melt into a dim and airy distance, as the prospect of ever beholding them again grew fainter; but, as they receded, she had loved and panted for them more.

"I must leave you somewhere for a few minutes," said the schoolmaster, at length breaking the silence into which they had fallen in their gladness. "I have a letter to present, and inquiries to make, you know. Where shall I take you? To the little inn yonder?"

"Let us wait here," rejoined Nell. "The gate is open. We will sit in the church porch till you come back."

"A good place, too," said the schoolmaster, leading the way towards it. "Be sure that I come back with good news, and am not long gone."

So the happy schoolmaster put on a brand-new pair of gloves which he had carried in a little parcel in his pocket all the way, and hurried off, full of ardor and excitement.

The child watched him from the porch until the intervening foliage hid him from her view, and then stepped softly out into the old churchyard—so solemn and quiet that every rustle of her dress upon the fallen leaves, which strewed the path and made her footsteps noiseless, seemed an invasion of its silence. It was an aged, ghostly place; the church had been built hundreds of years before; yet from this first glimpse the child loved it and felt that in some strange way she was a part of its crumbling walls and grass-grown churchyard.

After a time the schoolmaster reappeared, hurrying towards them and swinging a bunch of keys.

"You see those two houses?" he asked, pointing, quite out of breath. "Well, one of them is mine."

Without saying any more, or giving the child time to reply, the schoolmaster took her hand, and, his honest face quite radiant with exultation, led her to the place of which he spoke.

They stopped before its low, arched door. After trying several of the keys in vain, the schoolmaster found one to fit the huge lock, which turned back, creaking, and admitted them into the house.

It was a very old house, and, like the church, falling into decay, yet still handsome with high vaulted ceilings and queer carvings. It was not quite destitute of furniture. A few strange chairs, whose arms and legs looked as though they had dwindled away with age; a table, the very spectre of its race; a great old chest that had once held records in the church, with other quaintly fashioned domestic necessaries, and store of firewood for the winter, were scattered around, and gave evident tokens of its occupation as a dwelling-place, at no very distant time.

The child looked around her, with that solemn feeling with which we contemplate the work of ages that have become but drops of water in the great ocean of eternity. The old man had followed them, but they were all three hushed for a space, and drew their breath softly, as if they feared to break the silence, even by so slight a sound.

"It is a very beautiful place!" said the child, in a low voice.

"I almost feared you thought otherwise," returned the schoolmaster. "You shivered when we first came in, as if you felt it cold or gloomy."

"It was not that," said Nell, glancing around with a slight shudder. "Indeed, I cannot tell you what it was, but when I saw the outside, from the church porch, the same feeling came over me. It is its being so old and gray, perhaps."

"A peaceful place to live in, don't you think so?" said her friend.

"Oh, yes," rejoined the child, clasping her

hands earnestly. "A quiet, happy place—a place to live and learn to die in!"

"A place to live, and learn to live, and gather health of mind and body in," said the schoolmaster; "for this old house is yours."

"Ours!" cried the child.

"Aye," returned the schoolmaster, gaily, "for many a merry year to come, I hope. I shall be a close neighbor—only next door—but this house is yours."

Having now disburdened himself of his great surprise, the schoolmaster sat down, and drawing Nell to his side, told her how he had learned that the ancient tenement had been occupied for a long time by an old person, who kept the keys of the church, opened and closed it for the services, and showed it to strangers; how she had died not many weeks ago, and nobody had yet been found to fill the office; how, learning all this in an interview with the sexton, he had hurried to the clergyman and obtained the vacant post for Nell and her grandfather.

"There's a small allowance of money," said the schoolmaster. "It is not much, but still enough to live upon in this retired spot. By clubbing our funds together, we shall do bravely; no fear of that."

"Heaven bless and prosper you!" sobbed the child.

"Amen, my dear," returned her friend, cheerfully; "and all of us, as it will, and has, in leading us through sorrow and trouble to this tranquil life.  But we must look at *my* house now.
Come!"

They repaired to the other tenement; tried
the rusty keys as before; at length found the
right one; and opened the worm-eaten door.  It
led into a chamber, vaulted and old, like that
from which they had come, but not so spacious,
and having only one other little room attached.
It was not difficult to divine that the other house
was of right the schoolmaster's, and that he
had chosen for himself the least commodious, in
his care and regard for them.  Like the adjoining habitation, it held such old articles of furniture as were absolutely necessary, and had its
stack of firewood.

To make these dwellings as habitable and full
of comfort as they could, was now their pleasant care.  In a short time, each had its cheerful
fire glowing and crackling on the hearth, and
reddening the pale old walls with a hale and
healthy blush.  Nell, busily plying her needle,
repaired the tattered window-hangings, drew together the rents that time had worn in the
threadbare scraps of carpet, and made them
whole and decent.  The schoolmaster swept and
smoothed the ground before the door, trimmed

the long grass, trained the ivy and creeping plants, which hung their drooping heads in melancholy neglect; and gave to the outer walls a cheery air of home. The old man, sometimes by his side and sometimes with the child, lent his aid to both, went here and there on little patient services, and was happy. Neighbors, too, as they came from work, proffered their help; or sent their children with such small presents or loans as the strangers needed most. So it was not many days before they were quite cozy; and Nell felt again, in that strange way which had come over her at the church, that she had always been a part of the place.

And how she loved her work from the very first! Hour after hour she would spend in the old church, dusting off its pews or casements with reverent fingers, or more often, sitting quietly before some tablet or inscription looking at it or beyond it, with a dreamy light in her eyes.

Her grandfather noted her attitude anxiously. He saw that she grew more listless and frail, day by day, and he sought constantly—poor old man!—to lighten her few tasks. But it was not these which wearied her; it was merely the burden of all things earthly.

Every person in the village soon grew to love this frail, spiritual-looking child; but from the first she seemed a being apart from them. They were constantly showing her kindness, or pausing at the church gate to speak with her; but as they went their way, a sad smile or shake of the head told only too plainly of their fears. She was like some rare, delicate flower which, they knew, could not endure the frost of winter.

The good schoolmaster gently chided her for spending so much of her time in the church and among the graves, instead of out in the light and sunshine. But she only smiled and said she loved to tend the graves and keep them neat, for she could not bear to think that any lying there should be forgotten, or that she herself might be forgotten some day.

"There is nothing good that is forgotten," he replied kindly. "There is not an angel added to the host of Heaven but does its blessed work on earth in those that loved it here."

As the cold days of autumn and winter drew on, the child spent more and more time within doors, on a couch before the fire. The slightest task wearied her now, and her grandfather kept watch night and day to save her needless steps. He could scarcely bear her out of his sight; and often would creep to the side of her couch during the night, listening to her breathing or stroking her slender fingers softly. And if by chance she awoke and smiled on him, he would creep back to his own bed comforted.

But one chill morning in midwinter, when the snow lay thickly on the ground, it seemed to him that she slept more quietly than usual. The schoolmaster, coming in, found him crouched over a fire, muttering softly to himself and wondering why she slumbered so long. The two went softly into her chamber, and then the schoolmaster knew why she was so quiet.

For she was dead. Dear, gentle, patient, noble Nell was dead. No sleep so beautiful and calm, so free from trace of pain, so fair to look upon. She seemed a creature fresh from the hand of God, and waiting the breath of life; not one who had lived and suffered death.

The old man held one languid arm in his, and had the small hand tight folded to his breast, for warmth. It was the hand she had stretched out to him with her last smile—the hand that had led him on, through all their wanderings. Ever and anon he pressed it to his lips, then hugged it to his breast again, murmuring that it was warmer now; and, as he said it, he looked in agony to the schoolmaster, as if imploring him to help her.

She was dead, and past all help or need of it. The ancient rooms she had seemed to fill with life, even while her own was waning fast;

the garden she had tended; the eyes she had gladdened; the noiseless haunts of many a thoughtful hour; the paths she had trodden as it were but yesterday—could know her never-more.

"It is not," said the schoolmaster, as he bent down to kiss her on the cheek, and gave his tears free vent, "it is not on earth that Heaven's justice ends. Think what earth is, compared with the world to which her young spirit has winged its early flight, and say, if one deliberate wish expressed in solemn terms above this bed could call her back to life, which of us would utter it!"

The whole village, young and old, came to the churchyard when they laid her to rest—save only the old man. He could not realize that she was dead, and he had gone to pick winter berries to decorate her couch.

When he returned and could not find her, they were obliged to tell him the truth—that her body had been put away in the cold earth—and then his grief and distress were pitiful to see. He seemed at once to lose all power of thought or action, save as they concerned her alone.

Day by day he sought for her about the house or in the garden, calling her name wildly. At other times he sat before the fire staring dully, and did not seem to hear when they spoke to him.

At length, they found, one day, that he had risen early, and, with his knapsack on his back, his staff in his hand, her own straw hat, and little basket full of such things as she had been used to carry, was gone. As they were making ready to pursue him far and wide, a frightened school-boy came who had seen him, but a moment before, sitting in the church—upon her grave, he said.

They hastened there, and going softly to the door espied him in the attitude of one who waited patiently. They did not disturb him then, but kept a watch upon him all that day. When it grew quite dark, he rose and returned home, and went to bed, murmuring to himself, "She will come to-morrow!"

Upon the morrow he was there again from sunrise until night; and still at night he laid him down to rest, and murmured, "She will come to-morrow!"

And thenceforth, every day, and all day long, he waited at her grave for her. How many pictures of new journeys over pleasant country, of resting-places under the free broad sky, of rambles in the fields and woods, and paths not often trodden; how many tones of that one well-remembered voice; how many glimpses of

the form, the fluttering dress, the hair that
waved so gaily in the wind; how many visions
of what had been, and what he hoped was yet
to be—rose before him, in the old dull silent
church! He never told them what he thought,
or where he went. He would sit with them at
night, pondering with a secret satisfaction, they
could see, upon the flight that he and she would
take before night came again; and still they
would hear him whisper in his prayers, "Lord!
Let her come to-morrow!"

The last time was on a genial day in spring.
He did not return at the usual hour, and they
went to seek him. He was lying dead upon the
stone.

They laid him by the side of her whom he had
loved so well; and, in the church where they had
often prayed and mused and lingered hand in
hand, the child and the old man slept together.

# THE STORY OF

# Paul and Florence Dombey

## I.   THE HOUSE OF DOMBEY AND SON

PAUL DOMBEY was a boy born to achieve great things. His birth was the one historic event of the Dombey household—at least, so his father said. 'Tis true that Paul's sister Florence was six years older than he, but then Florence was only a girl. What Mr. Dombey had long wanted was a son who could grow up to carry on the business of the great export house, and who from his birth would make possible the imposing title of Dombey and Son.

So Florence, who had remained quietly neglected in her nursery, now came into notice only as the sister of Paul, or as a faithful little nurse who could help amuse him.

As for Mr. Dombey himself, he was a cold, haughty man, very proud of what he had done, and at all times exacting obedience from every one else. Paul's mother had died soon after he was born; and Mr. Dombey having engaged the best nurses he could find, expected them forthwith to bring the child through all the round of

infant ailments—of which the frail little fellow had more than his full share. Indeed, Mr. Dombey loved his son with all the love he had. If there were a warm place in his frosty heart, his son occupied it; though not so much as an infant or a boy, as a prospective man—the "Son" of the firm. Therefore he was impatient to have him grow up; feeling as if the boy had a charmed life, and *must* become the man around whom all his hopes centred.

Thus Paul grew to be nearly five years old. He was a pretty little fellow, though there was something wan and wistful in his small face, that gave occasion to many significant shakes of his nurse's head. His temper gave abundant promise of being imperious, like his father's, in after life. He was childish and sportive enough at times; but he had a strange, old-fashioned, thoughtful way at other times of sitting brooding in his miniature arm-chair, when he looked and talked like one of those terrible little beings in the fairy tales, who, at a hundred and fifty or two hundred years of age, fantastically represent the children for whom they have been substituted. He would frequently be stricken with this mood upstairs in the nursery, and would sometimes lapse into it suddenly, exclaiming that he was tired, even while playing with Florence, or driving his nurse in single harness.  But at no one time did he fall into it so surely, as when, his little chair being carried down into his father's room, he sat there with him after dinner by the fire.  They were the strangest pair at such a time that ever fire-light shone upon.  Mr. Dombey, so erect and solemn, gazing at the blaze; his little image, with an old, old face, peering into the red perspective with the fixed and rapt attention of a sage; the two so very much alike, and yet so monstrously contrasted.

On one of these occasions, when they had both been perfectly quiet for a long time, little Paul broke the silence thus:—

"Papa! what's money?"

The abrupt question had such immediate reference to the subject of Mr. Dombey's thoughts, that Mr. Dombey was quite disconcerted.

"What is money, Paul?" he answered. "Money?"

"Yes," said the child, laying his hands upon the elbows of his little chair, and turning the old face up towards Mr. Dombey's, "what is money?"

Mr. Dombey was in a difficulty.  He would have liked to give him some grown-up explanation; but looking down at the little chair, and seeing what a long way down it was, he answered:

"Gold, and silver, and copper. Guineas, shillings, halfpence. You know what they are?"

"Oh, yes, I know what they are," said Paul. "I don't mean that, papa. I mean what's money, after all."

"What is money, after all!" said Mr. Dombey, backing his chair a little, that he might the better gaze at the atom that made such an inquiry.

"I mean, papa, what can it do?" returned Paul.

Mr. Dombey drew his chair back to its former place, and patted him on the head. "You'll know better, by and by, my man," he said. "Money, Paul, can do anything."

"Anything, papa?"

"Yes. Anything—almost," said Mr. Dombey.

"Anything means everything, don't it, papa?" asked his son, not observing, or possibly not understanding the qualification.

"Yes," said Mr. Dombey.

"Why didn't money save me my mamma?" returned the child. "It isn't cruel, is it?"

"Cruel!" said Mr. Dombey, settling his neckcloth, and seeming to resent the idea. "No. A good thing can't be cruel."

"If it's a good thing, and can do anything," said the little fellow thoughtfully, as he looked back at the fire, "I wonder why it didn't save me my mamma."

Mr. Dombey having recovered from his surprise, not to say his alarm (for it was the very first occasion on which the child had ever broached the subject of his mother to him), expounded to him how that money, though a very potent spirit, could not keep people alive whose time was come to die; and how that we must all die, unfortunately, even in the city, though we were never so rich.

Paul listened to all this and much more with grave attention, and then suddenly asked a question which was still more alarming.

"It can't make me strong and quite well, either, papa, can it?"

"Why, you *are* strong and quite well," returned Mr. Dombey. "Are you not?"

Oh! the age of the face that was turned up again, with an expression, half of melancholy, half of slyness on it!

"You are as strong and well as such little people usually are, eh?" said Mr. Dombey.

"Florence is older than I am, but I'm not as strong and well as Florence, I know," returned the child; "but I believe that when Florence was as little as me, she could play a great deal longer at a time without tiring herself. I am so tired sometimes that I don't know what to do."

"But that's at night," said Mr. Dombey, drawing his own chair closer to his son's, and laying his hand gently on his back; "little people should be tired at night, for then they sleep well."

"Oh, it's not at night, papa," returned the child, "it's in the day; and I lie down in Florence's lap, and she sings to me. At night I dream about such cu-ri-ous things!"

Mr. Dombey was so astonished, and so perfectly at a loss how to pursue the conversation, that he could only sit looking at his son by the light of the fire.

Here they sat until Florence came timidly into the room to take Paul upstairs to bed; when he raised towards his father, in bidding him good-night, a countenance so much brighter, so much younger, and so much more childlike altogether, that Mr. Dombey, while he felt greatly reassured by the change, was quite amazed at it.

After they had left the room together, he thought he heard a soft voice singing; and remembering that Paul had said his sister sang to him, he had the curiosity to open the door and listen, and look after them. She was toiling up the great, wide staircase, with him in her arms; his head was lying on her shoulder, one of his arms thrown negligently round her neck.

So they went, toiling up; she singing all the way, and Paul sometimes crooning out a feeble accompaniment.

Mr. Dombey was so alarmed about Paul's remarks as to his health, that he called the family doctor in consultation the very next day. The doctor admitted that Paul was not as strong as he could hope, and suggested that sea air might benefit him. So the boy was sent to the home of a Mrs. Pipchin at Brighton. But he refused to go without Florence, much to the secret displeasure of Mr. Dombey, who did not like to see any one—especially this neglected daughter —gain more influence with Paul than he himself had.

Mrs. Pipchin was a cross-grained old lady who gained a livelihood by taking care of delicate children. But she was not unkind to Paul, whose patient little face and strange way of asking questions attracted her, as they did everybody else.

When he had been with her for some time and it was found that he did not gain in strength, a little carriage was hired for him, in which he could lie at his ease with his books and be wheeled down to the seaside.

Consistent in his odd tastes, the child set aside a ruddy-faced lad who was proposed as the drawer of his carriage, and selected, instead, the boy's grandfather—a weazen, old, crabfaced man in a suit of battered oilskin. With this attendant to pull him along, and Florence always walking by his side, he went down to the margin of the ocean every day; and there he would sit or lie in his carriage for hours together; never so distressed as by the company of children—Florence alone excepted, always.

Some small voice, near his ear, would ask him how he was, perhaps.

"I am very well, I thank you," he would answer. "But you had better go and play, if you please."

Then he would turn his head, and watch the child away, and say to Florence, "We don't want any others, do we? Kiss me, Floy."

His favorite spot was quite a lonely one, far away from most loungers; and with Florence sitting by his side at work, or reading to him, or talking to him, and the wind blowing on his face, and the water coming up among the wheels of his bed, he wanted nothing more.

"Floy," he said one day, "where's India?"

"Oh, it's a long, long distance off," said Florence, raising her eyes from her work.

"Weeks off?" asked Paul.

"Yes, dear. Many weeks' journey, night and day."

"If you were in India, Floy," said Paul, after

being silent for a minute. "I should—what is it that mamma did? I forget."

"Loved me?" answered Florence.

"No, no. Don't I love you now, Floy? What is it?—Died. If you were in India, I should die, Floy."

She hurriedly put her work aside, and laid her head down on his pillow, caressing him. And so would she, she said, if he were there. He would be better soon.

"Oh! I am a great deal better now!" he answered. "I don't mean that. I mean that I should die of being so sorry and so lonely, Floy!"

Another time, in the same place, he fell asleep, and slept quietly for a long time. Awaking suddenly, he started up, and sat listening.

Florence asked him what he thought he heard.

"I want to know what it says," he answered, looking steadily in her face. "The sea, Floy; what is it that it keeps on saying?"

She told him that it was only the noise of the rolling waves.

"Yes, yes," he said. "But I know that they are always saying something. Always the same thing. What place is over there?" He rose up, looking eagerly at the horizon.

She told him that there was another country

opposite, but he said he didn't mean that; he meant farther away—farther away.

Very often afterwards, in the midst of their talk, he would break off to try to understand what it was that the waves were always saying; and would rise up in his couch to look towards that invisible region far away.

But in spite of Paul's brooding fancies, the days in the open air, and with the salt spray blowing about him, began to have good effect. Little by little he grew stronger until he became able to do without his carriage; though he still remained the same old, quiet, dreamy child.

One day after he had been with Mrs. Pipchin about a year, Mr. Dombey came to see her. He informed Mrs. Pipchin that, as Paul was now six years old and much stronger, it was time his education was being considered; and so the child was to be sent to a certain Dr. Blimber, who lived near by and managed a select school of boys. Meanwhile, Florence could continue to live here, so that Paul need not be entirely separated from his sister.

Accordingly, a few days later, Paul stood upon the Doctor's doorsteps, with his small right hand in his father's, and his other locked in that of Florence. How tight the tiny pressure of that one, and how loose and cold the other!

The doctor was sitting in his portentous study, with a globe at each knee, books all round him, Homer over the door, and Minerva on the mantel-shelf.

"And how do you do, sir," he said to Mr. Dombey, when they had been ushered in, "and how is my little friend?"

Grave as an organ was the doctor's speech; and when he ceased, the great clock in the hall seemed (to Paul at least) to take him up, and to go on saying, "how–is–my–lit–tle–friend–how–is–my–lit–tle–friend," over and over and over again.

The little friend being something too small to be seen at all from where the doctor sat, over the books on his table, the doctor made several futile attempts to get a view of him round the legs; which Mr. Dombey perceiving, relieved the doctor from his embarrassment by taking Paul up in his arms and sitting him on another little table, over against the doctor, in the middle of the room.

"Ha!" said the doctor, leaning back in his chair with his hand in his breast. "Now I see my little friend. How do you do, my little friend?"

The clock in the hall wouldn't subscribe to this alteration in the form of words, but continued to repeat "how–is–my—lit–tle–friend—how–is–my–lit–tle–friend!"

"Very well, I thank you, sir," returned Paul, answering the clock quite as much as the doctor.

"Ha!" said Doctor Blimber. "Shall we make a man of him?"

"Do you hear, Paul?" added Mr. Dombey, Paul being silent.

"Shall we make a man of him?" repeated the doctor.

"I had rather be a child," replied Paul.

"Indeed!" said the doctor. "Why?"

The child sat on the table looking at him, with a curious expression of suppressed emotion in his face, and beating one hand proudly on his knee as if he had the rising tears beneath it, and crushed them. But his other hand strayed a little way the while, a little farther—farther from him yet—until it lighted on the neck of Florence. "This is why," it seemed to say, and then the steady look was broken up and gone, the working lip was loosened and the tears came streaming forth.

"Never mind," said the doctor, blandly nodding his head. "Ne-ver mind; we shall substitute new cares and new impressions, Mr. Dombey, very shortly. You would wish my little friend to acquire—"

"Everything, if you please, doctor," returned Mr. Dombey, firmly.

"Yes," said the doctor, who, with his half-shut eyes, and his usual smile, seemed to survey Paul with the sort of interest that might attach to some choice little animal he was going to stuff. "Yes, exactly. Ha! We shall impart a great variety of information to our little friend, and bring him quickly forward, I dare say. I dare say."

As soon as Mr. Dombey and Florence were gone, Dr. Blimber gave into the charge of his learned daughter Cornelia the little new pupil, saying, "Bring him on, Cornelia, bring him on."

Miss Blimber received her young ward from the doctor's hands; and Paul, feeling that the spectacles were surveying him, cast down his eyes.

"How old are you, Dombey?" said Miss Blimber.

"Six," answered Paul, wondering, as he stole a glance at the young lady, why her hair didn't grow long like Florence's, and why she was like a boy.

"How much do you know of your Latin Grammar, Dombey?" said Miss Blimber.

"None of it," answered Paul. Feeling that the answer was a shock to Miss Blimber's sensibility, he looked up and added timidly,—

"I haven't been well. I have been a weak child. I couldn't learn a Latin Grammar when I was out, every day, with old Glubb. I wish you'd tell old Glubb to come and see me, if you please."

"What a dreadfully low name!" said Miss Blimber. "Unclassical to a degree! Who is the monster, child?"

"What monster!" inquired Paul.

"Glubb."

"He's no more monster than you are," returned Paul.

"What!" cried the doctor, in a terrible voice. "What's that?"

Paul was dreadfully frightened; but still he made a stand for the absent Glubb, though he did it trembling.

"He's a very nice old man, ma'am," he said. "He used to pull my carriage for me, down along the beach. I wish you'd let him come to see me. He knows lots of things."

"Ha!" said the doctor, shaking his head; "this is bad, but study will do much."

Mrs. Blimber opined, with something like a shiver, that he was an unaccountable child; and, allowing for the difference of visage, looked at him pretty much as Mrs. Pipchin had been used to do.

As for Miss Blimber, she told him to come down to her room that evening at tea-time. When he did so he noticed a little pile of new books, which she was glancing over.

"These are yours, Dombey," she said.

"All of 'em, ma'am?" said Paul.

"Yes," returned Miss Blimber; "and Mr. Feeder will look you out some more very soon, if you are as studious as I expect you will be, Dombey."

"Thank you, ma'am," said Paul.

"I am going out for a constitutional," resumed Miss Blimber; "and while I am gone, that is to say, in the interval between this and breakfast, Dombey, I wish you to read over what I have marked in these books, and to tell me if you quite understand what you have got to learn. Don't lose time, Dombey, for you have none to spare, but take them downstairs, and begin directly."

"Yes, ma'am," answered Paul.

There were so many of them that although Paul put one hand under the bottom book and his other hand and his chin on the top book, and hugged them all closely, the middle book slipped out before he reached the door, and then they all tumbled down on the floor. Miss Blimber said, "Oh, Dombey, Dombey, this is really very careless!" and piled them up afresh for him; and this time, by dint of balancing them with great nicety, Paul got out of the room.

But if the poor child found them heavy to carry downstairs, how much harder was it to cram their contents into his head. Oh, how tired he grew! But always there was a never-ending round of lessons waiting for him during these long days and nights that Dr. Blimber and Cornelia tried to make a man of him. And all week long his aching head held but one long-ing desire—for Saturday to come.

Oh, Saturdays! Oh, happy Saturdays! when Florence always came at noon, and never would, in any weather, stay away.

And when Florence found how hard Paul's studies were for him, she quietly bought books just like his and studied them during the week, so that she might keep along with him and help him when they were together.

Not a word of this was breathed to Mrs. Pipchin; but many a night when she was in bed and the candles were spluttering and burn-ing low, Florence tried so hard to be a substitute for one small Dombey, that her fortitude and perseverance might have almost won her a free right to bear the name herself.

And high was her reward, when, one Satur-day evening, as little Paul was sitting down as usual to "resume his studies," she sat down by his side, and showed him all that was so rough made smooth, and all that was so dark made clear and plain before him. It was nothing but a startled look in Paul's wan face—a flush—a smile—and then a close embrace—but God knows how her heart leaped up at this rich payment for her trouble.

"Oh, Floy!" cried her brother, "how I love you! How I love you, Floy!"

"And I you, dear!"

"Oh! I am sure of that, Floy."

And so little Paul struggled on bravely under his heavy load, never complaining, but growing more old-fashioned day by day—and growing frailer, too.

Then came the holidays, and a grand party at the school, to which Florence came, looking so beautiful in her simple ball dress that Paul could hardly make up his mind to let her go again.

"But what is the matter, Floy?" he asked, almost sure he saw a tear on her face.

"Nothing, dear. We will go home together, and I'll nurse you till you are strong again."

"Nurse me!" echoed Paul.

Paul couldn't understand what that had to do with it, nor why the other guests looked on so seriously, nor why Florence turned away her face for a moment, and then turned it back, lighted up again with smiles.

"Floy," said Paul, holding a ringlet of her dark hair in his hand. "Tell me, dear. Do *you* think I have grown old-fashioned?"

His sister laughed and fondled him, and told him "No."

"Because I know they say so," returned Paul, "and I want to know what they mean, Floy."

Florence would have sat by him all night, and would not have danced at all of her own accord, but Paul made her, by telling her how much it pleased him. And he told her the truth, too; for his small heart swelled, and his face glowed, when he saw how much they all admired her, and how she was the beautiful little rosebud of the room.

Then after the party came the leave-taking, for Paul was going home. And every one was good to him—even the pompous doctor, and Cornelia—and bade him good-bye with many regrets; for they were afraid, as they looked upon his pinched, wan face, that he would not be able to come back and take up that load of heavy books ever again.

There was a great deal, the next day and afterwards, which Paul could not quite get clear in his mind. As, why they stopped at Mrs. Pipchin's for a while instead of going straight home; why he lay in bed, with Florence sitting by him; whether that had been his father in the room, or only a tall shadow on the wall.

He could not even remember whether he had often said to Florence, "Oh, Floy, take me home and never leave me!" but he thought he had. He fancied sometimes he had heard himself repeating, "Take me home, Floy! take me home!"

But he could remember, when he got home, and was carried up the well-remembered stairs, that there had been the rumbling of a coach for many hours together, while he lay upon the seat, with Florence still beside him, and Mrs. Pipchin sitting opposite. He remembered his old bed too, when they laid him down in it; but there was something else, and recent, too, that still perplexed him.

"I want to speak to Florence, if you please," he said. "To Florence by herself, for a moment!"

She bent down over him, and the others stood away.

"Floy, my pet, wasn't that papa in the hall, when they brought me from the coach?"

"Yes, dear."

"He didn't cry, and go into his room, Floy, did he, when he saw me coming in?"

Florence shook her head, and pressed her lips against his cheek.

"I'm very glad he didn't cry," said little Paul. "I thought he did. Don't tell them that I asked."

Paul never rose from his little bed. He lay there, listening to the noises in the street quite tranquilly; not caring much how time went, but watching everything about him with observing eyes. And when visitors or servants came softly to the door to inquire how he was, he always answered for himself, "I am better! I am a great deal better, thank you! Tell papa so!"

And sometimes when he awoke out of a feverish dream, in which he thought a river was bearing him away, he would see a figure seated motionless, with bowed head, at the foot of his couch. Then he would stretch out his hands and cry, "Don't be sorry for me, dear papa! Indeed, I am quite happy!"

His father coming, and bending down to him —which he did quickly, and without first pausing by the bedside—Paul held him round the neck, and repeated those words to him several times, and very earnestly; and Paul never saw him in his room at any time, whether it were day or night, but he called out, "Don't be so sorry for me! Indeed, I am quite happy!" This was the beginning of his always saying in the morning that he was a great deal better, and that they were to tell his father so.

Then one day he asked to see all his friends, and shook hands with each one quietly, and bade them good-bye. His father he clung to as though he felt more deeply for that proud man's sorrow and disappointment, than any unhappiness on his own account. For he was going to his mother—about whom he had often talked with Florence in these closing days.

"Now lay me down," he said, "and Floy, come close to me, and let me see you!"

Sister and brother wound their arms around each other, and the golden light came streaming in and fell upon them, locked together.

"How fast the river runs, between its green banks and the rushes, Floy! But it's very near the sea. I hear the waves! They always said so!"

Presently he told her that the motion of the boat upon the stream was lulling him to rest. How green the banks were now, how bright the flowers growing on them, and how tall the rushes! Now the boat was out at sea, but gliding smoothly on. And now there was a shore before him. Who stood on the bank!—

He put his hands together, as he had been used to do at his prayers. He did not remove his arms to do it; but they saw him fold them so behind her neck.

"Mamma is like you, Floy. I know her by the face. But tell them that the print upon the stairs at school is not divine enough. The light about the head is shining on me as I go!"

The golden ripple on the wall came back again, and nothing else stirred in the room.

The old, old fashion! The fashion that came in with our first garments, and will last unchanged until our race has run its course, and the wide firmament is rolled up like a scroll. The old, old fashion—Death!

Oh, thank God, all who see it, for that older fashion yet, of Immortality! And look upon us, angels of young children, with regards not quite estranged, when the swift river bears us to the ocean!

## II.   HOW FLORENCE CAME INTO HER OWN

The death of Paul, far from softening Mr. Dombey's heart toward his daughter, only served to widen the gap between them. He had been secretly hurt by Paul's preference for Florence, and now was more cold and distant with her than ever.

She, poor child, had this deep sorrow to bear in addition to the loss of Paul. Many and many a night when no one in the house was stirring, and the lights were all extinguished, she would softly leave her own room, and with noiseless feet descend the staircase, and approach her father's door. Against it, scarcely breathing, she would rest her face and head, and press her lips, in the yearning of her love. She crouched upon the cold stone floor outside it, every night, to listen even for his breath; and in her one absorbing wish to be allowed to show him some affection, to be a consolation to him, to win him over to some tenderness for her, his solitary child, she would have knelt down at his feet, if she had dared, in humble supplication.

No one knew it. No one thought of it. The door was ever closed, and he shut up within. He went out once or twice, and it was said in the house that he was very soon going on a journey; but he lived in those rooms, and lived alone, and never saw her or inquired for her. Perhaps he did not even know that she was in the house.

But one night Florence found the door slightly ajar. She paused a moment tremblingly, and then pushed it open and entered.

Her father sat at his old table in the middle room. He had been arranging some papers and destroying others, and the latter lay in fragile ruins before him. The rain dripped heavily upon the glass panes in the outer room, where he had so often watched poor Paul, a baby; and the low complainings of the wind were heard without.

He sat with his eyes fixed on the table, so immersed in thought that a far heavier tread than the light foot of his child could make, might have failed to rouse him. His face was turned towards her. By the waning lamp, and at that haggard hour, it looked worn and dejected; and in the utter loneliness surrounding him there was an appeal to Florence that struck home.

"Papa! papa! Speak to me, dear papa!"

He started at her voice.

"What is the matter?" he said sternly. "Why do you come here? What has frightened you?"

If anything had frightened her, it was the face he turned upon her. The glowing love within the breast of his young daughter froze before it, and she stood and looked at him as if stricken into stone. There was not one touch of tenderness or pity in it.

Did he see before him the successful rival of his son, in health and life? Did he look upon his own successful rival in that son's affection? Did a mad jealousy and withered pride poison sweet remembrances that should have endeared and made her precious to him? Could it be possible that it was gall to him to look upon her in her beauty and her promise: thinking of his infant boy!

Florence had no such thoughts. But love is quick to know when it is spurned and hopeless; and hope died out of hers, as she stood looking in her father's face.

"I ask you, Florence, are you frightened? Is there anything the matter, that you come here?"

"I came, papa—"

"Against my wishes. Why?"

She saw he knew why—it was written broadly on his face—and dropped her head upon her hands with one prolonged low cry.

He took her by the arm. His hand was cold and loose, and scarcely closed upon her.

"You are tired, I dare say," he said, taking up the light and leading her towards the door, "and want rest. We all want rest. Go, Florence. You have been dreaming."

The dream she had had was over then, God help her! and she felt that it could never more come back.

"I will remain here to light you up the stairs. The whole house is yours, above there," said her father, slowly. "You are its mistress now. Good-night!"

Still covering her face, she sobbed, and answered, "Good-night, dear papa," and silently ascended. Once she looked back as if she would have returned to him, but for fear. It was a momentary thought, too hopeless to encourage; and her father stood there with the light—hard, unresponsive, motionless—until her fluttering dress was lost in the darkness.

The days that followed were lonely and sad

indeed for the child. Her father went away upon a journey, and she was left entirely alone in the great house, but for the companionship of a faithful maid, Susan Nipper, and of her dog Diogenes.

Then some kind friends in the country took pity upon her loneliness and invited her to visit them.

When she came home she was amazed to find huge scaffolds built all around the house. It was being remodelled. Only her own little room had not been changed. The explanation for all this work came a few days later when her father came home accompanied by two ladies. One was old and greatly overdressed. The other— her daughter—was very beautiful, but with a cold, hard face.

"Mrs. Skewton," said her father, turning to the first, and holding out his hand, "this is my daughter Florence."

"Charming, I am sure," observed the lady, putting up her glass. "So natural! My darling Florence, you must kiss me, if you please."

Florence having done so, turned towards the other lady by whom her father stood waiting.

"Edith," said Mr. Dombey, "this is my daughter Florence. Florence, this lady will soon be your mamma."

Florence started, and looked up at the beautiful face in a conflict of emotions, among which the tears that name awakened struggled for a moment with surprise, interest, admiration, and an indefinable sort of fear. Then she cried out, "Oh, papa, may you be happy! may you be very, very happy all your life!" and then fell weeping on the lady's bosom.

There was a short silence. The beautiful lady, who at first had seemed to hesitate whether or not she should advance to Florence, held her to her breast, and pressed the hand with which she clasped her close about her waist, as if to reassure and comfort her. Not one word passed the lady's lips. She bent her head down over Florence, and she kissed her on the cheek, but said no word.

"Shall we go on through the rooms," said Mr. Dombey, "and see how our workmen are doing? Pray allow me, my dear madam."

He said this in offering his arm to Mrs. Skewton, and they turned and went up the staircase. The beautiful lady lingered a moment to whisper to the little girl.

"Florence," said the lady hurriedly, and looking into her face with great earnestness, "You will not begin by hating me?"

"By hating you, mamma!" cried Florence, winding her arm round her neck, and returning the look.

"Hush! Begin by thinking well of me," said the beautiful lady. "Begin by believing that I will try to make you happy and that I am prepared to love you, Florence."

Again she pressed her to her breast—she had spoken in a rapid manner, but firmly—and Florence saw her rejoin them in the other room.

And now Florence began to hope that she would learn from her new and beautiful mamma how to gain her father's love; and in her sleep that night, in her lost old home, her own mamma smiled radiantly upon the hope and blessed it. Dreaming Florence!

Very soon after this her new mamma came to live with them; and the gloomy house took on some semblance of life. But the marriage was not a happy one. Even Florence could see that. Mrs. Dombey's face did not belie her character. She was haughty and reserved—a fitting match for Mr. Dombey. He had married her out of a desire to have a suitable ornament for his home and position in society. She—it was whispered—had been lured into a "fine" marriage by her matchmaking mother. It was no wonder, then, that the marriage should be unhappy.

Only toward Florence did the proud lady unbend. The child's impulsive greeting had stirred her heart in a sudden and surprising way; and when Mrs. Dombey saw how lonely she was and how her life had been starved, she tried to make good her promise to the child to love her and be good to her always.

But once again poor Florence was misunderstood by her father.  He saw that his cold wife cared only for the child, and he thought that just as Florence had cheated him out of some of Paul's love she was now estranging his wife from him.  It was cruelly unjust, but Mr. Dombey was so arrogant that he could see things only in his own narrow way.

Thus matters went along in this unhappy house for several months.  Mr. and Mrs. Dombey met rarely, except at the table or in some social gathering, when the words which passed between them were of the coldest.

Then Mr. Dombey hit upon the meanest trick of his weak nature.  When he found that he could not "humble" his wife by ordinary means, he called in his business manager, Carker, a smooth, deceitful man whose hair was plastered down close to his white forehead and whose teeth shone in a continual sly smile.  To Carker Mr. Dombey would entrust various messages for Mrs. Dombey, as to the running of the house, the hiring of servants, and the like.  Mr. Dombey knew that she would resent such petty interference, especially through an outsider;

but he did not know that she submitted quietly to these indignities simply for the sake of Florence, whom she wished to protect.  And even her love for the girl was given in secret, for the same reason.

Florence, long since awakened from her dream, mournfully observed the estrangement between her father and new mother; and saw it widen more and more, and knew that there was greater bitterness between them every day. It had been very hard to have all her love repulsed, but it now seemed harder to be compelled to doubt her father, or choose between him and this mother, so affectionate and dear to her, yet whose other moods she could only witness with distrust or fear.

One great sorrow, however, was spared her. She never had the least suspicion that Mrs. Dombey, by her tenderness for her, widened the separation from her father, or gave him new cause of dislike.  If she had thought it, for a single moment, what grief she would have felt, what sacrifice she would have tried to make, poor loving girl!

No word was ever spoken between Florence and her mother now, on these subjects.  Mrs. Dombey had said there ought to be between them, in that wise, a silence like the grave itself; and Florence felt that she was right.

In this state of affairs her father was brought home suffering and ill, and gloomily retired to his own rooms, where he was tended by servants, not approached by his wife, and had no friend or companion but Mr. Carker, who always withdrew near midnight.

Every night Florence would listen out in the hall for news of him, after leaving her mother. But, late one evening, she was surprised to see a bright light burning in her room, and her mother sitting before the dying fire looking so fiercely at it that it terrified her.

"Mamma!" she cried, "what is the matter?"

Mrs. Dombey started; looking at her with such a strange dread in her face that Florence was more frightened than before.

"Mamma!" said Florence, hurriedly advancing. "Dear mamma! what is the matter?"

"I have not been well," said Mrs. Dombey, shaking, and still looking at her in the same strange way. "I have had bad dreams, my love."

"And have not yet been to bed, mamma?"

"No," she returned. "Half-waking dreams."

Her features gradually softened; and suffering Florence to come close to her, within her embrace, she said in a tender manner, "But what does my bird do here! What does my bird do here!"

"I have been uneasy, mamma, in not seeing you to-night, and in not knowing how papa was; and I—"

Florence stopped there, and said no more.

"Is it late?" her mother asked, fondly putting back the curls that mingled with her own dark hair, and strayed upon her face.

"Very late. Near day."

"Near day!" she repeated in surprise.

"Mamma!" said Florence. "Oh, mamma, what can I do, what should I do, to make us happier? Is there anything?"

"Nothing," she replied.

"Are you sure of that? Can it never be? If I speak now of what is in my thoughts, in spite of what we have agreed," said Florence, "you will not blame me, will you?"

"It is useless," she replied, "useless. I have told you, dear, that I have had bad dreams. Nothing can change them, or prevent their coming back."

"I do not understand," said Florence, gazing on her agitated face, which seemed to darken as she looked.

Her mother's clenched hand tightened on the trembling arm she had in hers, and as she looked down on the alarmed and wondering face, her own feelings subsided. "Oh, Florence!" she said, "I think I have been nearly mad to-night!" and humbled her proud head upon the girl's neck, and burst into tears.

"Don't leave me! be near me! I have no hope but in you!" These words she said a score of times.

Florence was greatly puzzled and distressed, and could only repeat her promise of love and trust.

Through six months that followed upon Mr. Dombey's illness and recovery, no outward change was shown between him and his wife. Both were cold and proud; and still Mr. Carker —a man whom she detested—bore his petty commands to her.

As for Florence, the little hope she had ever held for happiness in their new home was quite gone now. That home was nearly two years old, and even the patient trust that was in her could not survive the daily blight of such an experience.

Florence loved her father still, but by degrees had come to love him rather as some dear one who had been, or who might have been, than as the hard reality before her eyes. Something of the softened sadness with which she loved the memory of little Paul or her mother, seemed to enter now into her thoughts of him, and to make them, as it were, a dear remembrance. Whether it was that he was dead to her, and that partly for this reason, partly for his share in those old objects of her affection, and partly for the long association of him with hopes that were withered and tendernesses he had frozen, she could not have told; but the father whom she loved began to be a vague and dreamy idea to her; hardly more substantially connected with her real life than the image she would sometimes conjure up of her dear brother yet alive, and growing to be a man, who would protect and cherish her.

The change, if it may be called one, had stolen on her like the change from childhood to womanhood, and had come with it. Florence was almost seventeen, when, in her lonely musings, she was conscious of these thoughts.

She was often alone now, for the old association between her and her mamma was greatly changed. At the time of her father's illness, and when he was lying in his room downstairs, Florence had first observed that Edith avoided her. Wounded and shocked, and yet unable to reconcile this with her affection when they did meet, she sought her in her own room at night, once more.

"Mamma," said Florence, stealing softly to her side, "have I offended you?"

She answered "No."

"I must have done something," said Florence. "Tell me what it is. You have changed your manner to me, dear mamma. I cannot say how instantly I feel the least change; for I love you with my whole heart."

"As I do you," said Mrs. Dombey. "Ah, Florence, believe me never more than now!"

"Why do you go away from me so often, and keep away?" asked Florence. "And why do you sometimes look so strangely on me, dear mamma? You do so, do you not?"

"Dear Florence, it is for your good. Why, I cannot tell you now. But you will believe I have always tried to make you happy, dear, will you not?"

"Mamma," said Florence, anxiously, "there is a change in you, in more than what you say to me, which alarms me. Let me stay with you a little."

"No, dearest. I am best left alone now, and I do best to keep apart from you, of all else. Ask me no questions, but believe that what I am, I am not of my own will, or for myself. Forgive me for having ever darkened your dark home—I am a shadow on it, I know well—and let us never speak of this again."

"Mamma," sobbed Florence, "we are not to part?"

"We do this that we may not part," said her mother. "Ask no more. Go, Florence! My love and my remorse go with you!"

Thus did Mrs. Dombey hide from Florence one dark secret—that her husband was displeased with their love for each other. It was for Florence's welfare that she felt compelled to hide her affections.

From that hour Florence and she were as they had been no more. For days together they would seldom meet, except at table, and when Mr. Dombey was present. Then Mrs. Dombey, imperious, inflexible, and silent, never looked at her. Whenever Mr. Carker was of the party, as he often was during the progress of Mr. Dombey's recovery, she was more distant towards her than at other times. Yet she and Florence never encountered, when there was no one by, but she would embrace her as affectionately as of old, though not with the same relenting of her proud aspect; and often when she had been out late she would steal up to Florence's room as she had been used to do in the dark, and whisper "Good-night."

Then came a dreadful day not long afterwards when it was found that Mrs. Dombey had fled from her home. The day was the second anniversary of this ill-starred marriage; and the poor, misguided woman left a note for her husband telling him that she had gone away with the man whom he had trusted most (and whom she hated most) Mr. Carker. It was a foolish way to be revenged for the harsh treatment she had received, but it served her purpose. Mr. Dombey was wounded in his most vulnerable spot—his pride.

As for Florence, she was overcome with grief; yet in the midst of her own emotion she could realize her father's bitterness. Yielding at once to the impulse of her affection and forgetful of his past coldness, Florence hurried to him with her arms stretched out and crying, "Oh dear, dear papa!" tried to clasp him round the neck.

But in his wild despair he shook her off so roughly that she almost fell to the floor; telling her she could join her mother, for all he cared, as they had always been in league against him.

She did not sink down at his feet; she did not shut out the sight of him with her trembling hands; she did not weep nor speak one word of reproach. She only uttered a single low cry of pain and then fled from the house like a hunted animal.

Without a roof over her head—without father or mother, she was indeed an orphan.

While the days went by, after Florence's flight, what was the proud man doing? Did he ever think of his daughter or wonder where she had gone? Did he suppose she had come home again and was leading her old life in the weary house? He did not utter her name or make any search for her. He might have thought of her constantly, or not at all. It was all one for any sign he made.

But this was sure. He did *not* think that he had lost her. He had no suspicion of the truth that she had fled away from him. He had lived too long shut up in his pride, seeing her a patient, gentle creature in his path, to have any fear of that. And so he waited, day by day, until she should make her appearance on the stairs or at the table as before.

But the days dragged slowly by and she did not come.

The sea had ebbed and flowed through a whole year. Through a whole year the winds and clouds had come and gone; the ceaseless work of Time had been performed, in storm and sunshine. Through a whole year the famous House of Dombey and Son had fought a fight for life, against doubtful rumors, unsuccessful ventures, and most of all, against the bad judgment of its head, who would not contract its enterprises by a hair's breadth, and would not listen to a word of warning that the ship he strained so hard against the storm was weak, and could not bear it.

For Mr. Dombey had grown strangely indifferent and reckless, and plunged blindly into speculation.

The year was out, and the great House was down.

One summer afternoon there was a buzz and whisper, about the streets of London, of a great failure. A certain cold, proud man, well known there, was not there, nor was he represented there. Next day it was noised abroad that Dombey and Son had stopped, and next night there was a list of bankrupts published, headed by that name.

Nobody's opinion stayed the misfortune, lightened it, or made it heavier. It was understood that the affairs of the House were to be wound up as they best could be; that Mr. Dombey freely resigned everything he had, and asked for no favor from any one. That any resumption of the business was out of the question, as he would listen to no friendly negotiation having that compromise in view; that he had relinquished every post of trust or distinction he had held as a man respected among merchants; and that he was a broken man.

The old home where Paul had died and whence Florence had fled away was now empty and deserted—a wreck of what it had been. All the furniture and hangings had been sold to satisfy Mr. Dombey's creditors; and he now lived there alone in one cheerless room—a man without friends, without hope.

But at last he began to come to his senses; to see what a treasure he had cast away in Florence; to recall his own injustice and cruelty toward her.

In the miserable night he thought of it; in the dreary day, the wretched dawn, the ghostly, memory-haunted twilight, he remembered. In agony, in sorrow, in remorse, in despair!

"Papa! papa!" He heard the words again, and saw the face. He saw it fall upon the trembling hands, and heard the one prolonged, low cry go upward.

Oh! He did remember it! The rain that fell upon the roof, the wind that mourned outside the door, had foreknowledge in their melancholy sound. He knew now what he had done. He knew that he had called down that upon his head, which bowed it lower than the heaviest stroke of fortune. He knew now what it was to be rejected and deserted; now, when every loving blossom he had withered in his innocent daughter's heart was snowing down in ashes on him.

He thought of her as she had been that night when he and his bride came home. He thought of her as she had been in all the home events of the abandoned house. He thought now that of all around him, she alone had never changed. His boy had faded into dust, his proud wife had deserted him, his flatterer and friend had been transformed into the worst of villains, his riches had melted away, the very walls that sheltered him looked on him as a stranger; she alone had turned the same mild, gentle look upon him always. Yes, to the latest and the last. She had never changed to him—nor had he ever changed to her—and she was lost.

As, one by one, they fell away before his mind—his baby hope, his wife, his friend, his fortune—oh, how the mist through which he had seen her cleared, and showed him her true self! How much better than this that he had loved her as he had his boy, and lost her as he had his boy, and laid them in their early grave together!

As the days dragged by, it seemed to him that he should go mad with remorse and longing. He haunted Paul's room and Florence's room—so empty now—as though they were his only dwelling-place. He had meant to go away, but clung to this tie in the house as the last and only thing left to him. He would go to-morrow. To-morrow came. He would go to-morrow. Every night, within the knowledge of no human creature, he came forth, and wandered through the despoiled house like a ghost. Many a morning when the day broke, with altered face drooping behind the closed blind in his window, he pondered on the loss of his two children. It was one child no more. He reunited them in his thoughts, and they were never asunder.

Then, one day, when strange fancies oppressed him more than usual, he paused at Florence's door and gazed wildly down as though suddenly awakened from a dream.

He heard a cry—a loving, pleading voice— and there at his knees knelt Florence herself.

"Papa! Dearest papa! I have come back to ask forgiveness. I never can be happy more, without it!"

Unchanged still. Of all the world, unchanged. Raising the same face to his as on that miserable night Asking *his* forgiveness!

"Dear papa, oh, don't look strangely on me! I never meant to leave you. I never thought of it, before or afterwards. I was frightened when I went away and could not think. Papa, dear, I am changed. I am penitent. I know my fault. I know my duty better now. Papa, don't cast me off or I shall die!"

He tottered to his chair. He felt her draw his arms about her neck: he felt her put her own around his; he felt her kisses on his face; he felt her wet cheek laid against his own; he felt—oh, how deeply!— all that he had done.

Upon the breast that he had bruised, against the heart that he had almost broken, she laid his face, now covered with his hands, and said, sobbing,—

"I have been far away, dear papa, and could not come back before this. I have been across the seas, and I have a home of my own over there now. Oh, I want you to see it! I want to take you there; for my home is *your* home—always, always! Say you will pardon me, you will come to me!"

He would have said it if he could. He would have raised his hands and besought *her* for pardon, but she caught them in her own and put them down hurriedly.

"You will come, I know, dear papa! And I will know by that that you forgive me. And we will never talk about what is past and forgotten; never again!"

As she clung closer to him, in another burst of tears, he kissed her on the lips, and, lifting up his eyes, said, "Oh, my God, forgive me, for I need it very much!"

With that he dropped his head again, lamenting over and caressing her, and there was not a sound in all the house for a long, long time; they remaining clasped in one another's arms, in the glorious sunshine that had crept in with Florence.

# The Story of Pip

## AS TOLD BY HIMSELF

### I. HOW PIP HELPED THE CONVICT

MY father's family name being Pirrip, and
my Christian name Philip, my infant
tongue could make of both names nothing
longer than Pip. So I called myself Pip, and
came to be called Pip.

I give Pirrip as my father's family name, on
the authority of his tombstone and my sister—
Mrs. Joe Gargery, who married the blacksmith.
As I never saw my father or my mother, my first
fancies regarding what they were like were un-
reasonably derived from their tombstones.

Ours was the marsh country down by the
river, within twenty miles of the sea. My most
vivid memory of these early days was of a raw
evening about dusk. As such time I found out
for certain that this bleak spot where I chanced
to be wandering all alone was the churchyard;
that the low, leaden line beyond was the river;
and that the small bundle of shivers growing
afraid of it all and beginning to cry was myself
—Pip.

"Hold your noise!" cried a terrible voice, as

a man started up from among the graves at the side of the church porch.

He was a fearful looking man, clad in coarse gray, covered with mud and brambles, and with a great clanking chain upon his leg.

"Tell us your name!" said the man.  "Quick!"

"Pip, sir."

"Show us where you live," said the man. "P'int out the place!"

I pointed to where our village lay, on the flat in-shore among the trees a mile or more from the church.

The man, after looking at me for a moment, turned me upside-down and emptied my pockets. There was nothing in them but a piece of bread. When the church came to itself—for he was so sudden and strong that he made it go head-over-heels before me, and I saw the steeple under my feet—when the church came to itself, I say, I was seated on a high tombstone, trembling, while he ate the bread ravenously.

"You young dog," said the man, licking his lips, "what fat cheeks you ha' got."

I believe they were fat, though I was at that time undersized for my years, and not strong.

"Darn *me* if I couldn't eat 'em," said the man, with a threatening shake of his head, "and if I ha'nt half a mind to 't!"

I earnestly expressed my hope that he

wouldn't, and held tighter to the tombstone on which he had put me; partly to keep myself upon it; partly to keep myself from crying.

"Now lookee here!" said the man. "Where's your mother?"

"There, sir!" said I.

He started, made a short run, and stopped and looked over his shoulder.

"There, sir!" I timidly explained, pointing to an inscription on a stone; "that's my mother."

"Oh!" said he, coming back. "And is that your father alonger your mother?"

"Yes, sir," said I; "him too; 'late of this parish.'"

"Ha!" he muttered then, considering. "Who d' ye live with—supposin' you're kindly let to live, which I ha'nt made up my mind about?"

"My sister, sir—Mrs. Joe Gargery—wife of Joe Gargery, the blacksmith, sir."

"Blacksmith, eh?" said he, and looked down at his leg.

After darkly looking at his leg and at me several times, he came closer to my tombstone, took me by both arms, and lifted me back as far as he could hold me, so that his eyes looked most powerfully down into mine, and mine looked most helplessly up into his.

"Now lookee here," he said, "the question

being whether you're to be let to live. You know what a file is?"

"Yes, sir."

"And you know what wittles is?"

"Yes, sir."

After each question he tilted me over a little more, so as to give me a greater sense of help-lessness and danger.

"You get me a file." He tilted me again. "And you get me some wittles. If you don't—!"

He tilted me again and shook me till my teeth chattered.

"In—indeed—I will, sir," said I, "if you will only let me go. I'll run all the way home."

"Well, see that you come back. But to-morrow morning will do—early—before day. I'll wait for you here."

As he released me, I needed no second bidding, but scurried away as fast as I could, and soon reached the blacksmith shop.

My sister, Mrs. Joe Gargery, was more than twenty years older than I, and had established a great reputation with herself and the neighbors because she had brought me up "by hand." Having at that time to find out for myself what the expression meant, and knowing her to have a hard and heavy hand, and to be much in the habit of laying it upon her husband as well as upon me, I supposed that Joe Gargery and I were both brought up by hand.

She was not a good-looking woman, my sister; and I had a general impression that she must have made Joe Gargery marry her by hand. Joe was a fair man, with curls of flaxen hair on each side of his smooth face, and with eyes of such a very undecided blue that they seemed to have somehow got mixed with their own whites. He was a mild, good-natured, sweet-tempered, easy-going, foolish, dear fellow—a sort of Hercules in strength, and also in weakness.

My sister, Mrs. Joe, with black hair and eyes, had such a prevailing redness of skin that I sometimes used to wonder whether it was possible she washed herself with a nutmeg-grater instead of soap. She was tall and bony, and almost always wore a coarse apron, fastened behind with two loops, and having a bib in front that was stuck full of pins and needles.

Joe's forge adjoined our house, which was a wooden house, as many of the dwellings in our country were—most of them, at that time. When I ran home from the churchyard the forge was shut up, and Joe was sitting alone in the kitchen. Joe and I being fellow-sufferers, and having confidences as such, Joe imparted a confidence to me the moment I raised the latch of the door and peeped in at him opposite to it, sitting in the chimney corner.

"Mrs. Joe has been out a dozen times looking for you, Pip. And she's out now, making it a baker's dozen."

"Is she?"

"Yes, Pip," said Joe; "and what's worse, she's got Tickler with her."

At this dismal intelligence, I twisted the only button on my waistcoat round and round, and looked in great depression at the fire. Tickler was a wax-ended piece of cane, worn smooth by collision with my tickled frame.

"She sot down," said Joe, "and she got up, and she made a grab at Tickler, and she Rampaged out. That's what she did," said Joe, slowly clearing the fire between the lower bars with the poker, and looking at it; "she Rampaged out, Pip."

"Has she been gone long, Joe?" I always treated him as no more than my equal.

"Well," said Joe, glancing up at the Dutch clock, "she's been on the Rampage, this last spell, about five minutes, Pip. She's a coming! Get behind the door, old chap, and have the jack-towel betwixt you."

I took the advice. My sister, Mrs. Joe, throwing the door wide open, and finding an obstruction behind it, immediately divined the cause, and applied Tickler to its farther investigation.

"Where have you been?" she demanded, between tickles.

"I have only been to the churchyard," said I, crying and rubbing myself.

"Churchyard!" repeated my sister. "If it warn't for me you'd been to the churchyard long ago, and stayed there! Who brought you up by hand?"

My thoughts strayed from that question as I looked disconsolately at the fire. For the fugitive out on the marshes with the ironed leg, the file, the food, and the dreadful pledge I was under to steal, from under my sister's very roof, rose before me in the avenging coals.

"Ha!" said Mrs. Joe, restoring Tickler to his station. "Churchyard, indeed! You may well say churchyard, you two." (One of us, by the by, had not said it at all.) "You'll drive *me* to the churchyard betwixt you, one of these days, and oh, a pr-r-recious pair you'd be without me!"

As she applied herself to set the tea-things, Joe peeped down at me over his leg, as if he were mentally calculating what kind of pair we should make, under such circumstances. After that, he sat feeling his right-side flaxen curls and whisker, and following Mrs. Joe about with his blue eyes, as his manner always was at squally times.

My sister had a sudden, severe way of cutting and buttering bread, which never varied. Now she ripped me off a section of loaf, bidding me eat and be thankful. Though I was hungry, I dared not eat; for she was a strict housekeeper who would miss any further slices, and I must not let that dreadful man out in the churchyard go hungry. So I resolved to put my hunk of bread and butter down the leg of my trousers— a plan which I presently found the chance to carry out.

It was Christmas Eve, and I had to stir the pudding for next day with a copper-stick. I tried it with the load upon my leg (and that made me think afresh of the man with the load on *his* leg), and found the tendency of exercise to bring the bread-and-butter out at my ankle quite unmanageable. Happily, I slipped away and deposited that part of my conscience in my garret bedroom.

"Hark!" said I, when I had done my stirring and was taking my final warm in the chimney corner, before being sent up to bed; "was that great guns, Joe?"

"Ah!" said Joe. "There's another conwict off."

"What does that mean, Joe?" said I.

Mrs. Joe, who always took explanations upon herself, said snappishly, "Escaped. Escaped."

"There was a conwict off last night," added Joe, "after sunset-gun. And they fired warning of him. And now it appears they're firing warning of another."

"Who's firing?" said I.

"Drat that boy," interposed my sister, frowning at me over her work, "what a questioner he is. Ask no questions, and you'll be told no lies."

It was not very polite to herself, I thought, as she always answered. But she never was polite, unless there was company.

Presently Joe said to me in a quiet kind of whisper. "Hulks, Pip; prison ships. They're firing because one of the thieves on the hulks is got away."

Thieves! Prison ships! And here I was planning to rob my sister of the bread and butter; and honest Joe of a file! Truly conscience is a fearful thing, yet there was no turning back for me.

That night the rest of the dreadful deed was done. Just before daybreak I crept out, carrying the file which I had found among Joe's tools, the slice of bread, and a pie which was too convenient in the pantry, and which I took in the hope it was not intended for early use and would not be missed for some time.

I found the man with the iron waiting for me, crouched behind a tombstone.

"Are you alone?" he asked hoarsely.

"Yes, sir."

"No one following you?"

"No, sir."

"Well," said he. "I believe you. Give me them wittles, quick."

I had often watched a large dog of ours eating his food; and I now noticed a decided similarity between the dog's way of eating and the man's. The man took strong, sharp, sudden bites, just like the dog. He swallowed, or rather snapped up, every mouthful, too soon and too fast; and he looked sideways here and there while he ate, as if he thought there was danger in every direction of somebody's coming to take the pie away.

"Now give us hold of the file, boy," he said, when he had finished swallowing.

I did so, and he bent to the iron like a madman, and began filing it away in quick, fierce rasps. I judged this a good time to slip away, and he paid no further attention to me. The last I heard of him, the file was still going.

"And where the mischief ha' *you* been?" was Mrs. Joe's Christmas salutation, when I and my conscience showed ourselves.

I said I had been down to hear the chimes.

"Ah, well!" observed Mrs. Joe. "You might ha' done worse."

Not a doubt of that, I thought.

We were to have a superb dinner—so Joe slyly told me—consisting of a leg of pork and greens, a pair of roast stuffed fowls, and a handsome pie which had been baked the day before.

I started when he spoke about the pie, but his blue eyes beamed upon me kindly.

My sister having so much to do, was going to church vicariously; that is to say, Joe and I were going. In his working clothes, Joe was a well-knit characteristic-looking blacksmith; in his holiday clothes, he was more like a scarecrow in good circumstances, than anything else. Nothing that he wore then fitted him or seemed to belong to him. On the present festive occasion he emerged from his room, when the blithe bells were ringing, the picture of misery, in a full suit of Sunday penitentials. As to me, I think my sister must have had some general idea that I was a young offender who must be punished each holy-day by being put into clothes so tight that I could on no account move my arms and legs without danger of something bursting.

Joe and I going to church, therefore, must have been a moving spectacle for compassionate

minds.   Yet, what I suffered outside was nothing to what I underwent within.   The terrors
that had assailed me whenever Mrs. Joe had
gone near the pantry or out of the room, were
only to be equalled by the remorse with which
my mind dwelt on what my hands had done.
Under the weight of my wicked secret, I pondered whether even the Church would be powerful enough to shield me from the wrath to come.

Mr. Wopsle, the clerk at church, was to dine
with us; and Mr. Hubble, the wheelwright, and
Mrs. Hubble; and Uncle Pumblechook ( Joe's
uncle, but Mrs. Joe appropriated him), who was
a well-to-do cornchandler in the nearest town,
and drove his own chaise-cart.   The dinner
hour was half-past one.

When Joe and I got home, we found the table
laid, and Mrs. Joe dressed, and the dinner dressing, and the front door unlocked (it never was
at any other time) for the company to enter by,
and everything most splendid.   And still, not a
word of the robbery.

Oh, the agony of that festive dinner!   During
each helping of my plate I ate mechanically,
hardly daring to lift my eyes, and clutching
frantically at the leg of the table for support.
With each mouthful we drew nearer to that pie
—and discovery!   But as they chattered away,

I felt a faint hope that they might perhaps forget the pie.

They did not, for presently my sister said to Joe, "Clean plates—cold."

I got a fresh hold on the table leg. I foresaw I was doomed.

"You must taste," said my sister, addressing the guests with her best grace, "you must finish with a pie, in honor of Uncle Pumblechook."

The company murmured their compliments. Uncle Pumblechook, sensible of having deserved well of his fellow-creatures, said,—quite vivaciously, all things considered,—"Well, Mrs. Joe, we'll do our best endeavors; let us have a cut at this same pie."

My sister went out to get it. I heard her steps proceed to the pantry. I saw Mr Pumblechook balance his knife. I saw reawakening appetite in the Roman nostrils of Mr. Wopsle. I heard Mr. Hubble remark that "a bit of savory pie would lay atop of anything you could mention, and do no harm," and I heard Joe say "you shall have some, Pip." I have never been absolutely certain whether I uttered a shrill yell of terror, merely in spirit, or in the bodily hearing of the company. I felt that I could bear no more, and that I must run away. I released the leg of the table, and ran for my life.

But I ran no farther than the house door, for

there I ran headforemost into a party of soldiers
with their muskets, one of whom held out a pair
of handcuffs to me, saying, "Here you are, look
sharp, come on!"

The vision of a file of soldiers caused the dinner party to rise from the table in confusion, and
caused Mrs. Joe, re-entering the kitchen empty-
handed, to stop short and stare, in her wondering lament of "Gracious goodness, gracious me,
what's gone—with the—pie!"

"Excuse me, ladies and gentlemen," said the
sergeant, "but as I have mentioned at the door
to this smart young shaver" (which he hadn't),
"I am on a chase in the name of the king, and I
want the blacksmith."

"And pray, what might you want with him?"
retorted my sister, quick to resent his being
wanted at all.

"Missis," returned the gallant sergeant,
"speaking for myself, I should reply, the honor
and pleasure of his fine wife's acquaintance;
speaking for the king, I answer, a little job
done."

This was received as rather neat in the sergeant; insomuch that Mr. Pumblechook cried
audibly, "Good again!"

"You see, blacksmith," said the sergeant, who
had by this time picked out Joe with his eye,
"we have had an accident with these, and I find

the lock of one of 'em goes wrong, and the coupling don't act pretty. As they are wanted for immediate service, will you throw your eye over them?"

Joe threw his eye over them, and pronounced that the job would necessitate the lighting of his forge fire, and would take nearer two hours than one.

"Will it? Then will you set about it at once, blacksmith," said the off-hand sergeant, "as it's on his Majesty's service. And if my men can bear a hand anywhere, they'll make themselves useful." With that, he called to his men, who came trooping into the kitchen one after another, and piled their arms in a corner.

All these things I saw without then knowing that I saw them, for I was in an agony of apprehensions. But, beginning to perceive that the handcuffs were not for me, and that the military had so far got the better of the pie as to put it in the background, I collected a little more of my scattered wits.

The soldiers were out hunting for the convicts that had escaped. And as soon as Joe had mended the handcuffs, they fell in line and started again for the marshes. Joe caught an appealing look from me, and timidly asked if he and I might go along with them. The consent was given and away we went.

After a rough journey over bogs and through briars, a loud shout from the soldiers in front announced that one of the fugitives had been caught. We ran hastily up and peered into a ditch. It was my convict.

He was hustled into the handcuffs and hustled up a hill where stood a rough hut or sentry-box, and here we halted to rest.

My convict never looked at me, except once. While we were in the hut, he stood before the fire looking thoughtfully at it, or putting up his feet by turns upon the hob. Suddenly he turned to the sergeant and remarked:

"I wish to say something respecting this escape. It may prevent some persons laying under suspicion alonger me."

"You can say what you like," returned the sergeant, standing coolly looking at him with his arms folded, "but you have no call to say it here. You'll have opportunity enough to say about it, and hear about it, before it's done with, you know."

"I know, but this is another p'int, a separate matter. A man can't starve; at least *I* can't. I took some wittles, up at the village over yonder —where the church stands a'most out on the marshes."

"You mean stole," said the sergeant.

"And I'll tell you where from. From the blacksmith's."

"Hallo!" said the sergeant, staring at Joe.

"Hallo, Pip!" said Joe, staring at me.

"It was some broken wittle—that's what it was—and a dram of liquor, and a pie."

"Have you happened to miss such an article as a pie, blacksmith?" asked the sergeant, confidentially.

"My wife did, at the very moment when you came in. Don't you know, Pip?"

"So," said my convict, turning his eyes on Joe in a moody manner, and without the least glance at me; "so you're the blacksmith, are you? Then I'm sorry to say I've eat your pie."

"God knows you're welcome to it—so far as it was ever mine," returned Joe, with a saving remembrance of Mrs. Joe. "We don't know what you have done, but we wouldn't have you starve to death for it, poor miserable fellow-creatur. Would us, Pip?"

Something that I had noticed before clicked in the man's throat again, and he turned his back. The boat had returned, and his guard were ready, so we followed him to the landing-place made of rough stakes and stones, and saw him put into the boat, which was rowed by a crew of convicts like himself. No one seemed surprised to see him, but they looked at him stolidly and rowed him back to the hulks as a matter of course.

My state of mind regarding the pie was curious. I do not recall that I felt any tenderness of conscience in reference to Mrs. Joe, when the fear of being found out was lifted off me. But I loved Joe—perhaps for no better reason in those early days than because the dear fellow let me love him—and, as to him, my inner self was not so easily composed. It was much upon my mind (particularly when I first saw him looking about for his file) that I ought to tell Joe the whole truth. Yet I did not, and for the reason that I mistrusted that if I did he would think me worse than I was. The fear of losing Joe's confidence and of thenceforth sitting in the chimney corner at night staring drearily at my forever lost companion and friend, tied up my tongue. And so the whole truth never came out.

## II.   PIP AND ESTELLA

At this time I was only an errand boy around the forge, and my education was limited to spelling out the names on the tombstones. So in the evenings they sent me to school to Mr. Wopsle's aunt, a worthy woman, who used to go to sleep regularly from six to seven while her small class was supposed to study.

But I was lucky enough to find a friend in her granddaughter, Biddy.  She was about my own age, and, while her shoes were generally untied and her hands sometimes dirty, her heart was in the right place and she had a good head. So with her help I struggled through my letters as if they had been a bramble-bush, getting considerably worried and scratched by each letter in turn.  Then came the dreaded nine figures to add to my troubles.  But at last I learned to read and cipher.

I do not know which was the prouder, Joe or I, when I wrote him my first letter (which was hardly needed, as he sat beside me while I wrote it).

"I say, Pip, old chap!" he cried, opening his eyes very wide, "what a scholar you are!  Ain't you?"

"I should like to be," I answered, looking at the slate with satisfaction.

Mrs. Joe made occasional trips with Uncle Pumblechook on market-days, to assist him in buying such household stuffs and goods as required a woman's judgment; Uncle Pumblechook being a bachelor and reposing no confidences in his domestic servant.  On this particular evening she came home from such a trip, bringing Uncle Pumblechook with her.

"Now," said she, unwrapping herself with haste and excitement, and throwing her bonnet back on her shoulders where it hung by the strings, "if this boy ain't grateful this night, he never will be!"

I looked as grateful as any boy possibly could, who was wholly uninformed why he ought to assume that expression.

"You have heard of Miss Havisham up town, haven't you?" continued my sister, addressing Joe. "She wants this boy to go and play there. And of course he's going. And he had *better* play there," said my sister, shaking her head at me as an encouragement to be extremely light and sportive, "or I'll work him!"

I had heard of Miss Havisham up town— everybody for miles round had heard of Miss Havisham up town—as an immensely rich and grim lady who lived in a large and dismal house barricaded against robbers, and who led a life of seclusion.

"Well to be sure!" said Joe, astonished, "I wonder how she come to know Pip!"

"Noodle!" cried my sister. "Who said she knew him? Couldn't she ask Uncle Pumblechook if he knew of a boy to go and play there? And couldn't Uncle Pumblechook, being always

considerate and thoughtful of us, mention this
boy that I have been a willing slave to? And
couldn't Uncle Pumblechook, being sensible
that for anything we can tell, this boy's fortune
may be made by his going to Miss Havisham's,
offer to take him into town to-night in his own
chaise-cart, and to keep him to-night, and to
take him with his own hands to Miss Havisham's to-morrow morning? And Lor-a-mussy
me!" cried my sister, casting off her bonnet in
sudden desperation, "here I stand talking to
mere Mooncalfs, with Uncle Pumblechook waiting, and the mare catching cold at the door,
and the boy grimed with dirt from the hair of
his head to the sole of his foot!"

With that, she pounced upon me, like an eagle
on a lamb, and my face was squeezed into
wooden bowls in sinks, and my head was put
under taps of water-butts, and I was soaped and
kneaded, and towelled, and thumped, and har-
rowed, and rasped, until I really was quite beside myself.

When my ablutions were completed, I was
put into clean linen of the stiffest character, like
a young penitent into sackcloth, and was trussed
up in my tightest and fearfullest suit. I was
then delivered over to Mr. Pumblechook, who
formally received me as if he were the Sheriff,
saying pompously, "Boy, be forever grateful to

all friends, but especially unto them which brought you up by hand!"

"Good-bye, Joe!"

"God bless you, Pip, old chap!"

I had never parted from him before, and what with my feelings and what with soap-suds, I could at first see no stars from the chaise-cart. But they twinkled out one by one, without throwing any light on the questions as to why on earth I was going to play at Miss Havisham's, and what on earth I was expected to play at.

I spent the night at Uncle Pumblechook's, and the next morning after breakfast we proceeded to Miss Havisham's. It was a dismal looking house with a great many iron bars to it. Some of the windows had been walled up, and the others were rustily barred. There was a courtyard in front, which was also barred; so we had to wait, after ringing the bell, for some one to open it.

Presently a window was raised, and a clear voice demanded, "What name?"

"Pumblechook," was the reply.

The voice returned, "Quite right," and the window was shut again, and a young lady came across the courtyard, with keys in her hand.

"This," said Mr. Pumblechook, "is Pip."

"This is Pip, is it?" returned the young lady,

who was very pretty and seemed very proud; "come in, Pip."

Mr. Pumblechook was coming in also, when she stopped him with the gate.

"Oh!" she said. "Did you wish to see Miss Havisham?"

"If Miss Havisham wished to see me," returned Mr. Pumblechook, discomfited.

"Ah!" said the girl; "but you see she don't."

She said it so finally, and in such an undiscussible way, that Mr. Pumblechook, though in a condition of ruffled dignity, could not protest.

We went into the house by a side door—the great front entrance had two chains across it outside—and the first thing I noticed was that the passages were all dark, and that she had left a candle burning there. She took it up, and we went through more passages and up a staircase, and still was all dark, and only the candle lighted us.

At last we came to the door of a room and she said, "Go in."

I answered, more in shyness than politeness, "After you, miss."

To this she returned, "Don't be ridiculous, boy; I am not going in." And scornfully walked away, and—what was worse—took the candle with her.

This was very uncomfortable, and I was half

afraid.   However, the only thing to do being
to knock at the door, I knocked, and was told
from within to enter.   I entered, therefore, and
found myself in a pretty large room, well lighted
with wax candles.   No glimpse of daylight was
to be seen in it.   It was a dressing-room, as I
supposed from the furniture, though much of
it was of forms and uses then quite unknown to
me.   But prominent in it was a draped table
with a gilded looking-glass, and that I make out
at first sight to be a fine lady's dressing-table.

In an arm-chair, with an elbow resting on the
table and her head leaning on that hand, sat the
strangest lady I have ever seen, or shall ever see.

She was dressed in rich materials,—satins
and lace and silks,—all of white.   Her shoes
were white.   And she had a long white veil de-
pendent from her hair, and she had bridal flowers
in her hair, but her hair was white.   Some bright
jewels sparkled on her neck and on her hands,
and some other jewels lay sparkling on the table.
Dresses, less splendid than the dress she wore,
and half-packed trunks, were scattered about.
She had not quite finished dressing, for she had
but one shoe on,—the other was on the table
near her hand,—her veil was but half arranged,
her watch and chain were not put on, and her
handkerchief, gloves, some flowers, and a prayer-

book lay confusedly heaped about the looking-glass. "Who is it?" said the lady at the table.

"Pip, ma'am."

"Pip?"

"Mr. Pumblechook's boy, ma'am. Come—to play."

"Look at me," said Miss Havisham. "You are not afraid of a woman who has never seen the sun since you were born?"

I regret to state that I was not afraid of telling the enormous lie comprehended in the answer "No."

"I am tired," said Miss Havisham. "I want diversion, and I have done with men and women. Play."

I looked foolish and bewildered, not knowing what to do.

"I sometimes have sick fancies," she went on, "and I have a sick fancy that I want to see some play. There, there!" with an impatient movement of the fingers of her right hand; "play, play, play!"

For a moment, with the fear of my sister's working me before my eyes, I had a desperate idea of starting round the room in the assumed character of Mr. Pumblechook's chaise-cart. But I felt myself so unequal to the performance that I gave it up, and stood looking at Miss Havisham in what I suppose she took for a dogged manner, inasmuch as she said, when we had taken a good look at each other,

"Are you sullen and obstinate?"

"No, ma'am, I am very sorry for you, and very sorry I can't play just now. If you complain of me I shall get into trouble with my sister, so I would do it if I could; but it's so new here, and so strange, and so fine, and melancholy—" I stopped, fearing I might say too much.

"Call Estella," she commanded, looking at me. "You can do that."

To stand in a strange house calling a scornful young lady by her first name was almost as bad as playing to order. But she answered at last.

"My dear," said Miss Havisham, "let me see you play cards with this boy."

"What do you play, boy?" asked Estella, with the greatest disdain.

"Nothing but 'beggar my neighbor,' Miss."

"Beggar him," said Miss Havisham to Estella. So we sat down to cards.

It was then I began to understand that everything in the room had stopped, with the watch and the clock, a long time ago. I noticed that Miss Havisham put down the jewel exactly on the spot from which she had taken it up. As Estella dealt the cards, I glanced at the dressing-table again, and saw that the shoe upon it, once white, now yellow, had never been worn.

"He calls the knaves, Jacks, this boy!" said Estella with disdain, before our first game was out. "And what coarse hands he has! And what thick boots!"

I had never thought of being ashamed of my hands before; but now I began to consider them. Her contempt for me was so strong that I caught it.

She won the game, and I dealt. I misdealt, as was only natural, when I knew she was lying in wait for me to do wrong; and she denounced me for a stupid, clumsy laboring-boy.

"You say nothing of her," remarked Miss Havisham to me, as she looked on. "She says many hard things of you, but you say nothing of her. What do you think of her?"

"I don't like to say," I stammered.

"Tell me in my ear," said Miss Havisham, bending down.

"I think she is very proud," I replied, in a whisper.

"Anything else?"

"I think she is very pretty."

"Anything else?"

"I think she is very insulting," (She was looking at me then with a look of supreme aversion.)

"Anything else?"

"I think I should like to go home."

"You shall go soon," said Miss Havisham aloud; "play the game out."

I played the game to an end with Estella, and she beggared me. She threw the cards down on the table when she had won them all, as if she despised them for having been won of me.

"When shall I have you here again?" said Miss Havisham. "Let me think. I know nothing of days of the weeks, or of weeks of the year. Come again after six days. You hear?"

"Yes, ma'am."

"Estella, take him down. Let him have something to eat, and let him roam and look about him while he eats. Go, Pip."

I followed the candle down, as I had followed the candle up, and she stood it in the place where we had found it. Until she opened the side entrance, I had fancied, without thinking about it, that it must necessarily be night-time. The rush of the daylight quite confounded me, and made me feel as if I had been in the candle-light of the strange room many hours.

When I reached home, my sister was very curious to know all about Miss Havisham and what I had seen and done at her house. Uncle Pumblechook, too, came hurrying over, armed with many questions.

I was naturally a truthful boy—as boys go—
but I knew instinctively that I could not make
myself understood about that strange visit.  So
I didn't try.  When he fired his first question,
as to "What was Miss Havisham like?"

"Very tall and dark," I told him.

"Is she, Uncle?" asked my sister.

Mr. Pumblechook winked assent; from which
I at once inferred that he had never seen Miss
Havisham, for she was nothing of the kind.

"Good!" said Mr. Pumblechook conceitedly.
"Now, boy!  What was she a doing of when
you went in to-day?" he continued.

"She was sitting," I answered, "in a black
velvet coach."

Mr. Pumblechook and Mrs. Joe stared at one
another—as they well might—and both repeated,
"In a black velvet coach?"

"Yes," said I.  "And Miss Estella—that's
her niece, I think—handed her in cake and
wine at the coach-window, on a gold plate.  And
we all had cake and wine on gold plates.  And
I got up behind the coach to eat mine, because
she told me too."

"Was anybody else there?" asked Mr. Pumblechook.

"Four dogs," said I.

"Large or small?"

"Immense," said I "And they fought for veal cutlets out of a silver basket."

Mr. Pumblechook and Mrs. Joe stared at one another again in utter amazement. I was perfectly frantic—a reckless witness under the torture—and would have told them anything.

"Where *was* this coach, in the name of gracious?" asked my sister.

"In Miss Havisham's room." They stared again. "But there weren't any horses to it." I added this saving clause in the moment of rejecting four richly caparisoned coursers which I had had wild thoughts of harnessing.

"Can this be possible, uncle?" asked Mrs. Joe. "What can the boy mean?"

"I'll tell you, Mum," said Mr. Pumblechook. "My opinion is, it's a sedan-chair. She's flighty, you know—very flighty—quite flighty enough to pass her days in a sedan-chair."

"Did you ever see her in it, uncle?" asked Mrs. Joe.

"How could I?" he returned, forced to the admission, "when I never see her in my life. Never clapped eyes upon her!"

"Goodness, uncle! And yet you have spoken to her!"

"Just through the door," he replied testily. "Now, boy, what did you play?"

"We played with flags."

"Flags!" echoed my sister.

"Yes," said I. "Estella waved a blue flag, and I waved a red one, and Miss Havisham waved one sprinkled all over with little gold stars, out at the coach-window. And then we all waved our swords and hurrahed."

"Swords!" repeated my sister. "Where did you get swords from?"

"Out of a cupboard," said I. "And I saw pistols in it—and jam—and pills. And there was no daylight in the room, but it was all lighted up with candles."

"That's true, Mum," said Mr. Pumblechook, with a grave nod. "That's the state of the case, for that much I've seen myself." And then they both stared at me, and I at them, and plaited the right leg of my trousers with my right hand.

If they had asked me any more questions I should undoubtedly have betrayed myself, for I was even then on the point of mentioning that there was a balloon in the yard, and should have hazarded the statement but for my invention being divided between that phenomenon and a bear. They were so much occupied, however, in discussing the marvels I had already presented for their consideration, that I escaped. The subject still held them when Joe came in from his work to have a cup of tea. To whom my sister, more for the relief of her own mind than for the gratification of his, related my pretended experiences.

Now, when I saw Joe open his blue eyes and roll them all around the kitchen in helpless amazement, I was overtaken by penitence; but only as regarded him—not in the least as regarded the other two. Towards Joe and Joe only, I considered myself a young monster, while they sat debating what results would come to me from Miss Havisham's acquaintance and favor. They had no doubt that Miss Havisham would "do something" for me; their doubts related to the form that something would take. My sister stood out for "property." Mr. Pumblechook was in favor of a handsome premium for binding me apprentice to some genteel trade,—say, the corn and seed trade, for instance. Joe fell into the deepest disgrace with both, for offering the bright suggestion that I might only be presented with one of the dogs who had fought for the veal cutlets. "If a fool's head can't express better opinions that that," said my sister, "and you have got any work to do, you had better go and do it." So he went.

After Mr. Pumblechook had driven off, and when my sister was washing up, I stole into the forge to Joe, and remained by him until he had done for the night. Then I said, "Before the fire goes out, Joe, I should like to tell you something."

"Should you, Pip?" said Joe, drawing his shoeing-stool near the forge. "Then tell us. What is it, Pip?"

"Joe," said I, taking hold of his rolled up shirt sleeve, and twisting it between my finger and thumb, "you remember all that about Miss Havisham's?"

"Remember?" said Joe.  " I believe you! Wonderful!"

"It's a terrible thing, Joe; it ain't true."

"What are you telling of, Pip?" cried Joe, falling back in his greatest amazement. "You don't mean to say it's—"

"Yes, I do; it's lies, Joe."

"But not all of it?  Why sure you don't mean to say, Pip, that there was no black welwet co—ch?" For, I stood shaking my head. "But at least there was dogs, Pip?  Come, Pip," said Joe persuasively, "if there warn't no weal cut-lets, at least there was dogs?"

"No, Joe."

"A dog?" said Joe. "A puppy?  Come?"

"No, Joe, there was nothing at all of the kind."

As I fixed my eyes hopelessly on Joe, Joe contemplated me in dismay. "Pip, old chap!

This won't do, old fellow! I say! Where do you expect to go to?"

"It's terrible, Joe; ain't it?"

"Terrible?" cried Joe. "Awful! What possessed you?"

"I don't know what possessed me, Joe," I replied, letting his shirt sleeve go, and sitting down in the ashes at his feet, hanging my head; "but I wish you hadn't taught me to call knaves at cards, Jacks; and I wish my boots weren't so thick nor my hands so coarse."

And then I told Joe that I felt very miserable, and that I hadn't been able to explain myself to Mrs. Joe and Pumblechook, and that there had been a beautiful young lady at Miss Havisham's who was dreadfully proud, and that she had said I was common, and much more to that effect.

"There's one thing you may be sure of, Pip," said Joe, after some rumination, "namely, that lies is lies. Howsever they come, they didn't ought to come, and they come from the father of lies, and work round to the same. Don't you tell no more of 'em, Pip. *That* ain't the way to get out of being common, old chap. And as to being common, I don't make it out at all clear. You are oncommon in some things. You're oncommon small. Likewise you're a oncommon scholar."

"No, I am ignorant and backward, Joe."

"Why, see what a letter you wrote last night. Wrote in print even! I've seen letters—Ah! and from gentlefolks!—that I'll swear weren't wrote in print," said Joe.

"I have learnt next to nothing, Joe. You think much of me. It's only that."

"Well, Pip," said Joe, "be it so or be it so n't, you must be a common scholar afore you can be a oncommon one, I should hope! The king upon his throne, with his crown upon his 'ed, can't sit and write his acts of Parliament in print, without having begun, when he were a un-promoted prince, with the alphabet—Ah!" added Joe, with a shake of the head that was full of meaning, "and begun at A too, and worked his way to Z!"

There was some hope in this piece of wisdom, and it rather encouraged me.

"You're not angry with me, Joe?"

"No, old chap. But you might bear in mind about them dog fights and weal cutlets when you say your prayers to-night. That's all, old chap, and don't never do it no more."

III.    HOW PIP FELL HEIR TO GREAT EXPECTATIONS

The happy idea occurred to me a morning or two later when I woke, that probably the best step I could take towards making myself uncommon was to get out of Biddy everything she knew.  In pursuance of this idea, I mentioned to Biddy, when I went to Mr. Wopsle's aunt's at night, that I had a particular reason for wishing to get on in life, and that I should feel very much obliged to her if she would impart all her learning to me.  Biddy, who was the most obliging of girls, immediately said she would, and indeed began to carry out her promise within five minutes.

The books at the school were few and ragged, but we attacked them all valiantly during the course of the winter, and even refreshed our budding minds with newspaper scraps.  And with every new piece of knowledge I could fancy myself saying to Miss Estella, *"Now* am I common?"

At the appointed time I returned to Miss Havisham's, and my hesitating ring at the gate brought out Estella.

"You are to come this way to-day," she said after admitting me, and took me to quite another part of the house.

We went in at a door, which stood open, and

into a gloomy room with a low ceiling on the ground floor at the back. There was some company in the room, and Estella said to me as she joined it, "You are to go and stand there, boy, till you are wanted." "There," being the window, I crossed to it, and stood "there," in a very uncomfortable state of mind, looking out.

Presently she brought a candle and led the way down a dark passage to a staircase. As we went up the stairs we met a man coming down. He was large and bald, with bushy black eyebrows and deep-set eyes which were disagreeably keen. He was nothing to me at the time, and yet I couldn't help observe him.

He stopped and looked at me.

"How do *you* come here?" he asked.

"Miss Havisham sent for me, sir," I explained.

"Well! Behave yourself. I have a pretty large experience of boys, and you're a bad set of fellows. Now mind!" said he, biting the side of his great forefinger as he frowned at me, "you behave yourself!"

With those words he released me—which I was glad of, for his hand smelt of scented soap—and went his way downstairs. I wondered whether he could be a doctor; but no, I thought; he couldn't be a doctor, or he would have a quieter manner. There was not much time to consider the subject, for we were soon in Miss Havisham's room, where she and everything else were just as I had left them. Estella left me standing near the door, and I stood there until Miss Havisham cast her eyes upon me from the dressing-table.

"So!" she said, without being startled or surprised; "the days have worn away, have they?"

"Yes, ma'am. To-day is—"

"There, there, there!" with the impatient movement of her fingers. "I don't want to know. Are you ready to play?"

I was obliged to answer in some confusion, "I don't think I am, ma'am."

"Not at cards again?" she demanded with a searching look.

"Yes, ma'am; I could do that, if I was wanted."

"Since this house strikes you old and grave, boy," said Miss Havisham, impatiently, "and you are unwilling to play, are you willing to work?"

I could answer this inquiry with a better heart than I had been able to find for the other question, and I said I was quite willing.

"Then go into that opposite room," said she, pointing at the door behind me with her withered hand, "and wait there till I come."

I did so, and after hearing mice scamper about the faintly lighted room for a few minutes, Miss

Havisham entered and laid a hand upon my shoulder. In her other hand she had a crutch-headed stick on which she leaned, and she looked like the Witch of the place.

"This," said she, pointing to the long table with her stick, "is where I will be laid when I am dead. They shall come and look at me here."

With some vague misgivings that she might get upon the table then and there and die at once, the complete realization of the ghastly wax-work at the Fair, I shrank under her touch.

"What do you think that is?" she asked me, again pointing with her stick; "that, where those cobwebs are?"

"I can't guess what it is, ma'am."

"It's a great cake. A bride-cake. Mine!"

She looked all around the room in a glaring manner, and then said, leaning on me while her hand twitched my shoulder, "Come, come, come! Walk me, walk me!"

From this I made out that the work I had to do was to walk Miss Havisham round and round the room. So I started at once, she following at a fitful speed, twitching the hand upon my shoulder. After a while she said, "Call Estella," and I did so. Then the company I had noticed before filed in and paid their respects, which Miss Havisham hardly seemed to hear.

While Estella was away lighting them down,

Miss Havisham still walked with her hand on my shoulder, but more and more slowly. At last she stopped before the fire, and said, after muttering and looking at it some seconds,

"This is my birthday, Pip."

I was going to wish her many happy returns, when she lifted her stick.

"I don't suffer it to be spoken of. I don't suffer those who were here just now or any one to speak of it. They come here on the day, but they dare not refer to it."

Of course *I* made no further effort to refer to it.

"On this day of the year, long before you were born, this heap of decay," stabbing with her crutched stick at the pile of cobwebs on the table but not touching it, "was brought here. It and I have worn away together. The mice have gnawed at it, and sharper teeth than teeth of mice have gnawed at me."

She held the head of her stick against her heart as she stood looking at the table; she in her once white dress, all yellow and withered; the once white cloth, all yellow and withered; everything around, in a state to crumble under a touch.

"When the ruin is complete," said she, with a ghastly look, "and when they lay me dead, in my bride's dress on the bride's table—which shall be done, and which will be the finished curse upon him—so much the better if it is done on this day!"

She stood looking at the table as if she stood looking at her own figure lying there. I remained quiet. Estella returned, and she too remained quiet. It seemed to me that we continued thus a long time. In the heavy air of the room, and the heavy darkness that brooded in its remoter corners, I even had an alarming fancy that Estella and I might presently crumble to dust.

And thus passed my second visit to Miss Havisham's.

On my next visit, the following week, I saw a garden-chair—a light chair on wheels, that you pushed from behind. I entered, that same day, on a regular occupation of pushing Miss Havisham in this chair (when she was tired of walking with her hand upon my shoulder) round her own room, and across the landing, and round the other room. Over and over and over again, we would make these journeys, and sometimes they would last as long as three hours at a stretch. I insensibly fall into a general mention of these journeys as numerous, because it was at once settled that I should return every alternate day at noon for these purposes, and because I am now going to sum up a period of at least eight or ten months.

As we began to be more used to one another, Miss Havisham talked more to me, and asked me such questions as, what had I learned and what was I going to be. I told her I was going to be apprenticed to Joe, I believed; and I enlarged upon my knowing nothing and wanting to know everything, in the hope that she might offer some help towards that desirable end. But she did not; on the contrary, she seemed to prefer my being ignorant. Neither did she ever give me any money nor anything but my daily dinner.

Estella was always there to let me in and out. Sometimes she would coldly tolerate me; sometimes she would condescend to me; sometimes she would be quite familiar with me; sometimes she would say she hated me. But always my admiration for her grew apace, and I was the more firmly resolved not to be common.

There was a song Joe used to hum fragments of at the forge, of which the burden was Old Clem. This was not a very ceremonious way of rendering homage to a patron saint; for I believe Old Clem stood in that relation towards smiths. It was a song that imitated the measure of beating upon iron, and was a mere lyrical excuse for the introduction of Old Clem's re-

spected name.   Thus, you were to hammer boys
round—Old Clem!   With a thump and a sound
—Old Clem!   Beat it out, beat it out—Old
Clem!   With a clink for the stout—Old Clem!
Blow the fire, blow the fire—Old Clem!   Roaring dryer, soaring higher—Old Clem!   One day
soon after the appearance of the chair, Miss
Havisham suddenly saying to me, with the impatient movement of her fingers, "There, there,
there! Sing!"   I was surprised into crooning
this ditty as I pushed her over the floor.   It
happened so to catch her fancy that she took it
up in a low brooding voice as if she were singing
in her sleep.   After that, it became customary
with us to have it as we moved about, and Estella would often join in; though the whole
strain was so subdued, even when there were
three of us, that it made less noise in the grim
old house than the lightest breath of wind.

What could I become with these surroundings?   How could my character fail to be influenced by them?   Is it to be wondered at
if my thoughts were dazed, as my eyes were,
when I come out into the natural light from the
misty yellow rooms?

Perhaps I might have talked it all over with
Joe, had it not been for those enormous tales
about coaches, dogs, and veal cutlets.   But I
felt a natural shrinking from having Miss

Havisham and Estella discussed, which had come upon me in the beginning, and which grew much more potent as time went on. I reposed complete confidence in no one but Biddy; and so I told her everything. Why it came natural for me to do so, and why Biddy had a deep concern in everything I told her, I did not know then, though I think I know now.

We went on in this way for a long time, and it seemed likely that we should continue to go on in this way for a long time, when, one day, Miss Havisham stopped short as she and I were walking, she leaning on my shoulder; and said with some displeasure,

"You are growing tall, Pip!"

She said no more at the time; but she presently stopped and looked at me again; and presently again; and after that, looked frowning and moody. On the next day of my attendance, when our usual exercise was over, and I had landed her at her dressing-table, she stayed me with a movement of her impatient fingers:

"Tell me the name again of that blacksmith of yours."

"Joe Gargery, ma'am."

"Meaning the master you were to be apprenticed to?"

"Yes, Miss Havisham."

"You had better be apprenticed at once.

Would Gargery come here with you, and bring your indentures, do you think?"

I signified that I had no doubt he would take it as an honor to be asked.

"Then let him come."

"At any particular time, Miss Havisham?"

"There, there! I know nothing about times. Let him come soon, and come alone with you."

So, in my very next visit, I conducted Joe, stiffly arrayed in his Sunday clothes, into Miss Havisham's presence. She asked him several questions about himself and my apprenticeship, while the poor fellow twisted his hat in his hand and persisted in answering *me*. I am afraid I was a least bit ashamed of him, when I saw that Estella stood at the back of Miss Havisham's chair, and that her eyes laughed mischievously.

Miss Havisham glanced at him as if she understood what he really was, better than I had thought possible, seeing what an awkward figure he cut; and took up a little bag from the table beside her.

"Pip has earned a premium here," she said, "and here it is. There are five-and-twenty guineas in this bag. Give it to your master, Pip."

As if he were absolutely out of his mind with the wonder awakened in him by her strange figure and the strange room, Joe, even at this pass, persisted in addressing me.

"This is wery liberal on your part, Pip," said Joe, "and it is as such received and grateful welcome, though never looked for, far nor near nor nowheres. And now, old chap, may we do our duty! May you and me do our duty, both on us, by one and another, and by them which your liberal present—have—conweyed—to be— for the satisfaction of mind—of—them as never—" here Joe showed that he felt he had fallen into frightful difficulties, until he triumphantly rescued himself with the word, "and from myself far be it!" These words had such a round and convincing sound for him that he said them twice.

"Good-bye, Pip!" said Miss Havisham, after my papers were signed. "Let them out, Estella."

"Am I to come again, Miss Havisham?" I asked.

"No. Gargery is your master now. Gargery! One word!"

Thus calling him back as I went out of the door, I heard her say to Joe, in a distinct emphatic voice. "The boy has been a good boy here, and that is his reward. Of course, as an honest man, you will expect no other and no more."

How Joe got out of the room, I have never

been able to determine; but I know that when he did get out he was steadily proceeding up-stairs instead of coming down, and was deaf to all remonstrances until I went after him and laid hold of him. In another minute we were outside the gate, and it was locked, and Estella was gone. When we stood in the daylight alone again, Joe backed up against a wall, and said to me, "Astonishing!" And there he remained so long, saying, "Astonishing!" at intervals, so often, that I began to think his senses were never coming back. At length he prolonged his re-mark into "Pip, I do assure *you* this is as-TON-ishing!" and so, by degrees, became able to walk away.

It is a most miserable thing to feel ashamed of home. There may be black ingratitude in the thing, and the punishment may be retributive and well deserved; but that it is a miserable thing, I can testify.

Home had never been a pleasant place to me, because of my sister's temper. But, Joe had sanctioned it, and I believed in it. I had believed in the best parlor as a most elegant place; I had believed in the front door as a mysterious portal of the Temple of State whose solemn opening was attended with a sacrifice of roast fowls; I had believed in the kitchen as a chaste though not magnificent apartment; I had believed in the forge as the glowing road to manhood and independence. Within a single year all this was changed. Now, it was all coarse and common, and I would not have had Miss Havisham and Estella see it on any account.

How much of my ungracious condition of mind may have been my own fault, how much Miss Havisham's, how much my sister's, is now of no moment to me or to any one. The change was made in me; the thing was done.

Once, it had seemed to me that when I should at last roll up my shirt-sleeves and go into the forge, Joe's apprentice, I should be distinguished and happy. Now that the reality was here, I only felt that I was dusty with the dust of small-coal and that I had a weight upon my daily remembrance to which the anvil was a feather.

I remember that at a later period of my "time," I used to stand about the churchyard on Sunday evenings, when night was falling, comparing my own perspective with the windy marsh view, and making out some likeness between them by thinking how flat and low both were, and how on both there came an unknown way and a dark mist and then the sea. I was quite as dejected on the first working-day of my apprenticeship as in that after-time; but I am glad to know that I never breathed a murmur to Joe while my indentures lasted. It is

about the only thing I *am* glad to know of myself in that connection.

For, though it includes what I proceed to add,
all the merit was Joe's. It was not because
I was faithful, but because Joe was faithful, that
I never ran away and went for a soldier or a
sailor. It was not because I had a stronge sense
of the virtue of industry, but because of Joe,
that I worked with tolerable zeal against the
grain.

As I was getting too big for Mr. Wopsle's
aunt's room, my education under that lady
ended. Not, however, until Biddy had imparted
to me everything she knew, from the little cata-
logue of prices to a comic song she had once
bought for a half-penny. Although the only
coherent part of the latter piece were the opening lines:

> When I went to Lunnon town, sirs,
>   Too rul loo rul
>   Too rul loo rul
> Was't I done very brown, sirs?
>   Too rul loo rul
>   Too rul loo rul

—still, in my desire to be wiser, I got this composition by heart with the utmost gravity; nor
do I recollect that I questioned its merit, except
that I thought (as I still do) the amount of Too
rul somewhat in excess of the poetry.

Thus matters went until I reached the fourth year of my apprenticeship; and they bade fair to end that way, but for an unusual event.

I had gone with Joe one Saturday night to a neighboring tavern to join some friends. In the course of the conversation, a strange gentleman, who had been listening to us, stepped between us and the fire, and said:

"I understand that one of you is a blacksmith, by name, Joseph Gargery. Which is the man?"

"Here is the man," said Joe.

"You have an apprentice," pursued the stranger, "commonly known as Pip. Is he here?"

"Here," I answered.

The stranger did not recognize me, but I did recognize him as the man I had once met on the stair at Miss Havisham's.

"I wish to have a private talk with you both," he said. "Perhaps we had better go to your house."

So, in a wondering silence we left the inn and walked home, where Joe, vaguely recognizing the occasion to be important, opened the front door and ushered us into the state parlor.

The stranger told us that he was a lawyer in London, and was now acting as confidential agent for some one else. He wished to purchase my apprenticeship papers from Joe, if Joe were willing to release me.

"Lord forbid that I should want anything for not standing in Pip's way," said Joe, staring.

"Lord forbidding is pious, but not to the purpose," returned the lawyer. "The question is, Would you want anything? Do you want anything?"

"The answer is," returned Joe, sternly, "No."

"Then I am instructed to communicate to him," said Mr. Jaggers, throwing his finger at me, sideways, "that he will come into a handsome property. Further, that it is the desire of the present possessor of that property, that he be immediately removed from his present sphere of life and from this place, and be brought up as a gentleman—in a word, as a young fellow of great expectations."

My dream was out; my wild fancy was surpassed by sober reality; Miss Havisham was going to make my fortune on a grand scale!— at least, so I thought at the time.

"Now, Mr. Pip," pursued the lawyer, "I address the rest of what I have to say to you. You are to understand, first, that it is the request of the person from whom I take my instructions, that you always bear the name of Pip. You will have no objection, I dare say, to that easy condition. But if you have any objection, this is the time to mention it."

I gasped, but had no objection.

"The second condition," he resumed, "is that you are not to know the name of your benefactor, for the present. I will act as your guardian and see that you are educated properly. You desire an education, don't you?"

I replied that I had always longed for it.

"Good. Then we will see to getting you a tutor. But first you should have some new clothes to come away in. When will you be ready to leave? Say this day week. You'll want some money. Shall I leave you twenty guineas?"

He produced a long purse, with the greatest coolness, and counted them out on the table and pushed them over to me. This was the first time he had taken his leg from the chair. He sat astride of the chair when he had pushed the money over, and sat swinging his purse and eyeing Joe.

"Well, Joseph Gargery? You look dumbfoundered?"

"I *am!*" said Joe, in a very decided manner.

"It was understood that you wanted nothing for yourself, remember?"

"It were understood," said Joe. "And it *are* understood. And it ever will be similar according."

"But what," said the lawyer, swinging his purse, "what if it was in my instructions to make you a present, as compensation?"

"As compensation what for?" Joe demanded.

"For the loss of his services."

Joe laid his hand upon my shoulder with the touch of a woman. I have often thought of him since, like a steam-hammer, that can crush a man or pat an egg-shell, in his combination of strength with gentleness. "Pip is that hearty welcome," said Joe, "to go free with his services, to honor and fortun', as no words can tell him. But if you think as Money can make compensation to me for the loss of the little child— what come to the forge—and ever the best of friends—"

Oh, dear, good Joe, whom I was so ready to leave and so unthankful to, I see you again, with your muscular blacksmith's arm, before your eyes, and your broad chest heaving, and your voice dying away. Oh, dear, good, faithful, tender Joe, I feel the loving tremble of your hand upon my arm, as solemnly this day as if it had been the rustle of an angel's wing!

But at the time I was lost in the mazes of my future fortunes, and could not retrace the by-paths we had trodden together. I begged Joe to be comforted. Joe scooped his eyes with his disengaged wrist, as if he were bent on gouging himself, but said not another word.

After the lawyer had taken his leave, Joe and I went into the kitchen, where we found Biddy and my sister, and told them of my good fortune.

They dropped their sewing and looked at me. Joe held his knees and looked at me. I looked at them, in turn. After a pause they heartily congratulated me; but there was a certain touch of sadness in their congratulations that I rather resented.

Now that I was actually going away I became quite gloomy. I did not know why, but I sat in the chimney corner looking at the fire, my elbow on my knee; and while the others tried to make the conversation cheerful, I grew gloomier than ever.

But the bright sunlight of the next morning dispelled my doubts and fears, and I began to count the days eagerly. I went down to Trabb's, the tailor's, and got measured for a wonderful suit of clothes, much to the consternation of Trabb's boy, who thought himself equal to any blacksmith that ever lived. Then I went to the hatter's and the bootmaker's and the hosier's, and felt rather like Mother Hubbard's dog, whose outfit required the services of so many trades. I also went to the coach-office and took my place for seven o'clock Saturday morning. And everywhere about the village the news of my great expectations preceded me and I was heartily stared at.

Uncle Pumblechook was especially officious at this time. He acted as though he were the sole cause of all this.

"To think," said he, swelling up, "that I should have been the humble instrument of this proud reward."

He thought, like all the rest of us, that Miss Havisham was my unknown benefactor. It was a natural mistake, as she had been kind to me in her way; and I had seen the lawyer at her house. But it was a mistake after all and led to other unhappy blunders ere I learned the truth.

For, many years afterward, I found that "my convict"—the man I had helped down in the churchyard—was none other than the friend who had left me this fortune. He had escaped again from the hulks and, coming into a considerable property, had arranged with the lawyer to use it in making a gentleman out of the little boy he had found crying on the tombstone. But, as I say, none of us knew it or suspected it at first.

And now, those six days which were to have run out so slowly, had run out fast and were gone, and to-morrow looked me in the face more steadily than I could look at it. As the six evenings had dwindled away to five, to four, to three, to two, I had become more and more appreciative of the society of Joe and my sister and Biddy. On this last evening, I dressed myself out in my new clothes, for their delight, and sat in my splendor until bedtime. We had a hot supper on the occasion, graced by the inevitable roast fowl, and we had some flip to finish with. We were all very low, and none the higher for pretending to be in spirits.

It was a hurried breakfast, the next morning, with no taste in it. I got up from the meal, saying with a sort of briskness, as if it had only just occurred to me, "Well! I suppose I must be off!" and then kissed my sister, and kissed Biddy, and threw my arms around Joe's neck. Then I took up my little portmanteau and walked out. The last I saw of them was, when I presently heard a scuffle behind me, and looking back, saw Joe throwing an old shoe after me and Biddy throwing another old shoe. I stopped then, to wave my hat, and dear old Joe waved his strong right arm above his head, crying huskily "Hooroar!" and Biddy put her apron to her face.

I walked away at a good pace, thinking it was easier to go than I had supposed it would be, and reflecting that it would never have done to have an old shoe thrown after the coach, in

sight of all the High-street. I whistled and
made nothing of going. But the village was
very peaceful and quiet, and the light mists were
solemnly rising, as if to show me the world, and
I had been so innocent and little there, and all
beyond was so unknown and great, that in a
moment with a strong heave and sob I broke
into tears. It was by the finger-post at the end
of the village, and I laid my hand upon it, and
said, "Good-bye, oh, my dear, dear friend!"

So subdued was I by those tears, that when I
was on the coach, and it was clear of the town,
I deliberated with an aching heart whether I
would not get down when we changed horses,
and walk back, and have another evening at
home, and a better parting. But while I deliberated, we had changed and changed again, and
it was now too late and too far to go back, and
I went on. And the mists had all solemnly risen
now, and the world lay spread before me. My
boyhood was over. Henceforth I was to play a
man's part—a man with Great Expectations.

# THE STORY OF

# Little Dorrit

## I.  THE CHILD OF THE MARSHALSEA

SOME years ago when the laws of England
were  harsher  than  they  are  now,  there
were  debtors'  prisons,  or  big,  gloomy
jails into which men were put, if they couldn't
pay what they owed.  This was cruel and unjust, for the prisoner was of course cut off from
the chance to earn any more money; and so he
might linger there for years or even his whole
life long, if some friend did not come to his
relief.  But otherwise the prisoner was given
many liberties not found in ordinary jails.  His
family might live with him, if they chose, and
come and go as they pleased.

One of the largest of these debtors' prisons
was called the "Marshalsea."  One day a gentleman was brought there who had lost his money
in business; but so confident was he of speedily
regaining his liberty, that he would not unpack
his valise, at first.  His name was William
Dorrit, an easy-going man who had spent his
money freely and paid little attention to his
tradesmen's bills.  Now that he had fallen upon
evil days, he thought that his friends would be

glad to help him.   But as the days and weeks
passed with no prospect of aid, he was persuaded
not only to unpack his belongings but also to
have his wife and two children brought to live
with him.

The two children, Fanny and Edward—
commonly called "Tip"—were so young when
they were brought to the Marshalsea, that they
soon forgot any earlier life, and played very
happily with other children in the prison yard.
Not long after, a little sister was added to their
family.   She was christened Amy, but was so
tiny that everybody called her "Little Dorrit."

Being born in the prison, Little Dorrit was
petted and made much of.   Every one there
seemed to claim her, and visitors were proudly
shown "the Child of the Marshalsea."

The turnkey, who was a kind-hearted man,
took an especial interest in her.

"By rights," he remarked, when she was first
shown to him, "I ought to be her godfather."

Mr. Dorrit looked at the honest fellow for a
moment, and thought that he would suit better
than some of their false friends.

"Perhaps you wouldn't object to really being
her godfather?" he said.

"Oh, I don't object, if you don't," replied the
turnkey.

Thus it came to pass that she was christened

one Sunday afternoon, when the turnkey, being
relieved, went up to the font of Saint George's
church, and promised and vowed on her behalf,
as he himself related when he came back, "like
a good 'un."

This invested the turnkey with a new pro-
prietary share in the child, over and above his
former official one. When she began to walk
and talk, he became fond of her; bought a little
arm-chair and stood it by the high fender of
the lodge fireplace; liked to have her company
when he was on the lock; and used to bribe her
with cheap toys to come and talk to him. The
child, for her part, soon grew so fond of the
turnkey, that she would come climbing up the
lodge steps of her own accord at all hours of
the day. When she fell asleep in the little arm-
chair by the high fender, the turnkey would
cover her with his pocket handkerchief; and when
she sat in it dressing and undressing a doll—
which soon came to be unlike dolls on the other
side of the lock—he would contemplate her
from the top of his stool, with exceeding gentleness. Witnessing these things, the inmates
would express an opinion that the turnkey, who
was a bachelor, had been cut out by nature for
a family man. But the turnkey thanked them,
and said, "No, on the whole it was enough for
him to see other people's children there."

At what period of her early life the little creature began to perceive that it was not the habit of all the world to live locked up in narrow yards, surrounded by high walls with spikes at the top, would be a difficult question to settle. But she was a very, very little creature indeed, when she had somehow gained the knowledge, that her clasp of her father's hand was to be always loosened at the door which the great key opened; and that while her own light steps were free to pass beyond it, his feet must never cross that line. A pitiful and plaintive look, with which she had begun to regard him when she was still extremely young, was perhaps a part of this discovery.

Wistful and wondering, she would sit in summer weather by the high fender in the lodge, looking up at the sky through the barred window, until bars of light would arise, when she would turn her eyes away.

"Thinking of the fields," the turnkey said once, after watching her, "ain't you?"

"Where are they?" she inquired.

"Why, they're—over there, my dear," said the turnkey, with a vague flourish of his key. "Just about there."

"Does anybody open them, and shut them? Are they locked?"

The turnkey was at a loss. "Well!" he said, "not in general."

"Are they very pretty, Bob?" She called him Bob, by his own particular request and instruction.

"Lovely. Full of flowers. There's buttercups, and there's daisies, and there's"—the turnkey hesitated, being short of names—"there's dandelions, and all manner of games."

"Is it very pleasant to be there, Bob?"

"Prime," said the turnkey.

"Was father ever there?"

"Hem!" coughed the turnkey. "Oh, yes, he was there, sometimes."

"Is he sorry not to be there now?"

"N—not particular," said the turnkey.

"Nor any of the people?" she asked, glancing at the listless crowd within. "Oh, are you quite sure and certain, Bob?"

At this difficult point of the conversation Bob gave in, and changed the subject; always his last resource when he found his little friend getting him into a political, social, or theological corner. But this was the origin of a series of Sunday excursions that these two curious companions made together. They used to issue from the lodge on alternate Sunday afternoons with great gravity, bound for some meadows or great lanes that had been elaborately appointed by the turnkey in the course of the week; and there she picked grass and flowers to bring home, while he smoked his pipe. Afterwards they would come back hand in hand, unless she was more than usually tired, and had fallen asleep on his shoulder.

In those early days the turnkey first began profoundly to consider a question which cost him so much mental labor, that it remained undetermined on the day of his death. He decided to will and bequeath his little property of savings to his godchild, and the point arose how could it be so "tied up" that she alone should benefit by it. He asked the knotty question of every lawyer who came through the lodge gate on business.

"Settle it strictly on herself," the gentleman would answer.

"But look here," quoth the turnkey. "Supposing she had, say a brother, say a father, say a husband, who would be likely to make a grab at that property when she came into it—how about that?"

"It would be settled on herself, and they would have no more legal claim on it than you," would be the professional answer.

"Stop a bit," said the turnkey. "Supposing she was tender-hearted, and they came over her. Where's your law for tying it up then?"

The deepest character whom the turnkey sounded was unable to produce his law for tying such a knot as that.  So, the turnkey thought about it all his life, and died without a will after all.

But that was long afterwards, when his god-daughter was past sixteen.  She was only eight when her mother died, and from that time the protection that her wondering eyes had expressed towards her father became embodied in action, and the Child of the Marshalsea took upon herself a new relation.

At first, such a baby could do little more than sit with him, deserting her livelier place by the high fender, and quietly watching him.  But this made her so far necessary to him that he became accustomed to her, and began to be sensible of missing her when she was not there. Through this little gate she passed out of childhood into the care-laden world.

What her pitiful look saw, at that early time, in her father, in her sister, in her brother, in the jail; how much, or how little of the wretched truth it pleased God to make visible to her, lies hidden with many mysteries.  It is enough that she was inspired to be something which was not what the rest were, and for the sake of the rest.

And while the mark of the prison was seen only too clearly in her vain, selfish sister, and weak, wayward brother, Little Dorrit's life was singularly free from taint; her heart was full of service and love.

And so, in spite of her small stature and want of strength, she toiled and planned, and soon became the real head of this poor, fallen house.

At thirteen, she could read and keep accounts —that is, could put down in words and figures how much the bare necessaries that they wanted would cost, and how much less they had to buy them with.  She had been, by snatches of a few weeks at a time, to an evening school outside, and got her sister and brother sent to day schools during three or four years.  There was no instruction for any of them at home; but she knew well—no one better—that her broken-spirited father could no longer help them.

To these scanty means of improvement, she added another of her own contriving.  Once, among the curious crowd of inmates, there appeared a dancing-master.  Her sister Fanny had a great desire to learn to dance, and seemed to have a taste that way.  At thirteen years old, the Child of the Marshalsea presented herself to the dancing-master, with a little bag in her hand, and said timidly, "If you please, I was born here, sir."

"Oh!  You are the young lady, are you?" said

the man surveying the small figure and uplifted face.

"Yes, sir."

"And what can I do for you?"

"Nothing for me, sir, thank you," anxiously undrawing the strings of the little bag; "but if, while you stay here, you could be so kind as to teach my sister cheap—"

"My child, I'll teach her for nothing," said the dancing-master, shutting up the bag.

He was as good-natured a master as ever danced to the Insolvent Court, and he kept his word. Fanny was so apt a pupil, and made such wonderful progress that he continued to teach her after he was released from prison. In time, he obtained a place for her at a small theatre. It was at the same theatre where her uncle—who was also now a poor man—played a clarinet for a living; and Fanny left the Marshalsea and went to live with him.

The success of this beginning gave Little Dorrit courage to try again, this time on her own behalf. She had long wanted to learn how to sew, and watched and waited for a seamstress to come to the prison. At last one came, and Little Dorrit went to call upon her.

"I beg your pardon, ma'am," she said, looking timidly round the door of the milliner, whom she found in tears and in bed; "but I was born here."

Everybody seemed to hear of her as soon as they arrived; for the milliner sat up in bed, drying her eyes, and said, just as the dancing-master had said,

"Oh! *You* are the child, are you?"

"Yes, ma'am."

"I am sorry I haven't got anything for you," said the milliner, shaking her head.

"It's not that, ma'am. If you please I want to learn needlework."

"Why should you do that," returned the milliner, "with me before you? It has not done me much good."

"Nothing—whatever it is—seems to have done anybody much good who comes here," she returned in all simplicity; "but I want to learn, just the same.

"I am afraid you are so weak, you see," the milliner objected.

"I don't think I am weak, ma'am."

"And you are so very, very little, you see," continued the milliner.

"Yes, I am afraid I am very little indeed," returned the Child of the Marshalsea; and so began to sob over that unfortunate defect of hers, which came so often in her way. The milliner—who was not morose or hard-hearted, only newly insolvent—was touched, took her in hand with good-will, found her the most patient and earnest of pupils, and made her a cunning workwoman in course of time.

And so, presently, Little Dorrit had the immense satisfaction of going out to work by the day, and of supplying her father with many little comforts which otherwise he would not have enjoyed.

But her hardest task was in getting her brother out of prison and into some useful employment. The life there had been anything but good for him; and at eighteen he was idle and shiftless, not caring to lift a finger for himself. In her dilemma, Little Dorrit went to her old friend, the turnkey.

"Dear Bob," said she, "what is to become of poor Tip?"

The turnkey scratched his head. Privately he had a poor opinion of the young man.

"Well, my dear," he answered, "something ought to be done with him. Suppose I try to get him into the law?"

"That would be so good of you, Bob!"

The turnkey was as good as his word, and by dint of buttonholing every lawyer who came through the gate on business, he found Tip a place as clerk, where the pay was not large, but the prospects good.

Tip idled away in the law office for six months, then came back to the prison one evening with his hands in his pockets and told his sister he was not going back again.

"Not going back!" she exclaimed.

"I am so tired of it," said Tip, "that I have cut it."

Tip tired of everything. With intervals of Marshalsea lounging, his small second mother, aided by her trusty friend, got him into a variety of situations. But whatever Tip went into, he came out of tired, announcing that he had cut it.

Nevertheless, the brave little creature did so fix her heart on her brother's rescue, that while he was ringing out these doleful changes, she pinched and scraped enough together to ship him for Canada. When he was tired of nothing to do, and disposed in its turn to cut even that, he graciously consented to go to Canada. And there was grief in her bosom over parting with him, and joy in the hope of his being put in a straight course at last.

"God bless you, dear Tip. Don't be too proud to come and see us, when you have made your fortune."

"All right," said Tip, and went.

But not all the way to Canada; in fact, not farther than Liverpool. After making the voyage to that port from London, he found himself so strongly impelled to cut the vessel, that he resolved to walk back again. Carrying out which intention, he presented himself before her at the expiration of a month, in rags, without shoes, and much more tired than ever.

At length he found a situation for himself, and disappeared for months. She never heard from him but once in that time, though it was as well for her peace of mind that she did not. He was making trades for a tricky horse dealer.

One evening she was alone at work—standing up at the window, to save the twilight lingering above the wall—when he opened the door and walked in.

She kissed and welcomed him; but was afraid to ask him any question. He saw how anxious and timid she was, and appeared sorry.

"I am afraid, Amy, you'll be vexed this time. Upon my life I am!"

"I am very sorry to hear you say so, Tip. Have you come back?"

"Why—yes. But that's not the worst of it."

"Not the worst of it?"

"Don't look so startled, Amy. I've come back in a new way. I'm one of the prisoners now. I owe forty pounds."

For the first time in all those years, she sank under her cares. She cried, with her clasped hands lifted above her head, that it would kill their father if he ever knew it; and fell down at Tip's graceless feet.

It was easier for Tip to bring her to her senses, than for her to bring *him* to understand what a pitiable thing he had done.  But he agreed to help keep it a secret from their father; and Little Dorrit toiled harder than ever, in the hope of one day getting him out again.

Thus passed the life of the Child of the Marshalsea until she became a young woman.

## II.   HOW THE PRISON GATES WERE OPENED

Among the ladies for whom Little Dorrit sewed by the day was a certain Mrs. Clennam, a cold, stern person who lived in a cold, stern house.  Yet she gave the child plenty of work and paid her fairly well.  So Little Dorrit was often to be found in some gloomy corner there, sewing away busily and adding nothing at all to the few far-away sounds of the quiet old rooms.

Mrs. Clennam lived alone, except for a dried-up servant or two, and she herself had lost the use of her limbs.  So it is no wonder that the house was gloomy, and that Mrs. Clennam's son Arthur found it so, when he returned from a long visit in India. Arthur Clennam was a young man who had ideas of his own, and who had disappointed his mother by refusing to continue his father's business. They were not in sympathy—which made the house seem all the colder. But he was kind, open-hearted, and impulsive.

Though timid Little Dorrit kept as much in the dark corners as possible, Arthur soon noticed her, and asked one of the old servants who she was. He could learn nothing except that she was a seamstress who came by the day to sew, and who went away every night, no one knew where. The child interested him, and he resolved to follow her one evening and learn where she lived. He did so, and was amazed to see her enter the gate of a large forbidding building,—he did not know what building, as he had been long abroad.

Just then he saw an old man, in a threadbare coat, once blue, come tottering along, carrying a clarinet in a limp, worn-out case. As this old man was about to enter the same gate, Arthur stopped him with a question.

"Pray, sir," said he, "what is this place?"

"Ay! This place?" returned the old man, staying a pinch of snuff on its road, and pointing at the place without looking at it. "This is the Marshalsea, sir."

"The debtors' prison?"

"Sir," said the old man, with the air of deeming it quite necessary to insist upon that name, "the debtors' prison."

He turned himself about, and went on.

"I beg your pardon," said Arthur, stopping him once more, "but will you allow me to ask you another question? Can any one go in here?"

"Any one can *go in*," replied the old man; "but it is not every one who can go out."

"Pardon me once more. Are you familiar with the place?"

"Sir," returned the old man, squeezing his little packet of snuff in his hand, and turning upon his interrogator as if such questions hurt him, "I am."

"I beg you to excuse me. I am not impertinently curious, but have a good object. Do you know the name of Dorrit here?"

"My name, sir," replied the old man most unexpectedly, "is Dorrit."

Arthur pulled off his hat to him. "Grant me the favor of half a dozen words. I have recently come home to England after a long absence. I have seen at my mother's—Mrs. Clennam in the city—a young woman working at her needle, whom I have only heard addressed or spoken of as Little Dorrit. I have felt sincerely interested in her, and have had a great desire to

know something more about her.  I saw her,
not a minute before you came up, pass in at
that door."

The old man looked at him attentively.  "Are
you in earnest, sir?"

"I do assure you that I am."

"I know very little of the world, sir," returned the other, who had a weak and quavering
voice.  "I am merely passing on, like the shadow
over the sun-dial.  It would be worth no man's
while to mislead me; it would really be too
easy—too poor a success, to yield any satisfaction.  The young woman whom you saw go in
here is my brother's child.  My brother is William Dorrit; I am Frederick.  You say you have
seen her at your mother's (I know your mother
befriends her), you have felt an interest in her,
and you wish to know what she does here.  Come
and see."

He went on again, and Arthur accompanied
him.

"My brother," said the old man, pausing on
the step, and slowly facing round again, "has
been here many years; and much that happens
even among ourselves, out of doors, is kept
from him for reasons that I needn't enter upon
now.  Be so good as to say nothing of my niece's
working at her needle.  If you keep within our

bounds, you cannot well be wrong. Now! Come and see."

Arthur followed him down a narrow entry, at the end of which a key was turned, and a strong door was opened from within. It admitted them into a lodge, or lobby, across which they passed, and so through another door and a grating into the prison. The old man always plodding on before, turned round, in his slow, stiff, stooping manner, when they came to the turnkey on duty, as if to present his companion. The turnkey nodded; and the companion passed in without being asked whom he wanted.

The night was dark; and the prison lamps in the yard, and the candles in the prison windows faintly shining behind many sorts of wry old curtain and blind, had not the air of making it lighter. A few people loitered about, but the greater part of the population was within doors. The old man taking the right-hand side of the yard, turned in at the third or fourth doorway, and began to ascend the stairs.

"They are rather dark, sir, but you will not find anything in the way," he said.

He paused for a moment before opening the door on the second story. He had no sooner turned the handle, than the visitor saw Little Dorrit, and understood the reason of her dining alone, as she always preferred to do.

She had brought the meat home that she should have eaten herself, and was already warming it on a gridiron over the fire, for her father, who, clad in an old gray gown and a black cap, was awaiting his supper at the table. A clean cloth was spread before him, with knife, fork, and spoon, salt-cellar, pepper-box, glass, and pewter ale-pot. Such zests as his cayenne pepper and pickles in a saucer were not wanting.

She started, colored deeply, and turned white. The visitor, more with his eyes than by the slight impulsive motion of his hand, entreated her to be reassured and to trust him.

"I found this gentleman," said the uncle— "Mr. Clennam, William, son of Amy's friend —at the outer gate, wishful, as he was going by, of paying his respects, but hesitating whether to come in or not. This is my brother William, sir."

"I hope," said Arthur, very doubtful what to say, "that my respect for your daughter may explain and justify my desire to be presented to you, sir."

"Mr. Clennam," returned the other, rising, taking his cap off in the flat of his hand, and so holding it, ready to put on again, "you do me honor. You are welcome, sir." With a low bow. "Frederick, a chair. Pray sit down, Mr. Clennam."

He put his black cap on again as he had taken it off, and resumed his own seat. There was a wonderful air of benignity and patronage in his manner.

These were the ceremonies with which he received all visitors.

"You are welcome to the Marshalsea, sir. I have welcomed many gentlemen to these walls. Perhaps you are aware—my daughter Amy may have mentioned—that I am the Father of this place."

"I—so I have understood," said Arthur, dashing at the assertion.

"You know, I dare say, that my daughter Amy was born here. A good girl, sir, a dear girl, and long a comfort and support to me. Amy, my dear, put the dish on; Mr. Clennam will excuse the primitive customs to which we are reduced here. Is it a compliment to ask you if you would do me the honor, sir, to—"

"Thank you," returned Arthur. "I have dined."

She filled her father's glass, put all the little matters on the table ready to his hand, and then sat beside him while he ate his supper. She put some bread before herself, and touched his glass with her lips; but Arthur saw she was troubled and took nothing. Her look at her father, half admiring him and proud of him, half-ashamed for him, all devoted and loving, went to his inmost heart.

The Father of the Marshalsea condescended towards his brother as an amiable, well-meaning man; a private character, who had not arrived at distinction.

"Frederick," said he, "you and Fanny sup at your lodgings to-night, I know. What have you done with Fanny, Frederick?"

"She is walking with Tip."

"Tip—as you may know—is my son, Mr. Clennam. He has been a little wild, and difficult to settle, but his introduction to the world was rather"— he shrugged his shoulders with a faint sigh, and looked round the room—"a little adverse. Your first visit here, sir?"

"My first."

"You could hardly have been here since your boyhood without my knowledge. It very seldom happens that anybody—of any pretensions —any pretensions—comes here without being presented to me."

"As many as forty or fifty in a day have been introduced to my brother," said Frederick, faintly lighting up with a ray of pride.

"Yes!" the Father of the Marshalsea assented. "We have even exceeded that number. On a fine Sunday in term time, it is quite a reception!"

Thus the old man prattled on, proud of his

queer distinction, and yet showing traces of the
fine gentleman he once was.    And while he
listened, Arthur felt his heart throb with sympathy for the brave girl, sitting silent across the
table, who had so long borne the burdens of this
ruined family upon her frail shoulders.

He could not say anything to her, here, but
when he rose to take his leave, he asked her by
a look to come with him to the gate.    He felt
he must make some explanation for thus intrud-
ing and learning her secret.

"Pray forgive me," he said, when they paused
alone at the gate.    "I followed you to-night from
my mother's.    I should not have done so, but,
believe me, it was only in the hope of doing you
some service.    What I have seen here, in this
short time, has increased tenfold my heartfelt
wish to be a friend to you."

She seemed to take courage while he spoke
to her.

"You are very good, sir.    You speak very
earnestly to me.    But I—but I wish you had
not watched me."

He understood the emotion with which she
said it to arise in her father's behalf; and he
respected it, and was silent.

"Mrs. Clennam has been of great service to
me.    I don't know what we should have done
without the employment she has given me.    I

am afraid it may not be a good return to become secret with her. I can say no more to-night, sir. I am sure you mean to be kind to us. Thank you, thank you."

She was so agitated, and he was so moved by compassion for her, and by deep interest in her story as it dawned upon him, that he could scarcely tear himself away. But the stoppage of the bell, and the quiet in the prison, were a warning to depart; and with a few hurried words of kindness he left her gliding back to her father.

The next day, Arthur missed Little Dorrit at his home, and wondered if she might be ill. The weather was stormy, but she was not usually hindered by that. So he walked out toward the prison to look for her; and was presently rewarded by seeing her hurrying along in the face of the gale.

She had just reached the iron bridge, some distance from the gates, when his voice caused her to stop short. The wind blew roughly, the wet squalls came rattling past them, skimming the pools on the road and pavement, and raining them down into the river. The clouds raced on furiously in the lead-colored sky, the smoke and mist raced after them, the dark tide ran fierce and strong in the same direction. Little Dorrit seemed the least, the quietest and weakest of Heaven's creatures.

"Let me put you in a coach," said Arthur Clennam, very nearly adding, "my poor child."

She hurriedly declined, thanking him, and saying that wet or dry made little difference to her; she was used to go about in all weathers. He knew it to be so, and was touched with more pity, thinking of the slight figure, at his side, making its nightly way through the damp, dark, boisterous streets, to such a place of rest.

"But I am glad to have seen you, sir," she added shyly. "I did not want you to think that we were ungrateful for your interest and kindness, last night. And, besides, I had something else to say—"

She paused as if unable to go on.

"To say to me—" he prompted.

"That I hope you will not misunderstand my father. Don't judge him, sir, as you would judge others outside the gates. He has been there so long! I never saw him outside, but I can understand that he must have grown different in some things since."

"My thoughts will never be unjust or harsh towards him, believe me."

"Not," she said, with a prouder air, as the misgiving evidently crept upon her that she might seem to be abandoning him, "not that he has anything to be ashamed of for himself, or that I have anything to be ashamed of for him. He only requires to be understood. I only ask for him that his life may be fairly remembered. All that he said was quite true. He is very much respected. Everybody who comes in is glad to know him. He is more courted than any one else. He is far more thought of than the Marshal is." If ever pride were innocent, it was innocent in Little Dorrit when she grew boastful of her father.

"It is often said that his manners are a true gentleman's, and quite a study. He is not to be blamed for being in need, poor love. Who could be in prison a quarter of a century, and be prosperous!"

What affection in her words, what compassion in her repressed tears, what a great soul of fidelity within her, how true the light that shed false brightness round him!

"If I have found it best to conceal where my home is, it is not because I am ashamed of him. God forbid! Nor am I so much ashamed of the place itself as might be supposed. People are not bad because they come there. I have known many good friends there, and have spent many happy hours."

She had relieved the faithful fullness of her heart, and modestly said, raising her eyes appealingly to her new friend's, "I did not mean to say so much, nor have I ever but once spoken about this before. But it seems to set it more right than it was last night. I said I wished you had not followed me, sir. I don't wish it so much now, unless you should think—indeed I don't wish it at all, unless I should have spoken so confusedly, that—that you can scarcely understand me, which I am afraid may be the case."

He told her with perfect truth that it was not the case; and putting himself between her and the sharp wind and rain, sheltered her as well as he could.

"I feel permitted now," he said, "to ask you a little more concerning your father. Has he many creditors?"

"Oh! a great number."

"I mean detaining creditors who keep him where he is?"

"Oh, yes! a great number."

"Can you tell me—I can get the information, no doubt, elsewhere, if you cannot—who is the most influential of them?"

Little Dorrit was not sure of any names, but she had heard her father mention several people with whom he said he once had dealings. She told him these names, and Clennam made a careful note of them.

"It can do no harm," he thought, "to see some of these people."

The thought did not come so quietly but that she quickly guessed it.

"Ah," said Little Dorrit, shaking her head with the mild despair of a lifetime. "Many people used to think once of getting my poor father out, but you don't know how hopeless it is."

She forgot to be shy at the moment, in honestly warning him away from the sunken wreck he had a dream of raising; and looked at him with eyes which assuredly, in association with her patient face, her fragile figure, her spare dress, and the wind and rain, did not turn him from his purpose of helping her.

But presently an incident happened which showed him a new side of her life—still of helpfulness and service.

They were come into the High Street, where the prison stood, when a voice cried, "Little mother, little mother!"

Little Dorrit stopped, looking back, when an excited figure of a strange kind bounced against them, fell down, and scattered the contents of a large basket, filled with potatoes, in the mud.

"Oh, Maggy," said Little Dorrit, "what a clumsy child you are!"

Maggy was not hurt, but picked herself up immediately, and began to pick up the potatoes, in which both the others helped.  Maggy picked up very few potatoes, and a great quantity of mud. She was a curious, overgrown creature of about eight-and-twenty, with a vacant smiling face and a tattered shawl. She seemed twice as large as the child to whom she evidently looked for protection and called "little mother."

Arthur Clennam looked with the expression of one saying, "May I ask who this is?" Little Dorrit, whose hand Maggy had begun to fondle, answered in words. They were under a gateway into which the majority of the potatoes had rolled.

"This is Maggy, sir."

"Maggy, sir," echoed the personage presented. "Little mother!"

"She is the granddaughter—"

"Granddaughter," echoed Maggy.

"Of my old nurse, who has been dead a long time. Maggy, how old are you?"

"Ten, mother," said Maggy.

"You can't think how good she is, sir," said Little Dorrit, with infinite tenderness.

"Good *she* is," echoed Maggy, transferring the pronoun in a most expressive way from herself to her little mother.

"Or how clever," said Little Dorrit. "She goes on errands as well as any one." Maggy laughed. "And is as trustworthy as the Bank of England." Maggy laughed. "She earns her own living entirely. Entirely, sir!" in a lower and triumphant tone. "Really does!"

"What is her history!" asked Clennam.

"Think of that, Maggy!" said Little Dorrit, taking Maggy's two large hands and clapping them together. "A gentleman from thousands of miles away, wanting to know your history!"

"*My* history?" cried Maggy. "Little mother."

"She means me," said Little Dorrit, rather confused; "she is very much attached to me. Her old grandmother was not so kind to her as she should have been; was she, Maggy? When Maggy was ten years old," she continued, "she had a bad fever, sir, and has never grown any older since."

"Ten years old," said Maggy, nodding her head. "But what a nice hospital! So comfortable, wasn't it? Oh, so nice it was. Such a Ev'nly place!"

"She had never been at peace before, sir," continued the young girl, turning towards Arthur for an instant and speaking low, "and she always runs off upon that."

"Such beds there is there!" cried Maggy. "Such lemonades! Such oranges! Such d'licious broth and wine! Such Chicking! Oh, *ain't* it a delightful place to go and stop at!"

"So, Maggy stopped there as long as she

could," said Little Dorrit, in her former tone
of telling a child's story, the tone designed for
Maggy's ear; "and at last, when she could stop
there no longer, she came out. Then, because
she was never to be more than ten years old,
however long she lived—"

"However long she lived," echoed Maggy.

"And because she was very weak—indeed,
was so weak that when she began to laugh she
couldn't stop herself—which was a great pity—"

Maggy grew mighty grave of a sudden.

"Her grandmother did not know what to do
with her, and for some years was very unkind
to her indeed. At length, in course of time,
Maggy began to take pains to improve herself,
and to be very attentive and very industrious;
and by degrees was allowed to come in and out
as often as she liked, and got enough to do to
support herself, and does support herself. And
that," said Little Dorrit, clapping the two great
hands together again, "is Maggy's history, as
Maggy knows!"

Ah! that was all the history, as Little Dorrit
told it. But Arthur, reading between the lines,
saw in Maggy's absolute love and devotion the
weeks and months of toil and care on the part
of a pitying faithful child whose own burden
seemed great enough without carrying others.
The dirty gateway with the wind and rain whis-

tling through it, and the basket of muddy potatoes waiting to be spilt again or taken up, never seemed the common hole it really was, when he looked back to it by these lights.  Never, never!

Thereafter, Arthur Clennam, who was a man of some means, devoted a great part of his time to tracing out the Dorrit records.  He went from one government office to another—a long, weary round of them—before he could get any light on the matter.  He employed an agent whose specialty was to search out lost estates. And at last, after several months, their combined efforts were rewarded.

Mr. Dorrit was found to be heir-at-law to a large estate that had long lain unknown, unclaimed, and growing greater.  His right to it was cleared up by this skilful agent; so that all Mr. Dorrit had to do, now, would be to discharge his debts, and he would be a free man.

When Arthur was convinced of this surprising fortune, he hastened first to Little Dorrit, whom he wished to see alone.  But before he could say a word, his face told her that something unusual was afoot.

Hastily dropping her sewing, she cried, "Mr. Clennam!  What's the matter?"

"Nothing, nothing! That is—nothing bad. I have come to tell you good news."

"Good fortune?"

"Wonderful fortune!"

Her lips seemed to repeat the words, but no sound came.

"Dear Little Dorrit," he said, "your father—"

The ice of the pale face broke at the word, and little lights of expression passed over it. They were all expressions of pain. Her breath was faint and hurried. Her heart beat fast, but he saw that the eyes appealed to him to go on.

"Your father can be free within this week. He does not know it; we must go to him from here, to tell him of it. Your father will be free within a few days. Remember we must go to him, from here, to tell him of it!"

That brought her back. Her eyes were closing, but they opened again.

"This is not all the good fortune. This is not all the wonderful good fortune, Little Dorrit. Shall I tell you more?"

Her lips shaped "Yes."

"He will be a rich man. A great sum of money is waiting to be paid over to him as his inheritance; you are all henceforth very wealthy. Bravest and best of children, I thank Heaven that you are rewarded!"

She turned her head towards his shoulder,

and raised her arm towards his neck; then cried out, "Father! Father! Father!" and swooned away.

The housekeeper came running in at this, and Little Dorrit was soon revived, smiling bravely at her own weakness. But the news had been too much for her. It was the dream of her lifetime—come true!

"Come!" she exclaimed, "we must not lose a moment, but must hasten to my father!"

When the turnkey, who was on duty, admitted them into the lodge, he saw something in their faces which filled him with astonishment. He stood looking after them, when they hurried into the prison, as though he perceived that they had come back accompanied by a ghost apiece. Two or three debtors whom they passed, looked after them too, and presently joining the turnkey, formed a little group on the lodge steps, in the midst of which there originated a whisper that the Father was going to get his discharge. Within a few minutes it was heard in the remotest room in the prison.

Little Dorrit opened the door from without, and they both entered. Her father was sitting in his old gray gown, and his old black cap, in the sunlight by the window, reading his newspaper. His glasses were in his hand, and he had just looked round; surprised at first, no doubt, by her step upon the stairs, not expecting her until night; surprised again, by seeing Arthur Clennam in her company. As they came in, the same unwonted look in both of them, which had already caught attention in the yard below, struck him. He did not rise or speak, but laid down his glasses and his newspaper on the table beside him, and looked at them with his mouth a little open, and his lips trembling. When Arthur put out his hand, he touched it, but not with his usual state; and then he turned to his daughter, who had sat down close beside him with her hands upon his shoulder, and looked attentively in her face.

"Father! I have been made so happy, this morning!"

"You have been made so happy, my dear?"

"By Mr. Clennam, father. He brought me such joyful and wonderful intelligence about you!"

Her agitation was great, and the tears rolled down her face. He put his hand suddenly to his heart, and looked at Clennam.

"Compose yourself, sir," said Clennam, "and take a little time to think. To think of the brightest and most fortunate accidents of life. We have all heard of great surprises of joy. They are not at an end."

"Mr. Clennam? Not at an end? Not at an

end for—" He touched himself upon the breast, instead of saying "me."

"No," returned Clennam.

He looked at Clennam, and, so looking at him, seemed to change into a very old haggard man. The sun was bright upon the wall beyond the window, and on the spikes at the top. He slowly stretched out the hand that had been upon his heart, and pointed at the wall.

"It is down," said Clennam. "Gone!"

He remained in the same attitude, looking steadfastly at him.

"And in its place," said Clennam, slowly and distinctly, "are the means to possess and enjoy the utmost that they have so long shut out. Mr. Dorrit, there is not the smallest doubt that within a few days you will be free, and highly prosperous. I congratulate you with all my soul on this change of fortune, and on the happy future into which you are soon to carry the treasure you have been blessed with here—the best of all riches you can have elsewhere—the treasure in the dear child at your side."

With those words, he pressed Mr. Dorrit's hand and released it; and his daughter, laying her face against his, encircled him in the hour of his prosperity with her arms, as she had in the long years of his adversity encircled him with her love and toil and truth; and poured out her

full heart in gratitude, hope, joy, blissful ecstasy, and all for him.

"I shall see him, as I never saw him yet.  I
shall see my dear father, with the dark cloud
cleared away.  I shall see him, as my poor mother
saw him long ago.  Oh, my dear, my dear!  Oh,
father, father!  Oh, thank God, thank God!"

Mr. Dorrit came slowly out of the daze into
which he had seemed to fall.  To divert his mind,
Arthur told him how the good fortune had been
found through the skill of an agent.

"He shall be rewarded!" he exclaimed, starting up.  "Every one shall be—ha!—handsomely
rewarded!  Every cent I owe shall be paid.  Oh!
can this be true?  A free man, and all my debts
paid!  Give me my purse, Amy!"

He clutched it as if it were already overflow-
ing with gold, and paced rapidly up and down
the room.  Just then a great cheering arose in
the prison yard.

"The news has spread already," said Clennam, looking down from the window.  "Will
you show yourself to them, Mr. Dorrit?  They
are very earnest, and evidently wish it."

"I—hum—ha—I confess I could have desired,
Amy, my dear," he said, jogging about in a more
feverish flutter than before, "to have made some
change in my dress first, and to have bought a—
hum—a watch and chain.  But if it must be done

as it is, it—ha—it must be done. Fasten the collar of my shirt, my dear. Mr. Clennam, would you oblige me—hum—with a blue neckcloth you will find in that drawer at your elbow. Button my coat across at the chest, my love. It looks—ha—it looks broader, buttoned."

With his trembling hand he pushed his gray hair up, and then, taking Clennam and his daughter for supporters, appeared at the window leaning on an arm of each. The inmates cheered him very heartily, and he kissed his hand to them with great urbanity and protection. When he withdrew into the room again, he said "Poor creatures!" in a tone of much pity for their miserable condition.

Presently he said, unexpectedly:

"Mr. Clennam, I beg your pardon. Am I to understand, my dear sir, that I could—ha—could pass through the lodge at this moment, and—hum—take a walk?"

"I think not, Mr. Dorrit," was the unwilling reply. "There are certain forms to be completed; and although your detention here is now in itself a form, I fear it has to be observed for a few hours longer."

"A few hours, sir," he returned in a sudden passion. "You talk very easily of hours, sir! How long do you suppose, sir, that an hour is to a man who is choking for want of air?"

It was the cry of a man who had been imprisoned for nearly a quarter of a century.

Little Dorrit had been thinking too. After softly putting his gray hair aside, and touching his forehead with her lips, she looked towards Arthur, who came nearer to her, and pursued in a low whisper the subject of their thoughts.

"Mr. Clennam, will he pay all his debts before he leaves here?"

"No doubt. All."

"All the debts for which he has been imprisoned here, all my life and longer?"

"No doubt."

There was something of uncertainty and remonstrance in her look; something that was not all satisfaction. He wondered to detect it, and said:

"Are you not glad?"

"It seems to me hard," said Little Dorrit, "that he should have lost so many years and suffered so much, and at last pay all the debts as well. It seems to me hard that he should pay in life and money both."

"My dear child—" Clennam was beginning.

"Yes, I know I am wrong," she pleaded timidly, "don't think any worse of me; it has grown up with me here."

The prison, which could spoil so many things, had tainted Little Dorrit's mind no more than this.  It was the first speck Clennam had ever seen, it was the last speck Clennam ever saw, of the prison atmosphere upon her.

He thought this, and forebore to say another word.  With the thought, her purity and goodness came before him in their brightest light. The little spot made them the more beautiful.

# THE PERSONAL HISTORY OF

# David Copperfield

## I.   MY EARLIEST RECOLLECTIONS

THE first things that I seem to remember are the figure of my mother with her pretty hair and youthful face, and Peggotty, our faithful servant, large of figure, black of eye, and with cheeks and arms so hard and red that I wondered the birds didn't peck them in preference to apples.   I believe I can remember these two at a little distance apart, dwarfed to my sight by stooping down or kneeling on the floor, and I going unsteadily from the one to the other   My father I never saw, for he died before I was born.

What else do I remember?   Let me see. There comes to me a vision of our quaint cosy little home, the "Rookery."   On the ground floor is Peggotty's kitchen, opening into a back yard; with a pigeon-house on a pole, in the centre, without any pigeons in it; a great dog-kennel in a corner, without any dog; and a quantity of fowls that look terribly tall to me, walking about, in a ferocious manner.   There is one cock who gets upon a post to crow, and seems to take particular notice of me as I look at him through the kitchen window, who makes me shiver, he is so fierce. Of the geese outside the gate who come waddling after me with their long necks stretched out when I go that way, I dream fearfully at night.

Here is a long passage leading from Peggotty's kitchen to the front door. A dark storeroom opens out of it, and that is a place to be run past at night; for I don't know what may be among those tubs and jars and old tea-chests, in which there is the smell of soap, pickles, pepper, candles, and coffee, all at one whiff. Then there are the two parlors: the parlor in which we sit of an evening, my mother and I and Peggotty—for Peggotty is quite our companion, when her work is done and we are alone—and the best parlor where we sit on a Sunday; grandly but not so comfortably.

And now I see the outside of our house, with the latticed bedroom windows standing open to let in the sweet-smelling air, and the ragged old rook's-nests still dangling in the elm trees at the bottom of the front garden. Now I am in the garden at the back, beyond the yard where the empty pigeon-house and dog-kennel are—a very preserve of butterflies, as I remember it, with a high fence, and a gate and padlock; where the fruit clusters on the trees, riper and richer than

fruit has ever been since, in any other garden, and where my mother gathers some in a basket, while I stand by, bolting gooseberries slyly, and trying to look unmoved.

A great wind rises, and the summer is gone in a moment. We are playing in the winter twilight, dancing about the parlor. When my mother is out of breath and rests herself in an elbow-chair, I watch her winding her bright curls round her fingers and straightening her waist, and nobody knows better than I do that she likes to look so well, and is proud of being so pretty.

That is among my very earliest impressions, —that, and a sense that we were both a little afraid of Peggotty, and submit ourselves in most things to her direction.

Peggotty and I were sitting one night by the parlor fire, alone. I had been reading to Peggotty about crocodiles. I must not have read very clearly, for I remember she had a cloudy impression that they were a sort of vegetable. I was tired of reading, and sleepy; but having leave, as a high treat, to sit up until my mother came home from spending the evening at a neighbor's I would rather have died upon my post than have gone to bed.

We had exhausted the crocodiles, and begun with alligators, when the bell rang. We went out to the door; and there was my mother, looking unusually pretty, I thought, and with her a gentleman with beautiful black hair and whiskers, who had walked home with us from church last Sunday.

As my mother stooped down on the threshold to take me in her arms and kiss me, the gentleman said I was a more highly privileged little fellow than a monarch—or something like that.

"What does that mean?" I asked him, over her shoulder.

He patted me on the head; but somehow, I didn't like him or his deep voice, and I was jealous that his hand should touch my mother's in touching me—which it did. I put it away as well as I could. My mother gently chid me for being rude; and, keeping me close to her shawl, turned to thank the gentleman for bringing her home.

From the moment that I first saw the gentleman with the black whiskers, I held a deep instinctive dislike to him. And I am sure Peggotty agreed with me, from some remarks I chanced to hear her utter to my mother. But Mr. Murdstone—that was his name—began coming often to the Rookery, and exerted himself always to be agreeable to me, calling me a fine boy and patting me on the head; so I tried to think myself very ungrateful. But still I could not make myself like him. The sight of him made me fear that something was going to happen—I didn't know what.

Not long after that, when Peggotty and I were sitting alone, she darning and I reading farther in the crocodile book,—for my mother was out, as she often was, with Mr. Murdstone, —she bit off a thread and asked:

"Master Davy, how should you like to go along with me and spend a fortnight at my brother's at Yarmouth? Wouldn't *that* be a treat?"

"Is your brother an agreeable man, Peggoty?" I inquired doubtfully.

"Oh, what an agreeable man he is!" cried Peggotty, holding up her hands. "Then there's the sea; and the boats and ships; and the fishermen; and the beach; and 'Am to play with—"

Peggotty meant her nephew Ham, but she spoke of him as a morsel of English Grammar.

I was flushed by her summary of delights, and replied that it would indeed be a treat, but what would my mother say?

"Why, then, I'll as good as bet a guinea," said Peggotty, intent upon my face, "that she'll let us go. I'll ask her, if you like, as soon as ever she comes home. There now!"

"But what's *she* to do while we're away?" said I, putting my small elbows on the table to argue the point. "She can't live by herself."

If Peggotty were looking for a hole, all of a sudden, in the heel of that stocking it must have been a very little one indeed, and not worth darning.

"I say! Peggotty!  She can't live by herself, you know."

"Oh, bless you!" said Peggotty, looking at me again at last.  "Don't you know?  She's going to stay for a fortnight with Mrs. Grayper. Mrs. Grayper's going to have a lot of company."

Oh! If that was it, I was quite ready to go.  I waited, in the utmost impatience, until my mother came home from Mrs. Grayper's (for it was that identical neighbor), to ascertain if we could get leave to carry out this great idea. Without being nearly so much surprised as I had expected, my mother entered into it readily; and it was all arranged that night, and my board and lodging during the visit were to be paid for.

The day soon came for our going.  It was such an early day that it came soon, even to me, who was in a fever of expectation, and half afraid that an earthquake or a fiery mountain, or some other accident might stop the expedition. We were to go in a carrier's cart, which departed in the morning after breakfast.  I would have given any money to have been allowed to wrap myself up over-night, and sleep in my hat and boots.

It touches me nearly now, although I tell it lightly, to recollect how eager I was to leave my happy home; to think how little I suspected what I did leave for ever.

I am glad to recollect that when the carrier began to move, my mother ran out at the gate, and called to him to stop, that she might kiss me once more. I am glad to dwell upon the earnestness and love with which she lifted up her face to mine.

As we left her standing in the road, Mr. Murdstone came up to where she was, and chided her for being so moved. I was looking back round the awning of the cart, and wondered what business it was of his. Peggotty, who was also looking back on the other side, seemed anything but satisfied, as the face she brought back into the cart denoted.

The carrier's horse was the laziest horse in the world, I thought, as he shuffled along with his head down. But Peggotty had brought along a basket of refreshments which would have lasted us handsomely for a journey three times as long. And at last we drove up to the Yarmouth tavern, where we found Ham awaiting us. He was a huge, strong fellow, about six feet high, with a simple, good-natured face.

He put me upon his shoulder, and my box
under his arm, and trudged away easily down a
lane littered with shipbuilders' odds and ends,
past forges, yards and gas works, till we came
out upon an open waste of sand, with the sea
pounding upon it and eating away at it.  Then
Ham said,

"Yon's our house, Mas'r Davy!"

I looked in all directions, as far as I could,
and away at the sea, but no house could *I* make
out.  There was a black barge, or some other
kind of boat, not far off, high and dry on the
ground, with an iron funnel sticking out of it for
a chimney and smoking very cosily; but nothing else in the way of a house that was visible
to *me*.

"That's not it?" said I.  "That ship-looking
thing?"

"That's it, Mas'r Davy," returned Ham.

If it had been Aladdin's palace, roc's egg and
all, I suppose I could not have been more
charmed with the idea of living in it.  There
was a delightful door cut in the side, and it was
roofed in, and there were little windows in it;
but the charm of it was that it was a *real boat*
which had no doubt been upon the water hundreds of times, and which had never been intended to be lived in on dry land.

It was beautifully clean inside, and as tidy as

possible. There was a table, and a Dutch clock, and a chest of drawers, and a tea-tray with a painting on it. The tray was kept from tumbling down by a Bible; and the tray, if it had tumbled down, would have smashed a quantity of cups and saucers and a tea-pot around the book. On the walls there were some colored pictures, framed and glazed, of scripture subjects. There were some hooks in the beams of the ceiling whose use I did not know; and some lockers and boxes scattered around, which served for seats.

One thing I particularly noticed in this delightful house was the smell of fish, which was so searching that when I took out my pocket-handkerchief to wipe my nose, I found it smelt exactly as if it had wrapped up a lobster. On my whispering this to Peggotty, she informed me that her brother dealt in lobsters, crabs, and crawfish; and I afterwards found that a heap of these creatures, in a state of wonderful confusion with one another, and never leaving off pinching whatever they laid hold of, were usually to be found in a little wooden lean-to where the pots and kettles were kept.

We were welcomed by a very civil woman in a white apron, whom I had seen courtesying at the door when I was on Ham's back, about a quarter of a mile off; likewise by a most beautiful little girl with a necklace of blue beads, who wouldn't let me kiss her when I offered to, but ran away and hid herself.

By and by, when we had dined in a sumptuous manner off boiled fish, melted butter, and potatoes, with a chop for me, a hairy man with a very good-natured face came home. As he called Peggotty "Lass" and gave her a hearty smack on the cheek, I had no doubt that he was her brother; and so he turned out—being presently introduced to me as Mr. Peggotty, the master of the house.

"Glad to see you, sir," said Mr. Peggotty. "You'll find us rough, sir, but you'll find us ready."

I thanked him and replied that I was sure I should be happy in such a delightful place.

The civil woman with the white apron was Mrs. Gummidge, an old widowed lady who kept the boat-house in fine order. The little girl was Emily, a niece of Mr. Peggotty's. She had never seen her father, just as I had never seen mine—which was our first bond of sympathy. She had lost her mother, too; and as we played together happily in the sand, I told her all about *my* mother and how we had only each other and I was going to grow up right away to take care of her.

Of course I was quite in love with little Emily.

I am sure I loved her quite as truly as one could possibly love. And I made her confess that she loved me. So when the golden days flew by and the time of parting drew near, our agony of mind was intense. The farewells were very tearful; and if ever in my life I had a void in my heart, I had one that day.

I am ashamed to confess that the delightful fortnight by the sea had driven out all thoughts of home. But no sooner were we on the return journey, than the home longing came crowding in upon me tenfold. I grew so excited to see my mother, that it seemed as if I couldn't wait for that blundering old cart. But Peggotty, instead of sharing in these transports, tried to check them, though very kindly, and looked confused and out of sorts.

The Rookery would come, however, in spite of her, when the carrier's horse pleased—and did. How well I recollect it, on a cold, gray afternoon, with a dull sky threatening rain!

The door opened, and I sprang in, half laughing and half crying as I looked for my mother. It was not she who met me, but a strange servant.

"Why, Peggotty!" I said, ruefully, "isn't she come home?"

"Yes, yes, Master Davy," said Peggotty.

"She's come home. Wait a bit, Master Davy, and I'll—I'll tell you something."

"Peggotty!" said I, quite frightened. "What's the matter?"

"Nothing's the matter, bless you, Master Davy dear!" she answered, with an air of cheerfulness.

"Something's the matter, I'm sure. Where's mamma?"

"Master Davy," said Peggotty, untying her bonnet with a shaking hand, "what do you think? You have got a Pa!"

I trembled, and turned white. Something— I don't know what, or how—connected with my father's grave in the churchyard, and the raising of the dead, seemed to strike me like an unwholesome wind.

"A new one," said Peggotty.

"A new one?" I repeated.

Peggotty gave a gasp, as if she were swallowing something that was very hard, and, putting out her hand said,

"Come and see him."

"I don't want to see him."

"And your mamma," said Peggotty.

I ceased to draw back, and we went straight to the best parlor, where she left me. On one side of the fire, sat my mother; on the other,

Mr. Murdstone. My mother dropped her work, and arose hurriedly but timidly, I thought.

"Now, Clara, my dear," said Mr. Murdstone, "recollect! control yourself. Davy boy, how do you do?"

I gave him my hand. Then I went and kissed my mother; she kissed me, patted me gently on the shoulder, and sat down again to her work. I could not look at her, I could not look at him. I knew quite well that he was looking at us both; and I turned to the window and looked out there, at some shrubs that were drooping their heads in the cold.

As soon as I could, I crept upstairs. My old dear bedroom was changed, and I was to lie a long way off. I rambled downstairs to find anything that was like itself, so altered it all seemed; and roamed into the yard. I very soon started back from there, for the empty dog-kennel was filled up with a great dog—deep-mouthed and black-haired like Him—and he was very angry at the sight of me, and sprang out to get at me.

## II.    I FALL INTO DISGRACE

That first lonely evening when I crept off alone, feeling that no one wanted me, was the most miserable of my life. I rolled up in a corner of my bed and cried myself to sleep.

Presently I was awakened by somebody saying, "Here he is!" and uncovering my hot head. My mother and Peggotty had come to look for me, and it was one of them who had done it.

"Davy," said my mother, "what's the matter?"

I thought it very strange that she should ask me, and answered, "Nothing." I turned over on my face, I recollect, to hide my trembling lip, which answered her with greater truth.

"Davy," said my mother. "Davy, my child!"

I dare say, no words she could have uttered would have affected me so much, then, as her calling me her child. I hid my tears in the bedclothes, and pressed her from me with my hand, when she would have raised me up.

Then I felt the touch of a hand that I knew was neither hers nor Peggotty's, and slipped to my feet at the bedside. It was Mr. Murdstone's hand, and he kept it on my arm as he said:

"What's this? Clara, my love, have you forgotten? Firmness, my dear!"

"I am very sorry, Edward," said my mother. "I meant to be very good."

"Go below, my dear," he answered. "David and I will come down together."

When we two were left alone, he shut the door, and sitting on a chair, and holding me standing before him, looked steadily into my eyes.

"David," he said, making his lips thin, by pressing them together, "if I have an obstinate horse or dog to deal with, what do you think I do?"

"I don't know."

"I beat him. I make him wince and smart. I say to myself, 'I'll conquer that fellow'; and if it were to cost him all the blood he had, I should do it. What is that upon your face?"

"Dirt," I said.

He knew it was the mark of tears as well as I. But if he had asked the question twenty times, each with twenty blows, I believe my baby heart would have burst before I would have told him so.

"You have a good deal of intelligence for a little fellow," he said, with a grave smile that belonged to him, "and you understood me very well, I see. Wash that face, sir, and come down with me."

"Clara, my dear," he said, when I had done his bidding, and he walked me into the parlor, with his hand still on my arm; "you will not be made uncomfortable any more, I hope. We shall soon improve our youthful humors."

What a little thing will change the current of our lives! I might have been made another

creature perhaps by a kind word just then.   A
word of welcome home, of assurance that it *was*
home, might have made me respect my new
father instead of hate him.   But the word was
not spoken, and the time for it was gone.

From that time my life was a lonely one.   My
mother petted me in secret, but plainly stood in
awe of Mr. Murdstone; and even the dauntless
Peggotty must needs keep her peace.   His word
alone was law.

After a time his sister, Miss Murdstone, came
to live with us.   And from the second day of
her arrival she took charge of the household
keys, and managed things with a firmness second only to her brother himself.

There had been some talk of my going to
boarding-school.   Mr. and Miss Murdstone had
originated it, and my mother had of course
agreed with them.   Nothing, however was concluded on the subject yet, and in the meantime
I learned my lessons at home.

Shall I ever forget those lessons!   They were
presided over nominally by my mother, but
really by Mr. Murdstone and his sister, who
were always present, and found them a favorable
occasion for giving my mother lessons in that
miscalled firmness which was the bane of both
our lives.   I believe I was kept at home for that
purpose.   I had been apt enough to learn, and

willing enough, when my mother and I had lived alone together. I can faintly remember learning the alphabet at her knee. To this day, when I look upon the fat black letters in the primer, the puzzling novelty of their shapes and the easy good-nature of O and Q and S seem to present themselves again before me as they used to do. But they recall no feeling of disgust or reluctance. On the contrary, I seem to have walked along a path of flowers as far as the crocodile-book, and to have been cheered by the gentleness of my mother's voice and manner all the way.

But these solemn lessons which succeeded I remember as the death-blow to my peace, and a grievous daily drudgery and misery. They were very long, very numerous, very hard,—and I was generally as much bewildered by them as I believe my poor mother was herself.

Let me remember how it used to be, and bring one morning back again.

I come into the second-best parlor after breakfast with my books and an exercise-book and a slate. My mother is ready for me at her writing-desk, but not half so ready as Mr. Murdstone in his easy-chair by the window, though he pretends to be reading a book, or as Miss Murdstone, sitting near my mother, stringing steel beads. The very sight of these two has

such an influence over me that I begin to feel
the words I have been at infinite pains to get
into my head all sliding away and going I don't
know where.  I wonder where they *do* go, by
the bye?

I hand the first book to my mother.  Perhaps
it is a grammar, perhaps a history or geography.
I take a last drowning look at the page as I give
it into her hand, and start off aloud at a racing
pace while I have got it fresh.  I trip over a
word.  Mr. Murdstone looks up.  I trip over another word.  Miss Murdstone looks up.  I red-
den, tumble over half-a-dozen words, and stop.
I think my mother would show me the book if
she dared, but she does not dare, and she says
softly:

"Oh, Davy! Davy!"

"Now, Clara," says Mr. Murdstone, "be firm
with the boy.  Don't say 'Oh, Davy, Davy!'
That's childish.  He knows his lesson, or he does
not know it."

"He does *not* know it," Miss Murdstone inter-
poses awfully.

"I am really afraid he does not," says my
mother.

"Then you see, Clara," returns Miss Murdstone, "you should just give him the book back
and make him know it."

"Yes, certainly," says my mother; "that is

what I intend to do, my dear Jane. Now, Davy, try once more, and don't be stupid."

The natural result of this treatment was to make me sullen, dull, and dogged; and my temper was not improved by the sense that I was daily shut out from my mother.

One morning, after about six months of these lessons, when I went into the parlor with my books, I found my mother looking anxious, Miss Murdstone looking firm, and Mr. Murdstone binding something round the bottom of a cane, —a lithe and limber cane, which he left off binding when I came in, and poised and switched in the air.

"Now, David," he said, "you must be far more careful to-day than usual." He gave the cane another poise and another switch, and laid it down beside him with an expressive look and took up his book.

This was a good freshener to my presence of mind as a beginning. I felt the words of my lessons slipping off, not one by one, or line by line, but by the entire page. I tried to lay hold of them; but they seemed, if I may so express it, to have put skates on and to skim away from me with a smoothness there was no checking.

We began badly, and went on worse. I had come in, with an idea that I was very well prepared, but it turned out to be quite a mistake.

Book after book was added to the heap of failures, Miss Murdstone being firmly watchful of us all the time. And when we came to the last, my mother burst out crying.

"Clara!" said Miss Murdstone, in her warning voice.

Mr. Murdstone laid down his book and stood up, cane in hand.

"David, you and I will go upstairs," he said.

He walked me up to my room slowly and gravely, and when we got there, suddenly twisted my head under his arm.

"Mr. Murdstone! Sir!" I cried to him. "Don't! Pray don't beat me! I have tried to learn, sir, but I can't learn while you and Miss Murdstone are by. I can't indeed!"

"Can't you, indeed, David?" he said. "We'll try that."

He had my head as in a vise, but I twined round him somehow, and stopped him for a moment, entreating him not to beat me. It was only for a moment that I stopped him, for he cut me heavily an instant afterwards, and in the same instant I caught his hand in my mouth, and bit it through. It sets my teeth on edge to think of it!

He beat me then, as if he would have beaten me to death. Above all the noise we made, I heard them running up the stairs, and crying

out—I hear my mother crying out—and Peggotty. Then he was gone; and the door was
locked outside; and I was lying, torn and sore
and raging, upon the floor.

How well I recollect, when I became quiet,
what an unnatural stillness seemed to reign
through the whole house! How well I remember, when my smart and passion began to cool,
how wicked I began to feel!

I sat listening for a long while, but there was
not a sound. I crawled up from the floor, and
saw my face in the glass, so swollen, red, and
ugly that it almost frightened me. My stripes
were sore and stiff, and made me cry afresh,
when I moved; but they were nothing to the
guilt I felt. It lay like lead upon my breast.

For five days I was imprisoned thus within
my room, seeing no one except Miss Murdstone,
who came to bring me food. They live like
years in my remembrance. On the fifth night
I heard my name softly whispered through the
keyhole.

I groped my way to the door, and, putting my
own lips to the keyhole, whispered,

"Is that you, Peggotty, dear?"

"Yes, my own precious Davy," she replied.
"Be as soft as a mouse, or the Cat'll hear us."

I understood this to mean Miss Murdstone,
her room being close by.

"How's mamma, dear Peggotty? Is she very angry with me?"

I could hear Peggotty crying softly on her side of the keyhole, as I was doing on mine, before she answered, "No. Not very."

"What is going to be done with me, Peggotty, dear? Do you know?"

"School. Near London."

"When, Peggotty?"

"To-morrow."

"Sha'n't I see mamma?"

"Yes," said Peggotty. "Morning."

Then she stole away, fearful of surprises.

In the morning Miss Murdstone appeared as usual, and told me I was going to school, which was not altogether such news to me as she supposed. She also informed me that when I was dressed, I was to come down stairs into the parlor, and have my breakfast. There I found my mother, very pale and with red eyes, into whose arms I ran, and begged her pardon from my suffering soul.

"Oh, Davy!" she said. "That you could hurt any one I love! Try to be better, pray to be better! I forgive you; but I am so grieved, Davy, that you should have such bad passions in your heart."

They had persuaded her that I was a wicked fellow, and she was more sorry for that than for my going away. I felt it sorely. I tried to eat my parting breakfast, but my tears dropped upon my bread and butter, and trickled into my tea. I saw my mother look at me sometimes, and then glance at the watchful Miss Murdstone, and then look down, or look away.

"Master Copperfield's box there?" said Miss Murdstone, when wheels were heard at the gate.

I looked for Peggotty, but it was not she; neither she nor Mr. Murdstone appeared. My former acquaintance, the carrier, was at the door; the box was taken out to his cart and lifted in.

"Clara!" said Miss Murdstone, in her warning note.

"Yes, my dear Jane," returned my mother. "Good-bye, Davy. You are going for your own good. Good-bye, my child. You will come home in the holidays, and be a better boy. God bless you!"

Miss Murdstone was good enough to take me out to the cart, and to say on the way that she hoped I would repent, before I came to a bad end; and then I got into the cart, and the lazy horse walked off with it.

We had not gone half a mile when I was astonished to see Peggotty burst from a hedge and climb into the cart. Not a word did she say, but she squeezed me tight, crammed a bag of cakes into my pockets, and put a purse into my hand.   After a final squeeze she got down from the cart and ran away as quickly as she had come.

My pocket-handkerchief was now so wet that the carrier proposed spreading it out upon the horse's back to dry.  We did so, and I then had leisure to look at the purse.  It had three bright shillings in it from Peggotty, and—more precious still—two half-crowns folded together in a bit of paper, on which was written, in my mother's hand, "For Davy.  With my love."

I was so overcome by this that I asked the carrier to reach me my handkerchief again, but he said I had better let it dry first.  I thought so too, and wiped my eyes on my sleeve this time.

Then the cakes came in for consideration.  I offered the carrier one which he ate at a gulp, without the slightest change of expression.

"Did *she* make 'em?" asked the carrier, whose name, by the way, was Barkis.

"Peggotty, you mean, sir?"

"Ah!" said Mr. Barkis.  "Her."

"Yes, she makes all our pastry, and does all our cooking."

Mr. Barkis said nothing for some moments. Then—

"Perhaps you might be writin' to her, later on?"

"Yes, indeed," I said.

"Then you just say to her that Barkis is willin'. Would you?"

"Yes, sir," I replied, considerably puzzled by the message. And I did deliver it the very first time I wrote to Peggotty. I did not then know that the carrier meant, by being "willing," he wanted to marry my good Peggotty and was too shy to say so for himself.

### III.    THE FRIENDLY AND HELPFUL WAITER

I slept soundly until we got to Yarmouth, which place was so entirely new and strange to me that I abandoned a latent hope I had of meeting with some of Mr. Peggotty's family there, perhaps even with little Em'ly herself.

The coach was in the yard, shining very much all over, but without any horses to it as yet; and it looked in that state as if nothing was more unlikely than its ever going to London. I was thinking this, and wondering what would ultimately become of my box, which Mr. Barkis had put down on the yard-pavement by the pole (he having driven up the yard to turn his cart), and also what would ultimately become of me, when a lady looked out of a bow-window where some fowls and joints of meat were hanging up, and said:

"Is that the little gentleman from Blunderstone?"

"Yes, ma'am," I said.

"What name?"

"Copperfield, ma'am," I said.

"That won't do," returned the lady. "Nobody's dinner is paid for here, in that name."

"Is it Murdstone, ma'am?" I said.

"If you're Master Murdstone," said the lady, "why do you go and give another name, first?"

I explained to the lady how it was, who then rang a bell, and called out, "William! show the coffee-room!" Upon which a waiter came running out of a kitchen on the opposite side of the yard to show it, and seemed a good deal surprised when he found he was only to show it to me.

It was a large long room with some large maps in it. I doubt if I could have felt much stranger if the maps had been real foreign countries, and I cast away in the middle of them. I felt it was taking a liberty to sit down, with my cap in my hand, on the corner of the chair nearest the door; and when the waiter laid a cloth on purpose for me, and put a set of castors on it, I think I must have turned red all over with modesty.

He brought me some chops, and vegetables, and took the covers off in such a bouncing manner that I was afraid I must have given him some offence. But he greatly relieved my mind by putting a chair for me at the table, and saying very affably, "Now, six-foot! come on!"

I thanked him, and took my seat at the board; but found it extremely difficult to handle my knife and fork with anything like dexterity, or to avoid splashing myself with the gravy, while he was standing opposite staring so hard, and making me blush in the most dreadful manner every time I caught his eye. After watching me into the second chop, he said:

"There's half a pint of ale for you. Will you have it now?"

I thanked him and said "Yes." Upon which he poured it out of a jug into a large tumbler, and held it up against the light, and made it look beautiful.

"My eye!" he said. "It seems a good deal, don't it?"

"It does seem a good deal," I answered, with a smile. For, it was quite delightful to me to find him so pleasant. He was a twinkling-eyed, pimple-faced man, with his hair standing upright all over his head; and as he stood with one arm a-kimbo, holding up the glass to the light with the other hand, he looked quite friendly.

"There was a gentleman here yesterday," he said—"a stout gentleman by the name of Topsawyer—perhaps you know him?"

"No," I said, "I don't think—"

"In breeches and gaiters, broad-brimmed hat, gray coat, speckled choker," said the waiter.

"No," I said bashfully, "I haven't the pleasure—"

"He came in here," said the waiter, looking at the light through the tumbler, "ordered a glass of this ale—*would* order it—I told him not—drank it, and fell dead. It was too old for him. It oughtn't to be drawn, that's the fact."

I was very much shocked to hear of this melancholy accident, and said I thought I had better have some water.

"Why, you see," said the waiter, still looking at the light through the tumbler, with one of his eyes shut up, "our people don't like things being ordered and left. It offends 'em. But *I'*ll drink it, if you like. I'm used to it, and use is everything. I don't think it'll hurt me, if I throw my head back, and take it off quick. Shall I?"

I replied that he would much oblige me by drinking it, if he thought he could do it safely, but by no means otherwise. When he did throw his head back, and take it off quick, I had a horrible fear, I confess, of seeing him meet the fate of the lamented Mr. Topsawyer, and fall lifeless on the carpet. But it didn't hurt him. On the contrary, I thought he seemed the fresher for it.

"What have we got here?" he said, putting a fork into my dish. "Not chops?"

"Chops," I said.

"Lord bless my soul!" he exclaimed, "I didn't know they were chops. Why a chop's the very thing to take off the bad effects of that beer! Ain't it lucky?"

So he took a chop by the bone in one hand, and a potato in the other, and ate away with a very good appetite, to my extreme satisfaction. He afterwards took another chop, and another potato; and after that another chop and another potato. When we had done, he brought me a pudding, and having set it before me, seemed to ruminate, and to become absent in his mind for some moments.

"How's the pie?" he said, rousing himself.

"It's a pudding," I made answer.

"Pudding!" he exclaimed. "Why, bless me, so it is. What!" looking at it nearer. "You don't mean to say it's a batter-pudding!

"Why, a batter-pudding," he said, taking up a table-spoon, "is my favorite pudding! Ain't that lucky? Come on, little 'un, and let's see who'll get most."

The waiter certainly got most. He entreated me more than once to come in and win, but what with his table-spoon to my tea-spoon, his despatch to my despatch, and his appetite to my appetite, I was left far behind at the first mouthful, and had no chance with him. I never saw any one enjoy a pudding so much, I think; and he laughed, when it was all gone, as if his enjoyment of it lasted still.

Finding him so very friendly and companionable, it was then that I asked for the pen and ink and paper, to write Peggotty. He not only brought it immediately, but was good enough to look over me while I wrote the letter. When I had finished it, he asked me where I was going to school.

I said, "Near London," which was all I knew.

"Oh, my eye!" he said, looking very low-spirited, "I am sorry for that."

"Why?" I asked him.

"Oh, Lord!" he said, shaking his head, "that's the school where they broke the boy's ribs—two ribs—a little boy he was. I should say he was— let me see—how old are you, about?"

I told him between eight and nine.

"That's just his age," he said. "He was eight years and six months old when they broke his first rib; eight years and eight months old when they broke his second and did for him."

I could not disguise from myself, or from the waiter, that this was an uncomfortable coincidence, and inquired how it was done. His answer was not cheering to my spirits, for it consisted of two dismal words, "With whopping."

The blowing of the coach-horn in the yard was a seasonable diversion, which made me get up and hesitatingly inquire, in the mingled pride and diffidence of having a purse (which I took out of my pocket), if there were anything to pay.

"There's a sheet of letter-paper," he returned. "Did you ever buy a sheet of letter-paper?"

I could not remember that I ever had.

"It's dear," he said, "on account of the duty. Threepence. That's the way we are taxed in this country. There's nothing else, except the waiter. Never mind the ink. *I* lose by that."

"What should you—what should I—how much ought I to—what would it be right to pay the waiter, if you please?" I stammered, blushing.

"If I hadn't a family, and that family hadn't the cow-pock," said the waiter, "I wouldn't take a sixpence. If I didn't support a aged pairint, and a lovely sister,"—here the waiter was greatly agitated—"I wouldn't take a farthing. If I had a good place, and was treated well here, I should

beg acceptance of a trifle, instead of taking of
it.   But I live on broken wittles—and I sleep
on the coals"—here the waiter burst into tears.

I was very much concerned for his misfor-
tunes, and felt that any recognition short of
ninepence would be mere brutality and hard-
ness of heart.  Therefore I gave him one of my
three bright shillings, which he received with
much humility and veneration, and spun up with
his thumb, directly afterwards, to try the goodness of.

It was a little disconcerting to me, to find,
when I was being helped up behind the coach,
that I was supposed to have eaten all the dinner
without any assistance.  I discovered this, from
overhearing the lady in the bow-window, say to
the guard, "Take care of that child, George, or
he'll burst!" and from observing that the
woman-servants who were about the place came
out to look and giggle at me as a young phenomenon.  My unfortunate friend the waiter,
who had quite recovered his spirits, did not appear to be disturbed by this, but joined in the
general admiration without being at all confused.
If I had any doubt of him, I suppose this half-
awakened it; but I am inclined to believe that
with the simple confidence of a child, and the
natural reliance of a child upon superior years,

I had no serious mistrust of him on the whole, even then.

I felt it very hard, I must own, to be made, without deserving it, the subject of jokes between the coachman and guard as to the coach drawing heavy behind, on account of my sitting there, and as to the greater expediency of my travelling by wagon. The story of my supposed appetite getting wind among the outside passengers, they were merry upon it likewise, and asked me whether I was going to be paid for, at school, as two brothers or three, and whether I was contracted for, or went upon the regular terms; with other pleasant questions. But the worst of it was, that I knew I should be ashamed to eat anything, when an opportunity offered, and that, after a rather light dinner, I should remain hungry all night—for I had left my cakes behind, at the hotel, in my hurry. My apprehensions were realized. When we stopped for supper I couldn't muster courage to take any, though I should have liked it very much, but sat by the fire and said I didn't want anything. This did not save me from more jokes, either; for a husky-voiced gentleman with a rough face, who had been eating out of a sandwich-box nearly all the way, except when he had been drinking out of a bottle, said I was like a boa-constrictor who took enough at one meal to last him a long time; after which he actually brought a rash out upon himself with boiled beef.

We had started from Yarmouth at three o'clock in the afternoon, and reached London about eight next morning. There the stage set me down and an official from the school took charge of me. A fresh leaf of my life was begun.

IV.    SCHOOL.    STEERFORTH AND TRADDLES

Salem House was a square brick building with wings on each side. The schoolroom was very long, with three rows of desks running the length of it and bristling all around with pegs for hats and slates. Scraps of copy-books and exercises littered the floor. The other students had not yet returned from their holidays when I took my first peep into this room, in company with Mr. Mell, one of the tutors.

Presently I chanced to see a pasteboard sign lying upon a desk and bearing these words:
"TAKE CARE OF HIM
HE BITES"
I hurriedly climbed upon the desk, fearful of a dog underneath; but saw none.

"What are you doing there?" asked Mr. Mell.

"I beg your pardon, sir," I replied. "If you please, I'm looking for the dog."

"Dog? What dog?"

I pointed to the sign.

"No, Copperfield," he said gravely. "That's not a dog; that's a boy. My instructions are to put this sign on your back. I'm sorry to do so, but must do it."

With that, he took me down, and tied the placard, which was neatly constructed for the purpose, on my shoulders like a knapsack; and wherever I went, afterwards, I had the consolation of carrying it.

What I suffered nobody can imagine. Whether it was possible for people to see me or not, I always fancied that somebody was reading it. It was no relief to turn round and find nobody; for wherever my back was, there I imagined somebody always to be, until at last I positively began to have a dread for myself as the boy who *did* bite.

Mr. Creakle, the master of the school, was a short, thick-set man, and bald on the top of his head. He had a little nose and large chin. He had lost his voice and spoke almost in a whisper, which surprised me greatly, for his face always looked angry, and the exertion of talking made his thick veins stick out so that he looked angrier still.

When the boys began to come back I found my ordeal, on account of the sign on my back, not quite so great as I had feared; and it was chiefly on account of the first fellow to arrive, Tommy Traddles. Dear Tommy Traddles! You made a friend of a poor, lonesome, frightened boy that day, who will always be loyal to you so long as he lives.

Traddles was a jolly looking boy who laughed heartily when he first saw the card, as at a great joke; and he saved me from any further shyness by introducing me to every boy and saying gaily, "Look here! Here's a game!" Happily, too, most of the boys came back low-spirited, and were not very boisterous at my expense. Some of them certainly did dance about me like wild Indians and could not resist patting me, lest I should bite, and saying, "Lie down, sir!" and calling me Towzer. But on the whole I got through rather easily.

I was not considered as being formally received into the school, however, until J. Steerforth arrived. Before this boy, who was reputed to be a great scholar, and was very good-looking, and at least half-a-dozen years my senior, I was carried as before a magistrate. He inquired, under a shed in the playground, into the particulars of my punishment, and was pleased to express his opinion that it was "a jolly shame"; for which I became bound to him ever afterwards.

Then Steerforth asked how much money I had; and when I told him, he suggested that it was the proper thing for a new boy to stand treat to the others. I agreed, but felt helpless; whereupon he kindly volunteered to get the things for me and smuggle them into my room. I was a little uneasy about spending my mother's half-crowns, but didn't dare say so. I handed them over to him and he procured the feast and laid it out on my bed, saying,

"There you are, young Copperfield, and a royal spread you've got!"

I couldn't think of doing the honors of the feast, at my time of life, while he was by; my hand shook at the very thought of it. I begged him to do me the favor of presiding; and my request being seconded by the other boys he acceded to it, and sat upon my pillow, handing round the viands with perfect fairness, I must say. As to me, I sat on his left hand, and the rest were grouped about us, on the nearest beds and on the floor.

How well I recollect our sitting there, talking in whispers, or their talking, and my respectfully listening, I ought rather to say; the moonlight falling a little way into the room, through the window, painting a pale window on the floor, and the greater part of us in shadow, except when Steerforth struck a match, when he wanted to look for anything on the board, and shed a blue glare over us that was gone directly.

I heard all kinds of things about the school. I heard that Mr. Creakle was a tartar and thrashed the boys unmercifully—all except Steerforth, upon whom he didn't dare lay his hand. I heard that Mr. Creakle was very ignorant, and that Mr. Mell, who was not a bad sort of fellow, was poorly paid. All this and much more I heard in the whispers of that moon-lit room, before we finally betook ourselves to bed.

From that time on, big handsome Steerforth took me under his protection, and, for my part, I was his willing slave. I would tell him tales which I had imbibed from my early reading, while he would help me do my sums and keep the other boys from tormenting me. Why he, the fine head-boy, should have taken notice of me at all, I don't know. But I remember I all but worshipped him with his easy swagger and lordly air.

The other boy to whom I always owed allegiance was Traddles. Poor jolly Traddles! In a tight, sky-blue suit that made his arms and legs look like German sausages, he was at once

the merriest and most miserable of all boys.
He was always being caned by that fierce Mr.
Creakle, who made all our backs tingle, except
Steerforth's.   After Traddles had got his daily
caning he would cheer up somehow and get
comfort by drawing skeletons all over his slate.
He was always drawing these skeletons, just as
he was always being caned.   And they did
comfort him somehow, for presently he would
begin to laugh again before his tears were dry.

He was very honorable, Traddles was, and
held it as a solemn duty in the boys to stand by
one another.   He suffered for this on several
occasions; and particularly once, when Steerforth laughed in church, and the Beadle thought
it was Traddles, and took him out.   I see him
now, going away in custody, despised by the
congregation.   He never said who was the real
offender, though he smarted for it next day, and
was imprisoned so many hours that he came
forth with a whole churchyard full of skeletons
swarming all over his Latin Dictionary.   But
he had his reward.   Steerforth said there was
nothing of the sneak in Traddles, and we all
felt that to be the highest praise.   For my part,
I could have gone through a good deal to have
won such a reward.

Although Mr. Creakle's school was not noted
for scholarship, I can confess without vanity

that I did make good progress. I was naturally fond of books and a great reader; and now I had the first fair chance at learning things. In this I found Mr. Mell, the quiet, gentle tutor, a constant friend to me. I shall always remember him with gratitude.

But Steerforth, I am sorry to say, did not like the tutor and took no pains to hide his poor opinion. Since many of the other boys followed Steerforth's lead, poor Mr. Mell was not popular. Still, nothing especial came of it until one memorable day when Mr. Creakle was absent. The boys seized the chance to be uproarious, and Mr. Mell could not control them. Finally even his patience was exhausted, and he sprang to his feet and pounded his desk with a book.

"Silence!" he cried. "This noise must cease! It's maddening! How can you treat me this way, boys?"

It was my book that he struck his desk with; and as I stood beside him, following his eye as it glanced round the room, I saw the boys all stop, some suddenly surprised, some half afraid, and some sorry perhaps.

Steerforth's place was at the bottom of the school, at the opposite end of the long room. He was lounging with his back against the wall, and his hands in his pockets, and looked at Mr.

Mell with his mouth shut up as if he were whistling, when Mr. Mell looked at him.

"Silence, Mr. Steerforth!" said Mr. Mell.

"Silence yourself," said Steerforth, turning red. "Whom are you talking to?"

"Sit down," said Mr. Mell.

"Sit down yourself," said Steerforth, "and mind your business."

There was a titter, and some applause; but Mr. Mell was so white that there was silence.

"If you think, Steerforth," said Mr. Mell, "that you can make use of your position of favoritism here to disobey rules and insult a gentleman—"

"A what?—where is he?" said Steerforth.

Here somebody cried out, "Shame, J. Steerforth! Too bad!" It was Traddles, whom Mr. Mell instantly routed by bidding him hold his tongue.

—"To insult one who is not fortunate in life, sir, and who never gave you the least offence," continued Mr. Mell, his lip trembling, "you commit a mean and base action. You can sit down or stand up as you please, sir. Copperfield, go on."

"Young Copperfield," said Steerforth, coming forward, "stop a bit. I tell you what, Mr. Mell, once for all. When you take the liberty of calling men mean and base, or anything of that sort, you are an impudent beggar. You are always a beggar, you know; but when you do that, you are an impudent beggar."

I am not clear whether he was going to strike Mr. Mell, or Mr. Mell was going to strike him, or there was any such intention on either side. I saw a rigidity come upon the whole school as if they had been turned into stone, and found Mr. Creakle in the midst of us. Mr. Mell, with his elbows on his desk and his face in his hands, sat for some moments quite still.

"Mr. Mell," said Mr. Creakle, shaking him by the arm; and his whisper was very audible now; "you have not forgotten yourself, I hope?"

"No, sir," said Mr. Mell.

Mr. Creakle looked hard at him and then turned to Steerforth.

"Now, sir, will you tell me what this is about?"

Steerforth evaded the question for a little while; looking in scorn and anger on his opponent, and remaining silent. I could not help thinking what a fine-looking fellow he was, and how homely and plain Mr. Mell looked opposed to him.

"What did he mean by talking about favorites, then?" said Steerforth at length.

"Favorites?" repeated Mr. Creakle, with the

veins in his forehead swelling quickly. "Who talked about favorites?"

"He did," said Steerforth.

"And pray, what did you mean by that, sir?" demanded Mr. Creakle, turning angrily on his assistant.

"I meant, Mr. Creakle," he returned, in a low voice, "as I said; that no pupil had a right to avail himself of his position of favoritism to degrade me."

"To degrade *you?*" said Mr. Creakle. "My stars! But give me leave to ask you, Mr. What's your name, whether, when you talk about favorites, you showed proper respect to me? To *me,* sir," said Mr. Creakle, darting his head at him suddenly and drawing it back again, "the principal of this establishment and your employer."

"It was not judicious, sir, I am willing to admit," said Mr. Mell. "I should not have done so if I had been cool."

Here Steerforth struck in.

"Then he said I was mean, and then he said I was base, and then I called him a beggar. If *I* had been cool, perhaps I shouldn't have called him a beggar. But I did, and I am ready to take the consequences of it."

Without considering, perhaps, whether there were any consequences to be taken, I felt quite in a glow at this gallant speech. It made an impression on the boys, too, for there was a low stir among them, though no one spoke a word.

"I am surprised, Steerforth,—although your candor does you honor," said Mr. Creakle, "does you honor, certainly,—I am surprised, Steerforth, I must say, that you should attach such an epithet to any person employed and paid in Salem House, sir."

Steerforth gave a short laugh.

"That's not an answer, sir," said Mr. Creakle, "to my remark. I expect more than that from you, Steerforth."

If Mr. Mell looked homely in my eyes before the handsome boy, it would be quite impossible to say how homely Mr. Creakle looked.

"Let him deny it," said Steerforth.

"Deny that he is a beggar, Steerforth?" cried Mr. Creakle. "Why, where does he go a begging?"

"If he is not a beggar himself, his near relation's one," said Steerforth. "It's all the same."

"What do you mean?"

"Since you expect me, Mr. Creakle, to justify myself," said Steerforth, "and to say what I mean,—what I have to say is, that his mother lives on charity in an almshouse."

Mr. Creakle turned to his assistant with a severe frown and labored politeness:

"Now you hear what this gentleman says, Mr. Mell. Have the goodness, if you please, to set him right before the assembled school."

"He is right, sir, without correction," returned Mr. Mell, in the midst of a dead silence; "what he has said is true."

"Be so good then as to declare publicly, will you," said Mr. Creakle, putting his head on one side and rolling his eyes round the school, "whether it ever came to my knowledge until this moment?"

"I believe not directly," he returned.

"Why, you *know* not," said Mr. Creakle. "Don't you, man?"

"Sir, I think you knew my circumstances when I came here, and that a bare living wage—"

"I think, if you come to that," said Mr. Creakle, with his veins swelling again bigger than ever, "that you've been in a wrong position altogether, and mistook this for a charity school. Mr. Mell, we'll part if you please. The sooner the better."

"There is no time," answered Mr. Mell, rising, "like the present."

"Sir, to you!" said Mr. Creakle.

"I take my leave of you, Mr. Creakle, and of all of you," said Mr. Mell, glancing round the room and patting me gently on the shoulder. "James Steerforth, the best wish I can leave you is that you may come to be ashamed of what you have done to-day. At present I would prefer to see you anything rather than a friend to me or to any one in whom I feel an interest."

Then Mr. Mell walked out with his property under his arm.

Mr. Creakle made a speech, in which he thanked Steerforth for asserting (though perhaps too warmly) the independence and respectability of Salem House; and which he wound up by shaking hands with Steerforth, while we gave three cheers,—I did not quite know what for, but I suppose for Steerforth, and so joined in them ardently, though I felt miserable. Mr. Creakle then caned Tommy Traddles for being discovered in tears instead of cheers on account of Mr. Mell's departure: and went back to his sofa or wherever he had come from.

When he had gone there was an awkward silence. Somehow we all felt uncomfortable or ashamed. As for Steerforth, he said he was angry with Traddles and glad he had caught it.

Poor Traddles, who was relieving himself as usual with a burst of skeletons, said he didn't care. Mr. Mell was ill-used.

"Who has ill-used him, you girl?" said Steerforth.

"Why *you* have," returned Traddles.

"What have I done?" said Steerforth.

"What have you done?" retorted Traddles. "Hurt his feelings and lost him his situation."

"His feelings!" repeated Steerforth, disdainfully. "His feelings will soon get the better of it, I'll be bound. His feelings are not like yours, Miss Traddles. As to his situation,—which was a precious one, wasn't it?—do you suppose I am not going to write home and take care that he gets some money? Polly?"

We thought this intention very noble in Steerforth, whose mother was a widow, and rich, and would do almost anything, it was said, that he asked her. We were all extremely glad to see Traddles so put down, and exalted Steerforth to the skies. But as I look back at it now, I should rather have been Traddles that day than any other boy in the room. And I think the other boys will say so too.

I pass over all that happened at school, until the anniversary of my birthday came round in March. Except that Steerforth was more to be admired than ever, I remember nothing. He was going away at the end of the half-year, if not sooner, and was more spirited and independent that ever; but beyond this I remember nothing. The great event by which that time is marked in my mind, seems to have swallowed up all lesser recollections, and to exist alone.

It was after breakfast, and we had been summoned in from the playground, when Mr. Creakle entered and said:

"David Copperfield is to go into the parlor."

I expected a hamper from Peggotty, and brightened at the order. Some of the boys about me put in their claim not to be forgotten in the distribution of the good things, as I got out of my seat with great alacrity. But when I reached the parlor I saw no one except Mrs. Creakle, who held an open letter in her hand and looked at me gravely.

"You are too young to know how the world changes every day," said Mrs. Creakle, "and how the people in it pass away. But we all have to learn it, David! some of us when we are young, some of us when we are old, some of us at all times of our lives."

I looked at her earnestly.

"When you came away from home," said Mrs. Creakle, after a pause, "were they all well?" After another pause, "Was your mamma well?"

I trembled without distinctly knowing why, and still looked at her earnestly, making no attempt to answer.

"Because," said she, "I grieve to tell you that I hear this morning your mamma is very ill."

A mist arose between Mrs. Creakle and me, and her figure seemed to move in it for an instant. Then I felt the burning tears run down my face, and it was steady again.

"She is very dangerously ill," she added.

I knew all now.

"She is dead."

There was no need to tell me so. I had already broken out into a desolate cry, and felt an orphan in the wide world.

She was very kind to me. She kept me there all day, and left me alone sometimes; and I cried and wore myself to sleep, and awoke and cried again.

The next night I left Salem House, after a tender adieu to Steerforth, Traddles, and all the rest. I little thought that I left the school never to return.

When I reached home I was in Peggotty's arms before I got to the door, and she took me into the house. Her grief burst out when she first saw me; but she controlled it soon, and spoke in whispers, and walked softly, as if the dead could be disturbed. She had not been in bed, I found, for a long time. She sat up at night still, and watched. As long as her poor dear pretty was above the ground, she said, she would never desert her.

Mr. Murdstone took no heed of me when I went into the parlor where he was, but sat by the fireside, weeping silently, and pondering in his elbow-chair.  Miss Murdstone, who was busy at her writing-desk, which was covered with letters and papers, gave me her cold finger-nails, and asked me, in an iron whisper, if I had been measured for my mourning.

I will not dwell upon the dull, sorrowful days before and after my dear mother's funeral.  The house had been cold and quiet enough before, but was now almost terrifying.  And had it not been for Peggotty I do not know how I should have stood it.

But soon even she was denied me.  Miss Murdstone had never liked her, and now lost no time in dismissing her from our service.  The single ray of light in this gloomy time is a little visit I was allowed to make with her to Yarmouth, to our old friends, Mr. Peggotty, Ham, and Emily.  The latter was much grown now, and prettier than ever, and shyer about letting me kiss her.

And Barkis, the honest carrier, after having been "willing" all this time, was hugely gratified to gain a favorable answer from Peggotty.  They were married while I was was there, and I was glad to leave my faithful old nurse so well provided for.

Then I returned home—no, I cannot say that word—to Mr. and Miss Murdstone.

### V.   I BEGIN LIFE ON MY OWN ACCOUNT

And now I fell into a state of neglect, which I still cannot look back upon without deep sorrow. I was as one alone—apart from all friendly notice, apart from the society of all other boys my own age, apart from all companionship but my own spiritless thoughts,—which seems to cast its gloom upon this paper as I write.

What would I have given to have been sent to the hardest school that ever was kept—to have been taught something, anyhow, anywhere? No such hope dawned upon me. They disliked me; and they steadily overlooked me. I think Mr. Murdstone's means were straitened at about this time; but it is little to the purpose. He could not bear me; and in putting me from him he tried, as I believe, to put away the notion that I had any claim upon him—and succeeded.

I was not actively ill-used. I was not beaten, or starved; but day by day I was made to feel that I was in the way, and an altogether useless member of society. Finally Mr. Murdstone called me to him one day, and told me that he could not afford to send me to school, but that I must go to work for myself. He had a partner in the wine trade in London, and I was to be given a position there.

Accordingly, Miss Murdstone packed me off without loss of time; and I went to work—at ten years old—washing bottles in a vile-smelling warehouse down by the water-side.

There were three or four of us boys, counting me; and I was shown how to work by an older lad whose name was Mick Walker, and who wore a ragged apron and paper cap. He introduced me to another boy by the queer name of Mealy Potatoes. I discovered, later, that this youth had started out with another name, but had been given this one on account of a pale, mealy complexion.

No words can express the secret agony of my soul as I sank into this companionship; compared these associates with those of my happier childhood—not to say with Steerforth, Traddles, and the rest of those boys; and felt my hopes of growing up to be a learned and distinguished man crushed in my bosom. The feeling of being utterly without hope; of the shame I felt in my position; of the misery it was to believe that what I had learned would pass away from me, little by little, never to be brought back any more; cannot be written. As often as Mick Walker went away in the course of that forenoon, I mingled my tears with the water in which I was washing the bottles. But I was careful never to let the others see me in tears.

I was given the splendid salary of seven shillings[1] a week for my services, and out of that I had to feed and clothe myself. My lodgings were provided for, at the home of Mr. Micawber, a portly, dignified man with a large, shiny bald head and rusty, genteel clothes. Mr. Micawber was perpetually dodging creditors while he waited for "something to turn up," as he expressed it. But in his way he was kind to me.

Still I had not one upon earth to go to for friendship or advice. I must needs skimp and save to be sure of having enough bread and cheese to eat; and no one lifted a finger to help me, a frightened little stranger in a large, terrifying city. I look back upon it now as a horrible dream. I know that I worked from morning till night with common men and boys, a shabby child. I know that I lounged about the streets poorly clothed and half starved. I know that but for the mercy of God, I might easily have been—for any other care that was taken of me— a little thief or vagabond.

But in these darkest days a bright idea came to me—I don't know when or how, but come it did, and refused to depart. I remembered having heard of an aunt, Miss Betsey Trotwood, my dear father's sister. I had heard both my mother and Peggotty speak of her, with some

[1] About $1.68

awe, it is true, as being a rather eccentric
woman, who did not like boys, but still I resolved to find her.  So I wrote to Peggotty and
asked the address, and also for the loan of half
a guinea.  I had resolved to run away and appeal
to my aunt for protection.

Peggotty's answer soon came with much love
and the half guinea.  She told me that Miss Betsey lived near Dover, but she couldn't say exactly
where.  This was vague enough, but didn't deter
me in the slightest.  I worked my week out at
the warehouse, and, bidding Mick Walker and
Mealy Potatoes good-bye, ran away forthwith.

I may have had the notion of running all the
way to Dover when I started.  I had a small
box of clothes and the half guinea, but a carter
robbed me of both of them the first day.  So,
reduced to a few odd pence, I made but slow
progress on foot, and sleeping out in the open
by night.

For six days I trudged my weary way, pawn-
ing my coat for food. and not daring to ask aid
from any one, for fear of being seized and sent
back to London.  But at last I limped in upon
the bare white downs near Dover, sunburnt and
in rags.

By dint of inquiries I was directed to Miss
Betsey Trotwood's house, and I lost no time in
going there—a sorry enough figure, as you may

imagine. It was a neat little cottage looking out from some cliffs upon the sea.

As I stood at the gate peeping in and wondering how I had best proceed, a tall, slim lady came out of the house. She had a handkerchief tied over her cap, a pair of gardener's gloves on her hands, and carried a pruning-knife.

"Go away!" said Miss Betsey (for it was none other), shaking her head when she saw me, and making a distant chop in the air with her knife. "Go along! No boys here!"

I watched her, with my heart at my lips, as she marched to a corner of her garden, and stooped to dig a root. Then without a scrap of courage, but with a great deal of desperation, I went softly in and stood beside her, touching her with my finger.

"If you please, ma'am," I began.

She started and looked up.

"If you please, aunt."

"EH?" exclaimed Miss Betsey, in a tone of amazement I have never heard approached.

"If you please, aunt, I am your nephew."

"Oh, Lord!" said my aunt, and sat flat down in the garden-path.

"I am David Copperfield, of the Rookery. I used to hear my dear mamma speak of you before she died. I have been neglected and mistreated, and so I ran away and came to you. I

was robbed at first setting out, and have walked
all the way, and have never slept in a bed since
I began the journey."

Here my self-support gave away all at once;
and with a movement of my hands, intended to
show her my ragged state, and call it to witness
that I had suffered something, I broke into a
passion of crying, which I suppose had been
pent up within me all the week.

My aunt, with every sort of expression, sat
on the gravel, staring at me, until I began to
cry; when she got up in a great hurry, collared
me, and took me into the parlor.  Her first
proceeding there was to unlock a tall press,
bring out several bottles, and pour some of the
contents of each into my mouth.  I think they
must have been taken out at random, for I am
sure I tasted aniseed water, anchovy sauce, and
salad dressing.  Then she rang the bell.

"Janet," she said, when her servant came in,
"Go upstairs, give my compliments to Mr. Dick
and say I wish to speak to him."

Mr. Dick proved to be a pleasant-faced man
of whimsical ways, but upon whose advice my
aunt greatly relied.  As he proposed now that
I be given a bath and put to bed, my aunt lost
no time in following these ideas.

Janet had gone away to get the bath ready,
when my aunt, to my great alarm, became in

one moment rigid with wrath, and had hardly voice to cry out, "Janet! Donkeys!"

Upon which, Janet came running up the stairs as if the house were in flames, darted out on a little piece of green in front, and warned off two donkeys that had presumed to set hoof upon it; while my aunt, rushing out of the house, seized the bridle of the third animal, led him forth from those sacred precincts, and boxed the ears of the unlucky urchin in attendance.

To this hour I don't know whether my aunt had any lawful right of way over that patch of green; but she had settled it in her own mind that she had, and it was all the same to her. The one great outrage of her life, demanding to be constantly avenged, was the passage of a donkey over that spot. No matter what she was doing or saying, a donkey turned the current of her ideas in a moment, and she was upon him straight. Jugs of water and watering-pots were kept in secret places ready to be discharged on the offending boys; sticks were laid in ambush behind the door; sallies were made at all hours; and incessant war prevailed.

Perhaps this was an agreeable excitement to the donkey-boys; or perhaps the more sagacious of the donkeys, understanding how the case stood, stubbornly delighted in coming that way.

I only know that there were three alarms before
the bath was ready; and that on the occasion
of the last and most desperate of all, I saw my
aunt engage, single-handed, with a sandy-headed
lad of fifteen, and bump his sandy head against
her own gate, before he realized what was the
matter.   These interruptions were the more
ridiculous to me, because she was giving me
broth out of the tablespoon at the time (having
firmly persuaded herself that I was actually
starving, and must receive food at first in very
small quantities), and, while my mouth was yet
open to receive the spoon, she would put it back
into the basin, cry "Janet! Donkeys!" and go
out to the assault.

The bath was a great comfort.  For I began
to be sensible of acute pains in my limbs from
living out in the fields, and was now so tired
and low that I could hardly keep myself awake
for five minutes together.  When I had bathed
they enrobed me in a shirt and a pair of trousers
belonging to Mr. Dick, and tied me up in two
or three great shawls.  What sort of bundle I
looked like, I don't know, but I felt a very hot
one.  Feeling also very faint and drowsy, I soon
fell asleep.

The next morning at breakfast my aunt said,
with a determined shake of her head, "Well,
I've written to him."

"To whom?" I ventured.

"To Mr. Murdstone."

"Does he know where I am, aunt?" I inquired, alarmed.

"I have told him," said my aunt, with a nod.

"Shall I—be—given up to him?" I faltered.

"I don't know," said my aunt. "We shall see."

"Oh! I can't thing what I shall do," I exclaimed, "if I have to go back to Mr. Murdstone!"

"I don't know anything about it," said my aunt, shaking her head. "I can't say, I am sure. We shall see."

My spirits sank under these words, and I became very downcast and heavy of heart.

For the next few days I felt like a criminal condemned to die; although my aunt and Mr. Dick both were very kind to me. Finally the day of the expected visit from Mr. Murdstone arrived, but without bringing him till late in the afternoon. Our dinner had been postponed; but it was growing so late that my aunt had ordered it to be got ready, when she gave a sudden alarm of donkeys, and to my consternation, I beheld Miss Murdstone, on a side-saddle, ride deliberately over the sacred piece of green, and stop in front of the house, looking about her.

"Go along with you!" cried my aunt, shaking her head and her fist out of the window. "You have no business there. How dare you trespass? Go along! Oh, you bold-faced thing!"

My aunt was so exasperated by the coolness with which Miss Murdstone looked about her, that I really believe she did not know what to do. I hastened to tell her who it was, and that Mr. Murdstone was following behind, but it made no difference. She glared at them as they approached in a most terrible way.

"Shall I go away, aunt?" I asked, trembling.

"No, sir," said my aunt, "Certainly not!" with which she pushed me into a corner near her, and fenced me in with a chair, as if it were a prison or a bar of justice. This position I continued to occupy during the whole interview which presently ensued.

"Oh!" said my aunt, "I was not aware at first to whom I had the pleasure of objecting. But I don't allow anybody to ride over that turf. I make no exceptions. I don't allow anybody to do it."

"Your regulation is rather awkward to strangers," said Miss Murdstone.

"*Is* it!" said my aunt.

Mr. Murdstone here cleared his throat and began, "Miss Trotwood—"

"I beg your pardon," observed my aunt, with a keen look. "You are the Mr. Murdstone."

"I am," said Mr. Murdstone.

"You'll excuse my saying, sir," returned my aunt. "that I think it would have been a much better and happier thing if you had left that poor child alone."

Mr. Murdstone colored, and Miss Murdstone looked as though she could bite nails.

"I received your letter, " said Mr. Murdstone, "and thought it best to see you personally about this unhappy boy who has run away from his friends and his position. I need not tell you that he has always given us great trouble and uneasiness. He is sullen and stubborn and has a violent temper. I thought it best that you should know this."

"It can hardly be necessary for me to confirm anything stated by my brother," said Miss Murdstone; "but I beg to observe, that of all the boys in the world, I believe this is the worst boy."

"Strong!" said my aunt, shortly.

"But not at all too strong for the facts," returned Miss Murdstone.

"Ha!" said my aunt. "Well, sir?"

"Upon the death of his mother," continued Mr. Murdstone, scowling, "I obtained a respectable place for him—"

"Was it the sort of place you would have put a boy of your own in?" asked my aunt.

"If he had been my brother's own boy," returned Miss Murdstone, striking in, "his character, I trust, would have been altogether different."

"Or, if the poor child, his mother, had been alive, he would still have gone into the respectable business, would he?" said my aunt.

"I believe," said Mr. Murdstone, with a nod of his head, "that Clara would have disputed nothing which myself and my sister were agreed was for the best."

"Humph!" said my aunt. "Well, sir, what next?"

"Merely this, Miss Trotwood," he returned. "I am here to take David back—to take him back unconditionally, and to deal with him as I think right. I am not here to make any promise to anybody. You may possibly have some idea, Miss Trotwood, of abetting him in his running away. Your manner induces me to think it possible. Now I must caution you that if you abet him once, you abet him for good and all. I cannot trifle, or be trifled with. I am here, for the first and last time, to take him away. Is he ready to go? If he is not, my doors are shut against him henceforth, and yours, I take it for granted, are opened to him."

To this address my aunt had listened with the closest attention, sitting perfectly upright, with her hands folded on one knee, and looking grimly on the speaker. When he had finished, she turned her eyes so as to command Miss Murdstone, and said,

"Well, ma'am, have *you* got anything to remark?"

"Indeed, Miss Trotwood," said Miss Murdstone, "all that I could say has been so well said by my brother, that I have nothing to add except my thanks for your politeness."

This ironical remark, however, was wholly lost.

"And what does the boy say?" said my aunt. "Are you ready to go, David?"

I answered no, and entreated her not to let me go. I said that neither Mr. nor Miss Murdstone had ever liked me, or had ever been kind to me. That they had made my mamma, who always loved me dearly, unhappy about me, and that I knew it well and that Peggotty knew it. And I begged and prayed my aunt—I forget in what terms now but I remember that they affected me very much then—to befriend and protect me, for my father's sake.

"Mr. Dick," said my aunt, "what shall I do with this child?"

"Have him measured for a suit of clothes,

directly," said Mr. Dick, in his usual sudden way.

"Mr. Dick," said my aunt, triumphantly, "give me your hand, for your common sense is invaluable."

Having shaken it with great cordiality, she pulled me towards her, and said to Mr. Murdstone:

"You can go when you like; I'll take my chance with the boy. If he's all you say he is, at least I can do as much for him then as you have done. But I don't believe a word of it."

"Miss Trotwood," rejoined Mr. Murdstone, shrugging his shoulders, as he rose, "if you were a gentleman—"

"Bah! stuff and nonsense!" said my aunt. "Don't talk to me!"

"How exquisitely polite!" exclaimed Miss Murdstone, rising. "Overpowering, really!"

"Do you think I don't know," said my aunt, turning a deaf ear to the sister, and continuing to address the brother, and to shake her head at him, "what kind of life you must have led that poor, little woman you cajoled into marrying you? Do you think I don't know what a woeful day it was for her and her boy when *you* first came in her way?"

And thereupon she read him such a lecture as I warrant he had never listened to before in

his life, nor ever would again.  He bit his lip
in silence while she lectured, and all the color
left his face.  Miss Murdstone tried to inter-
rupt the flow of words repeatedly, with no success at all.  When she had ended—

"Good day, sir," said my aunt, "and good-
bye!  Good day to you, too, ma'am," turning suddenly upon his sister.  "Let me see you ride a
donkey over *my* green again, and as sure as you
have a head upon your shoulders, I'll knock your
bonnet off, and tread upon it!"

It would require a painter, and no common
painter too, to depict my aunt's face as she
delivered herself of this very unexpected senti-
ment, and Miss Murdstone's face as she heard
it.  But the manner of the speech, no less than
the matter, was so fiery, that Miss Murdstone,
without a word in answer, discreetly put her
arm through her brother's, and walked haughtily
out of the cottage; my aunt remaining in the
window looking after them, prepared, I have no
doubt, to carry her threat into instant execution.

No attempt at defiance being made, however,
her face gradually relaxed, and became so pleasant that I was emboldened to kiss and thank
her; which I did with great heartiness, and with
both my arms clasped round her neck.  I then
shook hands with Mr. Dick, who shook hands
with me a great many times, and hailed this

happy close of the proceedings with repeated bursts of laughter.

"You'll consider yourself guardian, jointly with me, of this child, Mr. Dick," said my aunt.

"I shall be delighted," said Mr. Dick, "to be the guardian of David's son."

"Very good," returned my aunt, *"that's* settled. I have been thinking, do you know, Mr. Dick, that I might call him Trotwood?"

"Yes, to be sure. Trotwood Copperfield," said Mr. Dick.

My aunt took so kindly to the notion, that some ready-made clothes, which were purchased for me the next day, were marked "Trotwood Copperfield," in her own handwriting, and in indelible marking-ink, before I put them on.

Thus I began my new life, in a new name, and with everything new about me. Now that the state of doubt was over, I felt, for many days, like one in a dream. I never thought that I had a curious couple of guardians in my aunt and Mr. Dick. I never thought of anything about myself, distinctly. While a remoteness had come upon the old life—which seemed to lie in the haze of an immeasurable distance.

In my new life I was to realize some of my youthful ambitions. I was to struggle, perhaps, but I was to succeed. And I was to find that my aunt—for all her gruff exterior—had a heart of gold.

But whatever there was of happiness or of sorrow, of success or of failure, in my new life, does not belong to these pages. The identity of the child, and of the boy, David Copperfield, in now forever merged in the personality of Trotwood Copperfield, Esquire, the Prospective Man.

# Sissy Jupe,

## THE CHILD OF THE CIRCUS

### I.   THE NEW PUPIL

"**G**IRL number twenty, stand up."

The speaker was a stocky school overseer in a small town school in England. The speaker's square coat, square legs, square shoulders,—nay, his very neck-cloth trained to take him by the throat in a stubborn way,—all proclaimed a man who had set ideas about teaching and about everything else in life. Above all, he believed in Facts, spelled with a capital F.

Turning he addressed the new teacher.

"In this life we want nothing but Facts, sir; nothing but Facts!"

"Girl number twenty," repeated Mr. Gradgrind (for that was his name), squarely pointing with his square forefinger, "I don't know that girl.   Who is that girl?"

"Sissy Jupe, sir," explained number twenty, blushing, standing up, and courtesying.

"Sissy is not a name," said Mr. Gradgrind. "Don't call yourself Sissy.   Call yourself Cecilia."

"It's father as calls me Sissy, sir," returned the young girl in a trembling voice, and with another courtesy.

"Then he has no business to do it," said Mr. Gradgrind. "Tell him he mustn't. Cecilia Jupe. Let me see. What is your father?"

"He belongs to the horse-riding, the circus, if you please, sir."

Mr. Gradgrind frowned, and waved off the objectionable calling with his hand.

"We don't want to know anything about that, here. You mustn't tell us about that here. Your father breaks horses, don't he?"

"If you please, sir, when they get any to break, they do break horses in the ring, sir."

"You mustn't tell us about the ring, here. Very well, then. Describe your father as a horse-breaker. He doctors sick horses, I dare say?"

"Oh yes, sir."

"Very well, then. He is a veterinary surgeon, a farrier, and horse-breaker. Give me your definition of a horse."

(Sissy Jupe thrown into the greatest alarm by this demand.)

"Girl number twenty unable to define a horse!" said Mr. Gradgrind, for the benefit of all the other scholars. "Girl number twenty possessed of no facts, in reference to one of the

commonest of animals!   Some boy's definition
of a horse.   Bitzer, yours."

The square finger, moving here and there,
lighted suddenly on Bitzer, perhaps because he
chanced to sit in the same ray of sunlight which,
darting in at one of the bare windows of the
intensely whitewashed room, irradiated Sissy.
For, the boys and girls sat on the face of the inclined plane in two compact bodies, divided up
the centre by a narrow interval; and Sissy, being
at the corner of a row on the sunny side, came in
for the beginning of a sunbeam, of which Bitzer,
being at the corner of a row on the other side,
a few rows in advance, caught the end.   But,
whereas the girl was so dark-eyed and dark-
haired, that she seemed to receive a deeper and
more lustrous color from the sun, when it shone
upon her, the boy was so light-eyed and light-
haired that the selfsame rays appeared to draw
out of him what little color he ever possessed.
His cold eyes would hardly have been eyes, but
for the short ends of lashes which, by bringing
them into immediate contrast with something
paler than themselves, expressed their form.
His short-cropped hair might have been a mere
continuation of the sandy freckles on his forehead and face.   His skin was so unwholesomely
deficient in the natural tinge, that he looked as
though, if he were cut, he would bleed white.

"Bitzer," said Thomas Gradgrind. "Your definition of a horse."

"Quadruped. Graminivorous. Forty teeth, namely twenty-four grinders, four eye-teeth, and twelve incisive. Sheds coat in the spring; in marshy countries, sheds hoofs, too. Hoofs hard, but requiring to be shod with iron. Age known by marks in mouth."

Thus (and much more) Bitzer.

"Now, girl number twenty," said Mr. Gradgrind. "You know what a horse is."

She courtesied again, and would have blushed deeper, if she could have blushed deeper than she had blushed all this time. Bitzer, after rapidly blinking at Thomas Gradgrind with both eyes at once, put his knuckles to his freckled forehead, and sat down again.

The third gentleman now stepped forth. A mighty man at cutting and drying, he was; a government officer; likewise a school inspector.

"Very well," said this gentleman, briskly smiling, and folding his arms. "That's a horse. Now, let me ask you girls and boys, Would you paper a room with representations of horses?"

After a pause, one-half of the children cried in chorus, "Yes, sir!" Upon which the other half, seeing in the gentleman's face that "Yes" was wrong, cried out in chorus, "No, sir!"—as the custom is, in these examinations.

"Of course No.  Why wouldn't you?"

A pause.  One corpulent slow boy, with a wheezy manner of breathing, ventured the answer, Because he wouldn't paper a room at all, but would paint it.

"You *must* paper it," said the gentleman, rather warmly.

"You *must* paper it," said Thomas Gradgrind, "whether you like it or not.  Don't tell *us* you wouldn't paper it!  What do you mean, boy?"

"I'll explain to you, then," said the gentleman, after another and a dismal pause, "why you wouldn't paper a room with representations of horses.  Do you ever see horses walking up and down the sides of rooms in reality—in fact?  Do you?"

"Yes, sir!" from one-half.  "No, sir!" from the other.

"Of course not" said the gentleman, with an indignant look at the wrong half.  "Why, then, you are not to see anywhere, what you don't see in fact; you are not to have anywhere, what you don't have in fact.  What is called Taste, is only another name for Fact."

Thomas Gradgrind nodded his approbation.

"This is a new principle, a discovery, a great discovery," said the gentleman.  "Now, I'll try you again.  Suppose you were going to carpet a room. Would you use a carpet having a representation of flowers upon it?"

There being a general conviction by this time that "No, sir!" was always the right answer to this gentleman, the chorus of No was very strong. Only a few feeble stragglers said "Yes;" among them Sissy Jupe.

"Girl number twenty," said the gentleman, smiling in the calm strength of knowledge.

Sissy blushed, and stood up.

"So you would carpet your room—or your husband's room, if you were a grown woman, and had a husband—with representations of flowers, would you?" said the gentleman. "Why would you?"

"If you please, sir, I am very fond of flowers," returned the girl.

"And is that why you would put tables and chairs upon them, and have people walking over them with heavy boots?"

"It wouldn't hurt them, sir. They wouldn't crush and wither, if you please, sir. They would be pictures of what was very pretty and pleasant, and I would fancy"—

"Ay, ay, ay! But you mustn't fancy!" cried the gentleman, quite elated by coming so happily to his point. "That's it! You are *never* to fancy!"

"You are not, Cecilia Jupe," Thomas Gradgrind solemnly repeated, "to do anything of that kind."

"Fact, fact, fact!" said the gentleman. And "Fact, fact, fact!" repeated Thomas Gradgrind.

"You are to be in all things regulated and governed," said the gentleman, "by Fact. You must discard the word Fancy altogether. You have nothing to do with it. You are not to have, in any object of use or ornament, what would be a contradiction in fact. You don't walk upon flowers in fact; you cannot be allowed to walk upon flowers in carpets. You don't find that foreign birds and butterflies come and perch upon your crockery; you cannot be permitted to paint foreign birds and butterflies upon your crockery. You never meet with animals going up and down walls; you must not have animals represented upon walls. This is the new discovery. This is Fact. This is Taste."

The girl courtesied, and sat down. She was very young, and she looked as if she were frightened. But fortunately the three learned gentlemen on the platform were so busy expounding their new discovery of Fact, which meant the killing of all Fancy, that Sissy did not have to stand up any more, that day.

But on his way home, Thomas Gradgrind was troubled. He felt that in his model school, a child brought up in the circus had no place. He did not want her associating with his children, Thomas junior, and Louisa. That would never do. What was that circus doing here anyhow, he wondered, and why would folks waste their time over such trash?

He had reached the outskirts of the town, when his ears were invaded by the sound of music. The clashing and banging band attached to the circus which had there set up its wooden pavilion, was in full bray. A flag, floating from the summit of the temple, proclaimed to mankind that it was "Sleary's Horse-riding" which claimed their attention. Miss Josephine Sleary, as some very long and very narrow posters announced, was then presenting her graceful equestrian Tyrolean flower-act. Among the other pleasing but always strictly moral wonders which must be seen to be believed, Signor Jupe was that afternoon to "exhibit his highly trained performing dog, Merrylegs." The same Signor Jupe was to "enliven the varied performances at frequent intervals with his quips and retorts." Lastly, he was to wind them up by appearing in his favorite character of Mr. William Button, of Tooley Street, in "the highly novel and laughable comedy of The Tailor's Journey."

Thomas Gradgrind took no heed of these trivialities of course, but passed on as a practical man ought to pass on, either brushing the noisy insects from his thoughts, or consigning them to the House of Correction.  But, the turning of the road took him by the back of the booth, and at the back of the booth a number of children were congregated in a number of stealthy attitudes, striving to peep in at the hidden glories of the place.

This brought him to a stop.  "Now, to think of these vagabonds," said he, "attracting the young rabble from a model school!"

A space of stunted grass and dry rubbish being between him and the young rabble, he took his eyeglass out of his waistcoat to look for any child he knew by name, and might order off. What did he then behold but his own Louisa peeping with all her might through a hole in a deal board, and his own Thomas abasing himself on the ground to catch but a hoof of the graceful equestrian Tyrolean flower-act!

Dumb with amazement, Mr. Gradgrind crossed to the spot where his family was thus disgraced, laid his hand upon each erring child, and said,—

"Louisa!  Thomas!"

Both rose, red and disconcerted.  But Louisa looked at her father with more boldness than Thomas did.  Indeed Thomas did not look at him, but gave himself up to be taken home like a machine.

"In the name of wonder, idleness and folly!" said Mr. Gradgrind, leading each away by a hand; "what do you do here?"

"Wanted to see what it was like," returned Louisa, shortly.

"What it was like?"

"Yes, father," she repeated sullenly.

Mr. Gradgrind looked at the two culprits with a frown. It was all the fault of that circus—coming into their model town and corrupting his model children with the rest. He turned with sudden determination.

"Come," he said, taking each by the hand, "we shall have to see Mr. Bounderby about this."

Mr. Bounderby, be it known, was another eminently practical man, and a town officer. They met him, as it chanced, going in at Mr. Gradgrind's own gate, in company with Mrs. Gradgrind.

"Well!" blustered Mr. Bounderby—for he always blustered when he spoke—"what's the matter? What are the children in the dumps about?"

"We were peeping at the circus," muttered Louisa without lifting her eyes, "and father caught us."

"Why, Mrs. Gradgrind," said her husband in a lofty manner, "I should as soon have expected to find my children reading poetry!"

"Dear me!" whimpered Mrs. Gradgrind. "How can you, Louisa and Thomas! I wonder at you. I declare you're enough to make one regret ever having had a family at all. I have a great mind to say that I wish I hadn't. *Then* what would you have done, I should like to know."

Mr. Gradgrind did not seem favorably impressed by these cogent remarks. He frowned impatiently.

"As if, with my head in its present throbbing state, you couldn't go and look at the shells and minerals and things provided for you, instead of circuses!" said Mrs. Gradgrind. "You know, as well as I do, no young people have circus masters, or keep circuses in cabinets, or attend lecture about circuses. What can you possibly want to know of circuses then? I am sure you have enough to do, if that is what you want. With my head in its present state, I couldn't remember the mere names of half the facts you have got to attend to."

"That's the reason!" pouted Louisa.

"Don't tell me that's the reason, because it can be nothing of the sort," said Mrs. Gradgrind. "Go and be somethingological directly." Mrs. Gradgrind was not a scientific character, and usually dismissed her children to their studies with this general injunction to choose their pursuit.

"There certainly is no reason in looking with interest at a parcel of vagabonds," returned Bounderby. "When I was a vagabond myself, nobody looked with any interest at *me;* I know that."

"Then comes the question," said the eminently practical father, with his eyes on the fire, "in what has this vulgar curiosity its rise?"

"I'll tell you in what. In idle imagination."

"I hope not," said the eminently practical; "I confess, however, that the misgiving *has* crossed me on my way home."

"In idle imagination, Gradgrind," repeated Bounderby. "A very bad thing for anybody, but a cursed bad thing for a girl like Louisa."

"But what put such a notion in my children's heads?" mused Mr. Gradgrind. "I am sure, *I* never suggested it."

"Stop a bit!" cried Bounderby, "You have one of those strollers' children in the school, haven't you?"

"Cecilia Jupe, by name," said Mr. Gradgrind.

"Now, stop a bit!" cried Bounderby again. "How did she come there?"

"Why, the fact is, I saw the girl myself, for the first time, only just now. She especially applied here at the house to be admitted, as not regularly belonging to our town, and—yes, you are right, Bounderby, you are right."

"Now stop a bit!" cried Bounderby, once more. "Louisa saw her when she came?"

"Louisa certainly did see her, for she mentioned the application to me. But Louisa saw her, I have no doubt, in Mrs. Gradgrind's presence."

"Pray, Mrs. Gradgrind," said Bounderby, "what passed?"

"Oh, my poor health!" returned Mrs Gradgrind. "The girl wanted to come to the school, and Mr. Gradgrind wanted girls to come to the school, and Louisa and Thomas both said that the girl wanted to come, and that Mr. Gradgrind wanted girls to come, and how was it possible to contradict them when such was the fact!"

"Now I tell you what, Gradgrind!" said Mr. Bounderby. "Turn this girl to the rightabout, and there's an end of it."

"I am much of your opinion."

"Do it at once," said Bounderby, "has always been my motto from a child. When I thought I would run away from my grandmother, I did it at once. Do you the same. Do this at once!"

"Are you walking?" asked his friend. "I have the father's address. Perhaps you would not mind walking to town with me?"

"Not the least in the world," said Mr Bounderby, "as long as you do it at once!"

So, Mr. Bounderby threw on his hat—he always threw it on, as expressing a man who had been far too busily employed in making himself, to acquire any fashion of wearing his hat—and with his hands in his pockets, set forth briskly with his friend to find the circus people.

## II.  THE CIRCUS PEOPLE

As the two eminently practical friends made their way back to the spot where the flaunting banners and noisy drums proclaimed the circus, they were almost run down by a frightened girl who came dashing recklessly around a corner.

"Hello!" said Mr. Gradgrind in surprise, recognizing her as Sissy Jupe; "Stop! Where are you going!"

Girl number twenty stopped then, palpitating and made him a courtesy.

"Why are you tearing about the streets," said Mr. Gradgrind, "in this improper manner?"

"I was—I was run after, sir," the girl panted, "and I wanted to get away."

"Run after?" repeated Mr. Gradgrind. "Who would run after *you?*"

The question was unexpectedly and suddenly answered for her, by the colorless boy, Bitzer, who came round the corner with such blind speed and so little anticipating a stoppage on the pavement, that he brought himself up against Mr. Gradgrind's waistcoat and rebounded into the road.

"What do you mean, boy?" said Mr. Gradgrind. "What are you doing? How dare you dash against—everybody—in this manner?"

Bitzer picked up his cap, which the concussion had knocked off; and backing, and knuckling his forehead, pleaded that it was an accident.

"Was this boy running after you, Jupe?" asked Mr. Gradgrind.

"Yes, sir," said the girl reluctantly.

"No, I wasn't sir!" cried Bitzer. "Not till she run away from me. But the circus folks never mind what they say, sir; they're famous for it." Bitzer looked slyly at Mr. Bounderby.

"He frightened me so," said the girl, "with his cruel faces!"

"Oh!" cried Bitzer. "Oh! Ain't you one of the rest! Ain't you a horse-rider! I never looked at her, sir. I asked her if she would know how to define a horse to-morrow, and offered to tell her again, and she ran away, and I ran after her, sir, that she might know how to answer when she was asked. You wouldn't have thought of saying such mischief if you hadn't been a horse-rider!"

"Her being one of the circus people seems to be pretty well known among the rest of the school," observed Mr. Bounderby. "You'd have had the whole school peeping in a row, in a week."

"Truly, I think so," returned his friend. "Bitzer, turn you about and take yourself home. Jupe, stay here a moment. Let me hear of your running in this manner any more, boy, and you will hear of me through the master of the school. You understand what I mean. Go along."

The boy stopped in his rapid blinking, knuckled his forehead again, glanced at Sissy, turned about, and retreated.

"Now, girl," said Mr. Gradgrind, "take this gentleman and me to your father's; we are going there. What have you got in that bottle you are carrying?"

"Gin," said Mr. Bounderby.

"Dear, no sir! It's the nine oils."

"The what?" cried Mr. Bounderby.

"The nine oils, sir. To rub father with."

"Then," said Mr. Bounderby, with a loud short laugh, "what the deuce do you rub your father with nine oils for?"

"It's what our people always use, sir, when

they get any hurts in the ring," replied the girl, looking over her shoulder, to assure herself that her pursuer was gone. "They bruise themselves very bad sometimes."

"Serve 'em right," said Mr. Bounderby, "for being idle." She glanced up at his face, mingled astonishment and dread.

"By George!" said Mr. Bounderby, "when I was four or five years younger than you, I had worse bruises upon me than ten oils, twenty oils, forty oils, would have rubbed off. I didn't get 'em by circus acts, but by being banged about. There was no rope-dancing for me; I danced on the bare ground and was larruped with the rope."

Mr. Gradgrind, though hard enough, was by no means so rough a man as Mr. Bounderby. His character was not unkind, all things considered; it might have been a very kind one indeed if he had only made some round mistake in the arithmetic that balanced it, years ago. He said, in what he meant for a reassuring tone, as they turned down a narrow road, "And this is where you live, is it, Jupe?"

"This is it, sir, and—if you wouldn't mind, sir—this is the house."

She stopped, at twilight, at the door of a mean little public-house, with dim red lights in it. As haggard and as shabby, as if, for want of custom, it had itself taken to drinking, and

had gone the way all drunkards go, and was very near the end of it.

"It's only crossing the room sir, and up the stairs, if you wouldn't mind, and waiting there for a moment till I get a candle. If you should hear a dog, sir, it's only Merrylegs, and he only barks."

When she returned presently with the light, they followed the girl up some steep corner-stairs without meeting any one, and stopped in the dark while she went on. They expected every moment to hear Merrylegs give tongue, but the highly-trained performing dog had not barked when the girl and the candle appeared together.

"Father is not in our room, sir," she said, with a face of great surprise. "If you wouldn't mind walking in, I'll find him directly."

They walked in; and Sissy, having set two chairs for them, sped away with a quick light step. It was a mean, shabbily furnished room, with a bed in it. The white nightcap, embellished with two peacocks' feathers and a pigtail bolt upright, in which Signor Jupe had that very afternoon enlivened the varied performances with his quips and retorts, hung upon a nail; but no other portion of his wardrobe, or other token of himself or his pursuits, was to be seen anywhere.

They heard the doors of rooms above, opening and shutting as Sissy went from one to another in quest of her father; and presently they heard voices expressing surprise. She came bounding down again in a great hurry, opened a battered and mangy old hair trunk, found it empty, and looked round with her hands clasped and her face full of terror.

"Father must have gone down to the Booth, sir. I don't know why he should go there, but he must be there; I'll bring him in a minute!" She was gone directly, without her bonnet; with her long, dark childish hair streaming behind her.

"What does she mean?" said Mr. Gradgrind. "Back in a minute? It's more than a mile off."

Before Mr. Bounderby could reply, a young man appeared at the door, and introducing himself with the words, "By your leaves, gentlemen!" walked in with his hands in his pockets. His face, close-shaven, thin, and sallow, was shaded by a great quantity of dark hair, brushed into a roll all round his head, and parted up the centre. His legs were very robust, but shorter than legs of good proportions should have been. His chest and back were as much too broad, as his legs were too short. He was dressed in a Newmarket coat and tight-fitting trousers. This gentleman was mentioned in the bills of the day as Mr. E. W. B. Childers, so justly celebrated for his daring vaulting act as the Wild Huntsman of the North American Prairies. In this performance, a diminutive boy with an old face, who now accompanied him, assisted as his infant son: being carried upside down over his father's shoulder, by one foot, and held by the crown of his head, heels upwards, in the palm of his father's hand, according to the violent paternal manner in which wild huntsmen fondle their offspring. On the bills he was called Cupid.

"By your leaves, gentlemen," said Mr. Childers, glancing round the room. "It was you, I believe, that were wishing to see Jupe?"

"It was," said Mr. Gradgrind. "His daughter has gone to fetch him, but I can't wait; therefore, if you please, I will leave a message for him with you."

"You see, my friend," Mr. Bounderby put in, "we are the kind of people who know the value of time, and you are the kind of people who don't know the value of time."

"I have not," retorted Mr. Childers, after surveying him from head to foot, " the honor of knowing *you;* but if you mean that you can make more money of your time than I can of mine, I should judge from your appearance, that you are about right."

"And when you have made it, you can keep it too, I should think," said Cupid.

"Kidderminster, stow that!" said Mr. Childers. (Master Kidderminster was Cupid's mortal name.)

"What does he come here cheeking us for, then?" cried Master Kidderminster.

"Kidderminster," said Mr. Childers, raising his voice, " stow that!—Sir," to Mr. Gradgrind, "I was addressing myself to you. You may or you may not be aware (for perhaps you have not been much in the audience), that Jupe has missed his tip very often lately."

"Has—what has he missed?" asked Mr. Gradgrind, glancing at the potent Bounderby for assistance.

"Missed his tip."

"Offered at the Garters four times last night, and never done 'em once," said Master Kidderminster. "Missed his tip at the banners, too, and was loose in his ponging."

"Didn't do what he ought to do. Was short in his leaps and bad in his tumbling," Mr. Childers interpreted.

"Oh!" said Mr. Gradgrind, "that is tip, is it?"

"In a general way that's missing his tip," Mr. Childers answered.

"Nine oils, Merrylegs, missing tips, garters, banners, and Ponging, eh!" ejaculated Bounderby, "queer sort of company, too, for a man who has raised himself."

"Lower yourself, then," retorted Cupid, "oh Lord! if you've raised yourself so high as all that comes to, let yourself down a bit."

"This is a very obtrusive lad!" said Mr. Gradgrind, turning, and knitting his brows on him.

"We'd have had a young gentleman to meet you, if we had known you were coming," retorted Master Kidderminster, nothing abashed. "It's a pity you don't have a bespeak, being so particular. You're on the Tight-Jeff, ain't you?"

"What does this unmannerly boy mean," asked Mr. Gradgrind, eyeing him in a sort of desperation, "by Tight-Jeff?"

"There! Get out, get out!" said Mr. Childers, thrusting his young friend from the room, rather in the prairie manner. "Tight-Jeff or Slack-Jeff, it don't much signify: it's only tight-rope and slack-rope. You were going to give me a message for Jupe?"

"Yes, I was."

"Then," continued Mr. Childers, quickly, "my opinion is, he will never receive it. Do you know much of him?"

"I never saw the man in my life."

"I doubt if you ever *will* see him now. It's pretty plain to me, he's off."

"Do you mean that he has deserted his daughter?"

"Ay! I mean," said Mr. Childers, with a nod, "that he has cut. He was goosed last night, he was goosed the night before last, he was goosed to-day. He has lately got into the way of being always goosed, and he can't stand it."

"Why has he been—so very much—Goosed?" asked Mr. Gradgrind, forcing the word out of himself, with great solemnity and reluctance.

"His joints are turning stiff, and he is getting used up," said Childers. "He has his points as a Cackler still, but he can't get a living out of *them*."

"A Cackler!" Bounderby repeated. "Here we go again!"

"A speaker, if the gentleman likes it better," said Mr. Childers, superciliously. "Now it's a remarkable fact, sir, that it cut that man deeper, to know that his daughter knew of his being goosed, than to go through with it."

"Good!" interrupted Mr. Bounderby. "This is good, Gradgrind! A man so fond of his daughter, that he runs away from her! This is devilish good! Ha! ha!"

Eyeing Mr. Bounderby from head to foot Childers turned from him to Mr. Gradgrind.

"Jupe sent his daughter out on an errand not an hour ago, and then was seen to slip out himself, with his hat over his eyes and a bundle tied up in a handkerchief under his arms. She will never believe it of him, but he has cut away and left her."

"Pray," said Mr. Gradgrind, "why will she never believe it of him?"

"Because those two were one. Because they were never asunder. Because, up to this time, he seemed to dote upon her," said Childers, taking a step or two to look into the empty trunk. "Poor Sissy! He had better have apprenticed her," continued Childers, giving his hair a shake, as he looked up from the empty box. "Now, he leaves her without anything."

"When Sissy got into the school here," he pursued, "her father was as pleased as Punch. I couldn't altogether make out why, myself, as we were not stationary here, being but comers and goers anywhere. I suppose, however, he had this move in his mind—he was always half-cracked—and then considered her provided for. If you should happen to have looked in to-night for the purpose of telling him that you were going to do her any little service," said Mr. Childers stroking his face again, and repeating his look, "it would be very fortunate and well-timed; *very* fortunate and well-timed."

"On the contrary," returned Mr. Gradgrind. "I came to tell him that her connections made her not an object for the school, and that she must not attend any more. Still if her father really has left her,—Bounderby, let me have a word with you."

Upon this, Mr. Childers politely betook himself, with his equestrian walk, to the landing outside the door, and there stood stroking his face and softly whistling. While thus engaged, he overheard such phrases in Mr. Bounderby's voice as "No. *I* say no. I advise you not. I say by no means." While, from Mr. Gradgrind, he heard in his much lower tone the words, "But even as an example to Louisa, of what this pursuit which has been the subject of vulgar curiosity, leads to and ends in. Think of it, Bounderby, in that point of view."

Meanwhile the various members of Sleary's company gradually gathered together from the upper regions, where they were quartered, and, from standing about, talking in low voices to one another and to Mr. Childers, gradually insinuated themselves and him into the room. There were two or three handsome young women among them, with their two or three husbands, and their two or three mothers, and their eight or nine little children, who did the fairy business when required. The father of one of the families was in the habit of balancing the father of another of the families on the top of a great pole;

the father of a third family often made a pyramid of both those fathers, with Master Kidderminster for the apex, and himself for the base; all the fathers could dance upon rolling casks, stand upon bottles, catch knives and balls, twirl hand-basins, ride upon anything, jump over everything, and stick at nothing. All the mothers could (and did) dance, upon the slack wire and the tight rope, and perform rapid acts on bare-backed steeds; and one of them, alone in a Greek chariot drove six in hand into every town they came to.

They all assumed to be mighty rakish and knowing, they were not very tidy in their private dresses, they were not at all orderly in their domestic arrangements, and the combined literature of the whole company would have produced but a poor letter on any subject. Yet there was a remarkable gentleness and childishness about these people, a special inaptitude for any kind of sharp practice, and an untiring readiness to help and pity one another, deserving, often of as much respect, and always of as much generous construction, as the every-day virtues of any class of people in the world.

Last of all appeared Mr. Sleary: a stout man, with one fixed eye and one loose eye, a voice like the efforts of a broken old pair of bellows.

"Thquire!" said Mr. Sleary, who was troubled

with asthma, and whose breath came far too thick and heavy for the letter s, "Your thervant! Thith ith a bad piethe of bithnith, thith ith. You've heard of my Clown and ith dog having thkipped?"

He addressed Mr. Gradgrind, who answered "Yes."

"Well Thquire," he returned, taking off his hat, and rubbing the lining with his pocket-handkerchief, which he kept inside for the purpose. "Ith it your intenthion to do anything for the poor girl, Thquire?"

"I shall have something to propose to her when she comes back," said Mr. Gradgrind.

"Glad to hear it, Thquire. Not that I want to get rid of the child, any more than I want to thtand in her way."

Here his daughter Josephine—a pretty fair-haired girl of eighteen, who had been tied on a horse at two years old,—cried "Father, hush! she has come back!"

Then came Sissy Jupe, running into the room as she had run out of it. And when she saw them all assembled, and saw their looks, and saw no father there, she broke into a most deplorable cry, and took refuge on the bosom of the most accomplished tight-rope lady, who knelt down on the floor to nurse her, and to weep over her.

"Ith an infernal thame, upon my thoul it ith!" said Sleary.

"O my dear father, my good kind father, where are you gone? You are gone to try to do me some good, I know! You are gone away for my sake, I am sure. And how miserable and helpless you will be without me, poor, poor father, until you come back!"

It was so pathetic to hear her saying many things of this kind, with her face turned upward, and her arms stretched out as if she were trying to stop his departing shadow and embrace it, that no one spoke a word until Mr. Bounderby (growing impatient) took the case in hand.

"Now, good people all," said he, "this is wanton waste of time. Let the girl understand the fact. Let her take it from me, if you like, who have been run away from, myself. Here, what's your name! Your father has absconded—deserted you—and you mustn't expect to see him again as long as you live."

They cared so little for plain Fact, these people, and were in that advanced state of degeneracy on the subject, that instead of being impressed by the speaker's strong common sense, they took it in extraordinary dudgeon. The men muttered "Shame!" and the women "Brute!" and Sleary, in some haste, communi-

cated the following hint, apart to Mr. Bounderby.

"I tell you what, Thquire. To thpeak plain
to you, my opinion ith that you had better cut
it thort and drop it. They're a very good-
natured people, my people, but they're accuth-
tomed to be quick in their movementh; and if
you don't act upon my advithe, I'm afraid they'll
pitch you out o' winder."

Mr. Bounderby being restrained by this mild
suggestion, Mr. Gradgrind found an opening
for his eminently practical exposition of the
subject.

"It is of no moment," said he, "whether this
person is to be expected back at any time, or
the contrary. He is gone away, and there is
no present expectation of his return. That, I
believe, is agreed on all hands."

"Thath agreed, Thquire, thick to that!"
From Sleary.

"Well, then. I, who came here to inform the
father of the poor girl, Jupe, that she could not
be received at the school any more, in consequence of there being practical objections, into
which I need not enter, to the reception there
of the children of persons so employed, am prepared in these altered circumstances to make a
proposal. I am willing to take charge of you,
Jupe, and to educate you, and provide for you.

have performed without hith mathter, tho ith
ath broad ath ith long!"

With that he regarded her attentively with his
fixed eye, surveyed his company with his loose
one, kissed her, shook his head, and handed her
to Mr. Gradgrind as to a horse.

"There the ith, Thquire," he said, sweeping
her with a professional glance as if she were
being adjusted in her seat, "and the'll do you
uthtithe. Good-by, Thethilia!"

"Good-by, Cecilia!" "Good-by, Sissy!" "God
less you, dear!" In a variety of voices from
all the room.

But the riding-master eye had observed the
bottle of nine oils in her bosom, and he now in-
posed with "Leave the bottle, my dear; ith
rge to carry; it will be of no uthe to you now.
ve it to me!"

"No, no!" she said, in another burst of tears.
Oh no! Pray let me keep it for father till he
comes back! He will want it when he comes
ck. He had never thought of going away,
en he sent me for it. I must keep it for him,
you please!"

And keep it she did—hugging the small
ttle of liniment to her breast as though it were
something sacred. In her eyes it was the only
ble link between her father and herself.

The only condition (over and above your good
behavior) I make is, that you decide now, at
once, whether to accompany me or remain here.
Also that if you accompany me now, it is understood that you communicate no more with any
of your friends who are here present.

"The only other observation I will make to
you, Jupe, in the way of influencing your de-
cision, is, that it is highly desirable to have a
sound practical education, and that even your
father appears to have known and felt that
much."

The last words had a visible effect upon her.
She stopped in her wild crying, a little detached
herself from Emma Gordon, and turned her
face full upon her patron. The whole company
perceived the force of the change, and drew a
long breath together, that plainly said, "She
will go!"

"Be sure you know your own mind, Jupe,"
Mr. Gradgrind cautioned her; "I say no more.
Be sure you know your own mind!"

"When father comes back," cried the girl,
bursting into tears again after a minute's silence,
"how will he ever find me if I go away!"

"You may be quite at ease," said Mr. Gradgrind, calmly; he worked out the whole matter
like a sum: "you may be quite at ease, Jupe, on

that score.  In such a case, your father, I appre-
hend, must find out Mr."—

"Thleary.  Thath my name, Thquire.  Not
athamed of it.  Known all over England, and
alwayth paythe ith way."

"Must find out Mr. Sleary, who would then
let him know where you went.  I should have no
power of keeping you against his wish, and he
would have no difficulty at any time, in finding
Mr. Thomas Gradgrind of Coketown.  I am
well known."

"Well known," assented Mr. Sleary, rolling
his loose eye.

There was another silence; and then she exclaimed, sobbing with her hands before her face,
"Oh, give me my clothes, give me my clothes,
and let me go away before I break my heart!"

The women sadly bestirred themselves to get
the clothes together—it was soon done, for they
were not many—and to pack them in a basket
which had often travelled with them.  Sissy sat
all the time, upon the ground, still sobbing and
covering her eyes.  Mr. Gradgrind and his friend
Bounderby stood near the door, ready to take
her away.  Mr. Sleary stood in the middle of
the room, with the male members of the company about him, exactly as he would have stood
in the centre of the ring during his daughter

Josephine's performance.  He
but his whip.

The basket packed in silenc
her bonnet to her, and smoothe
hair, and put it on.  Then th
her, and bent over her kissin
her: and brought the children
her; and were a tender-hearte
set of women altogether.

"Now, Jupe," said Mr. Gr
are quite determined, come!"

But she had to take her fa
part of the company yet, and
had to unfold his arms (fo
the professional attitude whe
selves near Sleary), and giv
Mr. Sleary was reserved unt
his arms wide he took her
and would have sprung her
the riding-master manne
young ladies on their dism
act; but there was no rebo
only stood before him cryi

"Good-by, my dear!"
make your fortune, I hope
folkth will ever trouble
with your father hadn't ta
ith a ill-conwenienth to h
billth.  But on thecond

Sissy Jupe had not an easy time of it, between Mr. M'Choakumchild, the teacher of the model school, and Mrs. Gradgrind, and was not without strong impulses, in the first months of her probation, to run away. It hailed *Facts* all day long so very hard, and life in general was opened to her as such a closely ruled ciphering-book, that assuredly she would have run away, but for only one restraint. The girl believed that her father had not deserted her; she lived in the hope that he would come back, and in the faith that he would be made happier by her remaining where she was.

The wretched ignorance with which Sissy clung to this belief filled Mr. Gradgrind with pity. Yet, what was to be done? M'Choakumchild reported that she had a very dense head for figures; that, once possessed with a general idea of the globe, she took the smallest conceivable interest in its exact measurements; that she was extremely slow in the acquisition of dates, unless some pitiful incident happened to be connected therewith; that she would burst into tears on being required (by mental process) immediately to name the cost of two hundred and forty-seven muslin caps at fourteenpence halfpenny; that she was as low down, in the

school, as low could be; that after eight weeks of
induction into the elements of Political Econ-
omy, she had only yesterday been set right by
a prattler three feet high, for returning to the
question, "What is the first principle of this
science?" the absurd answer, "To do unto others
as I would that they should do unto me."

Mr. Gradgrind observed, shaking his head,
that all this was very bad; that it showed the
necessity of infinite grinding at the mill of
knowledge, as per system, schedule, blue book,
report, and tabular statements A to Z; and that
Sissy "must be kept to it." So Sissy was kept
to it, and became low-spirited, but no wiser.

"It would be a fine thing to be you, Miss
Louisa!" she said, one night, when Louisa had
endeavored to make her perplexities for the next
day something clearer to her.

"Do you think so?"

"I should know so much, Miss Louisa. All
that is difficult to me now, would be so easy
then."

"You might not be the better for it, Sissy."

Sissy submitted, after a little hesitation, "I
should not be the worse, Miss Louisa." To
which Miss Louisa answered, "I don't know
that."

There had been so little communication between these two—both because life at Stone

Lodge went monotonously round like a piece of machinery which discouraged human interference, and because of the prohibition relative to Sissy's past career—that they were still almost strangers.  Sissy, with her dark eyes wonderingly directed to Louisa's face, was uncertain whether to say more or to remain silent.

"You are more useful to my mother, and more pleasant with her than I can ever be," Louisa resumed.  "You are pleasanter to yourself, than *I* am to *my*self."

"But, if you please Miss Louisa," Sissy pleaded, "I am—O so stupid!"

Louisa, with a brighter laugh than usual, told her she would be wiser by and by.

"You don't know," said Sissy, half crying, "what a stupid girl I am.  All through school hours I make mistakes.  Mr. and Mrs. M'Choakumchild call me up, over and over again, regularly to make mistakes.  I can't help them.  They seem to come natural to me."

"Mr. and Mrs. M'Choakumchild never make any mistakes themselves, I suppose, Sissy?"

"O no!" she eagerly returned.  "They know everything."

"Tell me some of your mistakes."

"I am almost ashamed," said Sissy, with reluctance.  "But to-day, for instance, Mr.

M'Choakumchild was explaining to us about Natural Prosperity."

"National, I think it must have been," observed Louisa.

"Yes, it was.—But isn't it the same?" she timidly asked.

"You had better say, National, as he said so," returned Louisa, with her dry reserve.

"National Prosperity. And he said, Now, this schoolroom is a Nation. And in this nation, there are fifty millions of money. Isn't this a prosperous nation? Girl number twenty, isn't this a prosperous nation, and ain't you in a thriving state?"

"What did you say?" asked Louisa.

"Miss Louisa, I said I didn't know. I thought I couldn't know whether it was a prosperous nation or not, and whether I was in a thriving state or not, unless I knew who had got the money, and whether any of it was mine. But that had nothing to do with it. It was not in the figures at all," said Sissy, wiping her eyes.

"That was a great mistake of yours," observed Louisa.

"Yes, Miss Louisa, I know it was, now. Then Mr. M'Choakumchild said he would try me again. And he said, This schoolroom is an immense town, and in it there are a million of inhabitants, and only five and twenty are starved

to death in the streets, in the course of a year.
What is your remark on that proportion? And
my remark was—for I couldn't think of a better one—that I thought it must be just as hard
upon those who were starved, whether the others
were a million, or a million million. And that
was wrong, too."

"Of course it was."

'Then Mr. M'Choakumchild said he would try
me once more. And he said, Here are the stutterings"—

"Statistics," said Louisa.

"Yes, Miss Louisa—they always remind me
of stutterings, and that's another of my mistakes—of accidents upon the sea. And I find
(Mr. M'Choakumchild said) that in a given
time a hundred thousand persons went to sea
on long voyages, and only five hundred of them
were drowned or burnt to death. What is the
percentage? And I said, Miss;" here Sissy
fairly sobbed as confessing with extreme con-
trition to her greatest error; "I said it was
nothing."

"Nothing, Sissy?"

"Nothing, Miss—to the relations and friends
of the people who were killed. I shall never
learn," said Sissy. "And the worst of all is, that
although my poor father wished me so much to
learn, and although I am so anxious to learn,

because he wished me to, I am afraid I don't
like it."

Louisa stood looking at the pretty modest
head, as it drooped abashed before her, until it
was raised again to glance at her face. Then
she asked,—

"Did your father know so much himself, that
he wished you to be well taught too, Sissy?"

Sissy hesitated before replying, and so plainly
showed her sense that they were entering on for-
bidden ground, that Louisa added, "No one hears
us; and if any one did, I am sure no harm could
be found in such an innocent question."

"No, Miss Louisa," answered Sissy, upon this
encouragement, shaking her head: "father knows
very little indeed. It's as much as he can do to
write; and it's more than people in general can
do to read his writing. Though it's plain to *me*."

"Your mother?"

"Father says she was quite a scholar. She
died when I was born. She was," Sissy made
the terrible communication nervously; "she was
a dancer."

"Did your father love her?" Louisa asked these
questions with a strong, wild, wandering interest
peculiar to her; an interest gone astray like a
banished creature, and hiding in solitary places.

"O yes! As dearly as he loves me. Father
loved me, first, for her sake. He carried me

about with him when I was quite a baby. We have never been asunder from that time."

"Yet he leaves you now, Sissy?"

"Only for my good. Nobody understands him as I do; nobody knows him as I do. When he left me for my good—he never would have left me for his own—I know he was almost broken-hearted with the trial. He will not be happy for a single minute, till he comes back."

"Tell me more about him," said Louisa, "I will never ask you again. Where did you live?"

"We travelled about the country, and had no fixed place to live in. Father's a;" Sissy whispered the awful word, "a clown."

"To make the people laugh?" said Louisa, with a nod of intelligence.

"Yes. But they wouldn't laugh sometimes, and then father cried. Lately, they very often wouldn't laugh, and he used to come home despairing. Father's not like most. Those who didn't know him as well as I do, and didn't love him as dearly as I do, might believe he was not quite right. Sometimes they played tricks upon him; but they never knew how he felt them, and shrunk up, when he was alone with me. He was far, far timider than they thought!"

"And you were his comfort through everything?"

She nodded, with the tears rolling down her

face. "I hope so, father said I was. It was because he grew so scared and trembling, and because he felt himself to be a poor, weak, ignorant, helpless man (those used to be his words), that he wanted me so much to know a great deal, and be different from him. I used to read to him to cheer his courage, and he was very fond of that. They were wrong books—I am never to speak of them here—but we didn't know there was any harm in them."

"And he liked them?" said Louisa, with her searching gaze on Sissy all this time.

"O very much! They kept him, many times, from what did him real harm. And often and often of a night, he used to forget all his troubles in wondering whether the Sultan would let the lady go on with the story, or would have her head cut off before it was finished."

"And your father was always kind? To the last?" asked Louisa; contravening the great principle, and wondering very much.

"Always, always!" returned Sissy, clasping her hands. "Kinder and kinder than I can tell. He was angry only one night, and that was not to me, but Merrylegs. Merrylegs;" she whispered the awful fact; "is his performing dog."

"Why was he angry with the dog?" Louisa demanded.

"Father, soon after they came home from per-

forming, told Merrylegs to jump on the backs
of the two chairs and stand across them—which
is one of his tricks.  He looked at father, and
didn't do it at once.  Everything of father's had
gone wrong that night, and he hadn't pleased
the public at all.  He cried out that the very
dog knew he was failing, and had no compassion
on him.  Then he beat the dog, and I was frightened, and said, 'Father, father!  Pray don't hurt
the creature who is so fond of you!  O Heaven
forgive you, father, stop!'  And he stopped,
and the dog was bloody, and father lay down
crying on the floor with the dog in his arms, and
the dog licked his face."

Louisa saw that she was sobbing; and going
to her, kissed her, took her hand, and sat down
beside her.

"Finish by telling me how your father left
you, Sissy.  Now that I have asked you so much,
tell me the end.  The blame, if there is any
blame, is mine, not yours."

"Dear Miss Louisa," said Sissy, covering her
eyes, and sobbing yet; "I came home from the
school that afternoon, and found poor father
just come home too, from the booth.  And he
sat rocking himself over the fire, as if he was in
pain.  And I said, 'Have you hurt yourself,
father?' (as he did sometimes like they all did)
and he said, 'A little, my darling.'  And when

I came to stoop down and look up at his face, I saw that he was crying. The more I spoke to him, the more he hid his face; and at first he shook all over, and said nothing but 'My darling;' and 'My love!' "

Sissy stopped a moment, then resumed in a lower voice. "At last poor father said that he had given no satisfaction again, and never did give any satisfaction now, and that he was a shame and disgrace, and I should have done better without him all along. I said all the affectionate things to him that came into my heart, and presently he was quiet and I sat down by him, and told him all about the school and everything that had been said and done there. When I had no more left to tell, he put his arms round my neck, and kissed me a great many times. Then he asked me to fetch some of the stuff he used, for the little hurt he had had, and to get it at the best place, which was at the other end of town from there; and then, after kissing me again, he let me go. When I had gone downstairs, I turned back that I might be a little bit more company to him yet, and looked in at the door and said, 'Father, dear, shall I take Merrylegs?' Father shook his head and said, 'No, Sissy, no; take nothing that's known to be mine, my darling;' and I left him sitting by the fire. Then the thought must have come upon him, poor,

poor father! of going away to try something for my sake; for, when I came back, he was gone.

"There's no more to tell, Miss Louisa. I keep the nine oils ready for him, and I know he will come back. Every letter that I see in Mr. Gradgrind's hand takes my breath away and blinds my eyes, for I think it comes from father, or from Mr. Sleary about father. Mr. Sleary promised to write as soon as ever father should be heard of, and I trust to him to keep his word."

After this, whenever Sissy dropped a courtesy to Mr. Gradgrind in the presence of his family, and said in a faltering way, "I beg your pardon, sir, for being troublesome—but—have you had any letter yet about me?" Louisa would suspend the occupation of the moment, whatever it was, and look for the reply as earnestly as Sissy did. And when Mr. Gradgrind regularly answered, "No, Cecilia, nothing of the sort," the trembling of Sissy's lip would be repeated in Louisa's face, and her eyes would follow Sissy with compassion to the door.

Mr. Gradgrind usually improved these occasions by remarking when she was gone, that if Cecilia had been properly trained from an early age, she would have proved to herself the baselessness of such fantastic hopes. Yet it did seem as if fantastic hope would take as strong a hold as Fact.

Sissy Jupe was, indeed, never to give up her Fancy for Fact. She remained to the last an enigma to the practical Mr. Gradgrind.

"I fear, Cecilia," he said, two or three years later, "that your continuance at the school any longer would be useless."

"I am afraid it would, sir," she replied, blushing.

"I cannot disguise from you," continued Mr. Gradgrind, knitting his brow, "that the result of your probation there has disappointed me; has greatly disappointed me. You have not acquired, under Mr. and Mrs. M'Choakumchild, anything like that amount of exact knowledge which I looked for. You are extremely deficient in your facts. Your acquaintance with figures is very limited. You are altogether backward, and below the mark."

"I am sorry, sir," she returned, " but I know it is quite true. Yet I have tried hard, sir."

"Yes," said Mr. Gradgrind, "yes, I believe you have tried hard; I have observed you, and I can find no fault in that respect."

"Thank you, sir. I have thought sometimes;" Sissy replied timidly, "that perhaps I tried to learn too much, and that if I had asked to be allowed to try a little less, I might have"—

"No, Cecilia, no," said Mr. Gradgrind, shaking his head in his profoundest and most eminently practical way. "No. The course you pursued, you pursued according to the system —the system—and there is no more to be said about it. I can only suppose that the circumstances of your early life were too unfavorable to the development of your reasoning powers, and that we began too late. Still, as I have said already, I am disappointed."

"I wish I could have made a better acknowledgement, sir, of your kindness to a poor forlorn girl who had no claim upon you, and of your protection of her."

"Don't shed tears," said Mr. Gradgrind. "Don't shed tears. I don't complain of you. You are an affectionate, earnest, good girl and— and we must make that do."

"Thank you, sir, very much," said Sissy, with a grateful courtesy. "I should have nothing to wish, sir, if"—

"I understand you," said Mr. Gradgrind; "you still refer to your father. I have heard from Miss Louisa that you still preserve that bottle. Well! If your training in the science of arriving at exact results had been more successful, you would have been wiser on these points. I will say no more."

He really liked Sissy too well to have a contempt for her; otherwise he held her powers of reasoning in such slight estimation that he must have fallen upon that conclusion. Somehow or other, he had become possessed by an idea that there was something in this girl which could hardly be set forth in his scheme of education.

He did not know—till long after—that it was his scheme of education which was at fault, and not the warm, loving heart of Sissy Jupe.